CITY OF GOD

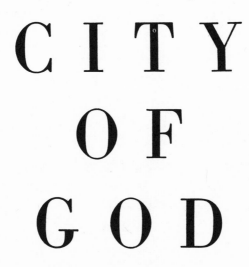

CITY OF GOD

A Novel of the Borgias

By Cecelia Holland

LONDON
VICTOR GOLLANCZ LTD
1979

Printed in Great Britain by
Lowe & Brydone Printers Limited, Thetford, Norfolk

FOR BOB GOTTLIEB, WITH LOVE

CITY OF GOD

straight nose and a jaw that flared back from the chin into a belligerent wedge. Nicholas enjoyed this beauty. He let the wine lie on his tongue before swallowing.

"Oh." The big man rose out of his chair, staring across the room. "That's clever—I never saw that until now."

He meant the Roman temple painted in among the olive trees on the west wall. Nicholas said, "I'm pleased it amuses you."

Stefano sat down again heavily in the chair. Something had put him on edge, perhaps Nicholas's tone of voice. He still held his empty glass and he set it down on the floor by his foot.

"I told you, I know nothing of Valentino."

"What is your opinion of him?"

The pale eyes opened wider. "Valentino? He is a man, that one."

"Ah."

"A few years ago, what was he? The bastard son of a Spanish Cardinal. Now—Gonfalonier of the Church, conqueror of the Romagna—"

"Nor is his father a mere Cardinal, now, but the Pope. There have been men before who shone like stars while their relatives were Pope, and went out like candles when their patrons died. Girolamo Riario, for instance."

Stefano shrugged. His clothes were badly cut of cheap fabric and did not suit him. "That is in the future," he said. "Now Valentino is the greatest man in Italy."

Nicholas propped his chin up on his fist, his elbow on the arm of the chair. "I want to know the gossip of the Trastevere. As much to know what folk believe as to learn what is true."

"I'll do anything I'm paid for."

Stefano put one hand on his coat, where the purse bulged. The door into the kitchen squealed and Juan returned, collected their glasses, and went out again.

"When you want to see me, leave word at the Fox and

room were painted with vistas of hills and olive trees, a sky half blue and half cloud. The small, light furniture was set well away from the walls, to keep from disturbing the effect. It was supposed to be as if they stood on a hillside in the country. Nicholas was so accustomed to it that he had forgotten how to be amused by it. He went to the sideboard and slid open the top drawer.

"This is magnificent," Stefano said.

"Do you think so?" Nicholas took a purse from the chest. "I used to enjoy it, but now it seems obvious. Fifty crowns."

He held out the purse, and after a moment Stefano crossed the room and took it. Nicholas had seen several members of the Baglione family but none as handsome as this one, with his red-brown hair and pale eyes, almost amber, and his fine sensuous mouth.

"Why are you doing this?" the fine mouth said.

"As I told you I am the resident secretary at the legation of the Signoria of Florence to the Papal Court. I collect news. I would pay to know the news of the Trastevere."

Stefano gave the humph of a half-formed laugh. The purse slipped away inside his coat. "Corn is dear and the wine is always watered. Why should the Trastevere interest Florence? No one lives there—no one great. Only whores and thieves and working folk."

"Cesare Borgia has a palace in the Trastevere," said Nicholas. "Sit down, if you please. We'll have some wine. Unwatered."

They sat in two facing chairs near the middle of the room. The old servant came silently in with wine in glasses.

Stefano sat perched uncomfortably on the edge of his chair. His gaze traveled over the painted walls. He held the wine a while in his hand before he drank it; then he drank it without tasting it, as if it were well water. He had no manner of a prince, for all his looks and name. His coloring was not that of a peasant. Wide-spaced, his eyes, above a large

"You could have let your friend knife me, back at the Tiber."

Nicholas went through the gate into the wild tangle of the garden. The previous owner of the house had planted vines and fruit trees and pruned and watered, but Nicholas had no interest in the plantings and for twenty years had let them all do as they would. It was a big garden, choked with weeds and brambles and fallen branches. The house was buried in the middle of it. A walk of flagstones led to it through the high grass and wild roses. There was no step or porch; the door was set plainly into the blank wall of the house.

"I have a proposal for you," Nicholas said. He tapped on the door.

"What?"

The door opened and Nicholas's old servant looked out at them over a candle. He said nothing, only backed away to let them in. Age had humped his shoulders so that he could not stand upright and his head jutted forward like a dog's on his rigid neck. While he went off around the room lighting the candles on the walls, Nicholas shed his coat, and Stefano Baglione at last removed his hat.

Nicholas laid his coat over the chair by the door, the seat still dented from the old man's weight. Stefano had come past him a step, as he entered, and Nicholas could look at him without effrontery. The Baglioni were known for their good looks. He was interested to see if that, too, supported this man's claim to the name.

"What proposal?" Stefano asked, turning.

Caught staring, Nicholas lowered his eyes. "Come sit down."

The old servant, Juan, had left the room. Nicholas turned to bolt the door. Stefano walked off around the room, looking at the paintings on the walls.

The ceiling was very high; the four ample walls of the

big thief, whose hat protected his face from the light of the lantern. "Who are you? You aren't from this quarter."

"Stefano Baglione," the thief said calmly. "I live in the Trastevere."

Nicholas kept his surprise from showing on his face. The Baglione family were lords of the city of Perugia. If this were a lie, it was a bold one. He glanced at the man beside him, his curiosity at full bloom. They were big men, the Baglioni. Perhaps it was true.

The watchman did not believe it; he gave a coarse hoot of derision. He smelled of wine. His eyes were red-veined. Probably he had just come from the wine shop in the next street. He said, "A Baglione? In the Trastevere?"

"Mind your tongue," Nicholas said.

"Your pardon, Messer Dawson."

The watchman nodded to him and walked off, his deputies trailing after him down the soggy stretch of meadow on the other side of the Colosseo. Nicholas started away into the pitch darkness the lantern left behind.

"Potlickers," Stefano Baglione said furiously. "They think they own the street."

"You should change your name."

"It's my name!"

"Still, folk can only be skeptical."

Stefano said no more. Nicholas took him down the lane that led to his house. They passed between two rows of little shops and across the paved square that opened up before the wine shop. Now on one side of the street was a pasture and on the other an abandoned warehouse. Puddles of filth stood in the gulley, and Nicholas watched where he put his feet. The warehouse's front wall came up flush with the edge of the street. At its corner a thick hedge of thorn began, eight feet high.

Midway along this hedge there was an iron gate. Nicholas took his key from his shirt and swung the gate open.

"You could have set the watch on me," Stefano said.

his army toward Florence. He says he means no harm, but his soldiers are looting the villages as they come on them, and who can believe a Borgia's word on his intentions?" The big man flicked his gaze at Nicholas. "You are the Florentine ambassador."

"Only the secretary," Nicholas said.

"We sent the note to the ambassador."

"The most excellent and illustrious Ercole Bruni does not meet folk late at night by the river." Nicholas touched the big man's arm, directing him to the left, through the dense evergreen trees. He drew his hand back. His fingertips grazed the cheap velvet sleeve of the thief's coat. "Would you have threatened an ambassador to the Court of the Pope? Risky."

"The dark cuts the risk," the thief said. "I need money."

Ahead the trees gave way to the wide meadows and pastures around the Colosseo. The cold wind rushed at them. Sheep grazed across the open ground, their bells tinkling. Nicholas led the thief past the terraces and broken columns that marked the edge of the Forum, where the fires of the lime kilns still burned. The two men went on around past the Colosseo itself, looming up under its coats of shrubs and climbing vines. None of the great of Rome claimed it, perhaps because it was known to be haunted. The Pierleone had once used it for a fortress, but now the inside was abandoned to the owls and cats and necromancers. Wretched hovels clung to the outside wall. Long poles set in chinks in the marble braced their walls of junk. The place looked evil to Nicholas, who knew what pastimes the ancients had engaged in there.

Halfway around it the watch hailed them.

"Messer Dawson," said the leader of the watch, recognizing him. On his shoulder he carried his pike; one of his followers bore the lantern on its long pole.

"Yes," Nicholas said. "My companion and I are going to my home. Is the place quiet?"

"Nothing stirring," the watchman said, squinting at the

his back. From every direction came the rolling peal of the bells of Rome, measuring the time.

Nicholas fought his way through a screen of brush and vines onto the broad well-traveled road that led by the Palatino. To the right, beyond some stone pines, was a little church, where folk would be gathering for Mass. The hand left his arm.

He unkinked his arm and the blood tingled back through the limb, going warm up to his armpit. He shook his hand to bring the life back into his numb fingers.

"Take me straight to this house of yours," the man in the hat said. "And no trouble." He threw a long look back into the darkness of the river.

"Did you hurt him?" Nicholas said. The word "kill" stuck on his tongue.

The other man laughed again. He was taller than Nicholas, heavy-set, or seemed so in his voluminous coat and hat. He said, "No—I just hit him. I don't cut people. There is too much risk in shedding blood. So move fast, he may wake up soon."

Nicholas began to walk faster, and the big thief gave another round gust of laughter. They were passing the churchyard. There folk were entering the church, their heads already bowed and their hands together in prayer. Beyond the church the long horizon of the hill stretched off, broken by the flat heads of pine trees and a ruined wall.

"Do you know anything of Duke Valentino?" Nicholas asked.

"No more than anyone else," the thief said. With both hands he adjusted the wide soft brim of his hat. There was a medal pinned to it, which he touched in passing, as if for luck. Nicholas watched these fastidious gestures, his interest piqued.

"Tell me what you know," he said, "about Cesare Borgia."

"Valentino has seized half the cities in the Romagna," the thief said. "Forli, Imola, Cesena . . . Now he has marched

"Who says I'm to fit in with this?" the tall man's voice rose. "You go in, and I wait forever in the street! Is that your scheme?"

Nicholas ran his gaze from one to the other of the thieves. Perhaps he would escape while they argued. He sidled away from the river. A flickering light caught his eye and he turned his head enough to see the light of a torch reflected in the water on the far side, and farther off the torch itself, leading the penitents' procession. The tight hold on his arm did not ease.

"I'll go with him," the man with the hat said to the tall man. "You go back to the Fox and Grapes—I'll meet you there later."

"Likely! Just likely!"

The knife flicked forward across the space between the two thieves. The man with the hat swung Nicholas around off balance and let him go. Nicholas fell to his knees on the stones. Scrambling up, he dashed away down the edge of the river. Behind him as he rushed away there was scuffling. Suddenly, like a voice in the sky, the first bell of midnight tolled. Nicholas slipped and slid on the damp shore, his lungs full of rotten river air.

As he clawed his way through the undergrowth along the marsh path, the man with the hat caught him.

"Not bad," he said, and twisted Nicholas's arm up between his shoulders. "But the next time you run foot races, wear better shoes."

Nicholas was out of breath. He glanced back the way he had run, looking for the other man.

"Don't worry about him," said the man with the hat. "You owe me fifty crowns."

"I'll pay," Nicholas said. "Please let go of my arm."

The other man laughed. He thrust Nicholas on ahead of him down the path. With one hand Nicholas fended off the weeds and thorny brambles that overhung the thread of the trail on either side. His aching arm was still curled up behind

They pressed close to him; he clenched his teeth, the river stench in his nostrils like an omen.

"Don't kill me. I will gladly give you the fifty crowns not to kill me."

The tall man moved abruptly in the dark. Nicholas flinched from the blow he expected, and nearly lost his balance. He flailed with his hands at the air. The man with the hat caught him by the arm and held him still, painfully gripped in a hand like a vise.

"You have no money," the tall man said. He had not moved to hit Nicholas, but to draw a knife.

Across the river fifty voices suddenly rose in a Lenten chant of penance. Nicholas touched his tongue to his lips. "Not here," he said. "I have a house—the other side of the Palatino. Near the Colosseo." With an effort he kept his voice low. His words rushed forth but he held himself calm and tried to speak evenly. He said, "I will take you there. Give you the money."

"Kill him," the tall man said.

"If you kill me you will get nothing."

The man in the hat reached between Nicholas and the tall man, pushing them apart. Nicholas saw the long thin blade of the knife as the tall man backed away. Across the river, the penitents were chanting a Miserere nobis. The man in the hat still held Nicholas by the arm in a hurtful twisting grip.

"If we go to this house of yours, you will set your men on us."

"I have no men," Nicholas said. "One of you could come inside to get the money. The other could wait outside."

"I'll go in with you," said the man in the hat.

Nicholas let out his breath, relieved. The wind touched his damp forehead. The man with the hat was between him and the knife.

The tall man said, "Yes, and I wonder how much of the money I'll ever see."

"Let's go," said the man with the hat.

He wished he had brought a sword, or at least his walking stick. He had no knowledge of fighting; yet he longed for something to put between himself and strangers.

There were two of them, two men coming single-file toward him along the edge of the water. Perhaps they were honest. Perhaps, in a few moments, Nicholas would know what all Italy longed to know of Valentino.

Thinking of Valentino made him eager. He called out to the two men coming near him: "Wait there! Come no closer. Who are you?"

They stopped in their file. The leader put his hand out to the side, holding the other man behind him. The leader was broad-shouldered and wore a great flopping hat. The other was taller and thin. Nicholas could see nothing of their faces.

"Who are you?" one called.

"I had a message," Nicholas said.

He wound his fingers in his coat. The back of his mouth was dry.

"You want to know where Cesare Borgia marches, and whom he will attack," said the man in the hat. "For which you will pay fifty crowns."

"Agreed," Nicholas said.

The stones crunched. The two men were moving toward him again. They separated, coming at him from either side, and his hackles rose. A trap. He wheeled, his shoes slipping on the mossy ground, but there was nowhere to run. On either side the strangers closed in on him.

"The money," said the man in the hat.

"I did not bring it," Nicholas said. "I have nothing with me."

The tall man swore a loutish country oath. He gripped Nicholas by the sleeve and pushed him to the bank—almost into the shallow sewage-ridden water. The other man passed his hands hard over Nicholas's coat, searching for his purse.

"I have no money with me," Nicholas said.

"Kill him," the tall man said.

Night had come. Nicholas Dawson, waiting on the stony shore of the Tiber, began to shiver in the cold. He tucked his hands into the folds of his coat and swayed a little from one foot to the other, and cast a look around him, from the river to the swampy meadow behind him, stinking of rot.

Usually he avoided this part of Rome even during the day, but the messenger had said, "Come alone." The messenger had also spoken a certain name to him. But for that name he would never have come here at night, by himself.

He had been waiting nearly an hour. The midnight bells would toll soon. He tried to control the shivering of his body. He began to think that he might leave—call it a hoax and leave. At that thought he stirred again, rocking on his feet set close together on the river stones. The Tiber rushed along in the dark; where its waters lapped on the shore a streak of garbage was cast up as the river passed. Ahead of him, the black smelly water broke white against the piers of an ancient bridge, broken with years, so that only two piers and one arch remained.

Near the bridge, in the tangled thickets of the swamp, something moved.

Nicholas Dawson stopped rocking on his feet. His eyes strained to pick out the shapes coming at him through the darkness. Stones clicked on the path. Nicholas stepped sideways, away from the water, toward the protecting shadows of the marshes, and he half-turned, ready to run away, but with his head twisted toward the men approaching him.

Grapes," Stefano said. "That's a taverna, near Santa Maria— do you know it?"

"I am somewhat acquainted with the Trastevere."

Juan returned with the glasses filled. Stefano's eyes turned to the old man as he crossed the room toward them. Nicholas touched his fingers to his cheek, softly, stroking his own skin. He wondered how Stefano would answer another proposal.

The old man brought his glass. Nicholas gave him a quick, weighted look and Juan left them. He would not come in again.

"I'm pleased you like my house," Nicholas said.

"Yes," Stefano said. He was sitting back in the chair, now, with the glass in his hand. "You must have a lot of money, to have a house like this."

"Would that were true. I would enjoy showing you the rest of it."

"Oh? Are there other rooms like this one?"

"Only the bedroom."

The younger man's head snapped back. His shocked stare met Nicholas's and the color rushed into his cheeks.

"So. You are that kind. I thought so, when first I saw you. Well, I am not!"

"Very well," Nicholas said.

"I enjoy women. Many women. I am very good with them, too—they adore me."

"I dislike women," Nicholas murmured.

"Yes, your kind does."

Nicholas muttered behind his hand. He regretted letting this talk happen.

"Still, as I told you," Stefano said, "I will do anything for money."

Nicholas smiled, relaxing. He stirred in his chair, one hand on the arm. He wondered why Stefano had changed his mind, or if he had: perhaps he had only been defending his honor.

"How much?"

"One hundred crowns."

"Per Baccho," Nicholas said. "This is Rome, after all. For ten crowns I could buy a red hat. Twenty crowns, which is generous."

"What am I—a whore? Besides, I am a virgin."

"That is no advantage to me."

"Forty crowns."

"Thirty."

Stefano looked away, casual, his attention going to the painted wall again. "Very well."

Nicholas stroked his fingertips lightly over the oiled wood of the chair. "We'll have some more wine," he said, and rose.

AT NINE THE NEXT MORNING Nicholas went into the Leonine City, across the river from the center of Rome, to attend Pope Alexander.

His walking stick tucked under his arm, he waited in a corridor of the Vatican Palace for his ambassador to arrive. The walls of the corridor were hung with indifferent paintings on mythological themes. Through an open window Nicholas looked out on a brick courtyard, half in sun, half in the shade of a tall stone pine; at the foot of the slender trunk there were piled several empty terra cotta wine jars. Nicholas stood admiring the accident of art in this scene through the window. He compared the sun-warmed colors of the brick and the pine with the lifeless painting of the Minotaur on the wall beside the window.

Bruni came, the Florentine legate to the Curia, a tall, solid man, smiling. "I am late," he said, as if that pleased him. "As usual. What happened last night at your tryst?"

Nicholas cleared his throat. "Nothing."

"No one came?" Bruni said sharply.

"They came. It was a trap, for the money."

"Did they get it?"

Nicholas aimed his gaze out the window, unable to meet Bruni's eyes. "Yes." The money had come out of Bruni's pocket.

"Fifty crowns!" said Bruni, in a rising voice.

"I could have refused to give it up," Nicholas said, "and had my throat cut. And lost the money anyway."

Bruni made a sound in his chest. Planting one fist on his hip, he glanced around them to see who might overhear. "How many were there?"

"Two."

"Only two? You couldn't have escaped? I knew this was a mistake from the beginning. Well, never mind, it can't be avoided, I suppose, in our position. Let's go in. Maybe there's something to be learned here."

Nicholas went after him down the corridor to the door at the end. They passed into a crowded, noisy room. Bruni sniffed. As his custom was in crowds, he thrust his head up and his chin into the air. "Get us through this mob," he said. He maneuvered his way to the nearest window, took a handkerchief from his coat, and stood looking out and fluffing the handkerchief before his nose. Nicholas went toward the head of the room.

This was only the antechamber; the Pope would keep his informal audience in the next room. At the door between the two, several pages were loitering, some wearing the livery of the Borgias, some in other colors, and Nicholas moved in among them to the doorway.

This room was dark, but the next room was full of a golden light: its windows faced the sun. The walls were painted with murals, court scenes and crowds, like the court scene and crowd moving around the room. Nicholas could not see the Pope for the milling men and women, but he knew everyone there, and before half a minute had passed he had caught the attention of three or four people. Turning away from the door, he moved off a few steps along the wall.

Bruni's remarks about the fifty crowns still ruffled him; he wished that he had spoken up more for himself. He steered his thoughts away from the uses he had made of Stefano Baglione, who now had Bruni's money. Bruni was standing framed against the window. He wore a splendid coat of Milanese stuff, green with an intricate pattern woven through it in silver thread. The Florentine Signory would frown at that. They wanted a sober, mercantile appearance in their orators. Someone tugged on Nicholas's sleeve.

It was a page in the Borgia colors, little bulls embroidered on his fluffed-up velvet cap. He said, "His Holiness will receive the legate from Florence."

Nicholas went to tell Bruni. The ambassador, putting on his smile, strode toward the door, Nicholas in his wake.

At this hour Pope Alexander saw only a few people outside his court. In fact he was not even in the golden room beyond the antechamber. The page led them through the scattering of people there; the chatter of voices made a complex music, and because of the painted courtiers on the walls they seemed many more than they were. Going out the far door, the page turned a corner and went through another door. Bruni and Nicholas waited in the tiny empty room where the page had left them. Nicholas could still hear the muffled voices in the sala grande.

"Are you coming in?" Bruni asked, between his teeth.

"Excellency, perhaps I could accomplish more without going in with you."

"Very good." Bruni waved at him, a vague salute, half blessing. The page returned and Bruni followed him away through the narrow door that led to the Pope.

Nicholas remained there, listening. Through the door he heard the patter of the page's announcement, and then the round jovial boom of Pope Alexander.

"There you are, Monsignor Bruni. What a shame you do not play tarocco, we might make a better game of it."

Nicholas wondered whom the Pope was playing cards

with and guessed it was his mistress, Giulia. The Pope's favorite partner, his daughter Lucrezia, was not in Rome. There was a screen across the door and he could hear very little of Bruni's peroration to the Pope. For months now the Florentine legation had been trying to persuade the Pope to release a prisoner from the dungeons of Sant' Angelo and this audience today was supposed to deal with that, not with the threat Valentino's army posed to Florence herself.

Nicholas wandered away from the door. He did not go back to the golden room full of courtiers; he went on deeper into the private apartments of the Borgias.

In the next room, which overlooked from another angle the pretty little courtyard he had admired from the corridor, kitchen servants in white scarves were setting out plates and glasses on a table. He turned toward the next room; he could hear music ahead of him, and a woman laughed. But before he could go on, a little page in pink satin ran out the door and all but collided with him.

The page blinked at him, round-eyed. "Messer Dawson!"

"Good morning, Piccolo."

The page shrugged, still looking surprised, but of course he would not expect to find Nicholas here. He said, "Come with me, please."

"I am looking for—"

"My mistress urgently wishes to see you."

Nicholas raised his eyebrows. He followed Piccolo into the next room. That explained the little boy's look of surprise, that he had found Nicholas already on his way. They crossed the next room, where a man in work clothes was scrubbing off the wall; the Pope intended to paint every room of his apartments, but the work was hardly well begun yet. The page took him toward the music.

It came from a narrow sunlit room, the music of flutes and a little harpsichord. Nicholas paused just inside the threshold. The floor was of black and white tiles, like a chessboard. Two people were dancing across it like errant chessmen. The page went off to the musicians, and Nicholas stood there waiting to be noticed.

"Ah." The woman abruptly stopped in the dance and turned out of her partner's arms. "Messer Nicholas." Her bell-shaped skirt, weighted with jewels and metallic thread, went on swaying around her in its own dance.

"You may kiss my foot," she said, and tittered and pulled her skirts up halfway to her knees to thrust out her slippered foot.

Nicholas bowed deeply over one knee. "As you have said it, Madonna Angela, consider I have done it."

"Show me some respect, now—" she said. "I keep one of the keys under my pillow. Cecco, you may go."

"Madonna." Her dancing partner bowed and went out, with the musicians trailing after in his wake.

"I require something of you," Angela Borgia said to Nicholas.

"Madonna, you need only ask."

"Do you still keep your secluded house by the Colosseo?"

"Yes, Madonna."

"I would like the use of it, tomorrow night."

Nicholas said, "I will bring you the key to it with my own hand. Shall you need my house servant?"

"No—remove him. And yourself, entirely, Nicholas."

"As Madonna wishes."

"I shall send Piccolo for the key." She sauntered closer to him; she had a little looking glass on a chain at her belt, and she took it and looked at herself in it, then turned it to look at him in it. "And you, my love, will you need some other place to stay? I can provide you one." She touched the enameled back of the mirror to his arm.

"I will stay at the embassy," Nicholas said.

She sniffed at him, her black brows tightening over her nose. She was the only one of the Borgias not fair and tall. Raising the mirror at arm's length, she watched herself in it, saying, "I shall send Piccolo." Slowly she began to dance again, her skirts swaying out, and observed her steps in the mirror.

Nicholas bowed again and went out. Before he had gone many steps the pink-satin page reappeared and led him back through the unpainted rooms to the painted ones.

In the sala grande Nicholas withdrew by himself to the wall and propped himself on his walking stick. Before him the other courtiers wandered around the room, pausing to talk to one another. Nicholas fell to musing over what Angela Borgia had asked of him. She would want use of his house for only the most obvious reason, having no real interests beyond herself and her pleasures. Yet for that same reason her own resources were sufficient. There was more to her request than what it seemed.

"Let us go," Bruni said, beside him.

Nicholas had not noticed him come up. He raised his head, frowning at Bruni's frown.

"What did he say?"

Bruni shrugged his shoulders, made broader by the heavy stuffing inside his coat. The chains he wore around his neck chimed together. "He said he can do nothing in the matter of the Lady of Forli, who is in his son's charge."

"Did you manage to get him onto the subject of Valentino's invasion of Tuscany?"

"I could not get him off! He never stopped talking—he said we ought to be asking rather for our own safety than for the Lady of Forli, since we have angered him by supporting his enemies in the past. Then he sent me out again." He looked fretfully around them at the other courtiers.

"What took so long, then?" Nicholas asked.

"I had to wait to talk to him until he had finis. ed his game of cards."

"Who was he playing with?"

Bruni gave him a sideways glance. "What does that matter? The divine Giulia." He drew out the name to make the epithet ironical.

Nicholas started toward the door leading out, Bruni at his side, keeping silent. They went out through the ante-chamber and into the corridor. Most of the people waiting to see the Pope had either gotten in or gone home. Three or four men in half-armor, carrying pikes with ribbons on the hafts, were leaning against the wall, waiting to go on sentry duty when the audience ended. Halfway down the corridor, near a sunny window, several other men were clumped to-gether talking. Nicholas touched Bruni's arm.

"The French."

Bruni straightened, his face keen. The Frenchmen began moving out of their council, coming down through the shad-ows toward the Florentines, and Bruni moved to plant him-self squarely in their path. Surrounded by his underlings in multicolored clothes, the Cardinal of Rouen saw Bruni, smiled, bowed his head without missing stride, and murmur-ing a vague greeting in French circled the Florentine to the doorway and went in.

"Our doom is sealed," Bruni said.

Nicholas got him by the arm and led him away. When they were on the steps going down to the courtyard, Bruni said, "They are all against us now. Did you see him? Not even the common courtesy of an inquiry after my health!"

In fact Rouen had inquired, but in French, which Bruni did not speak. Nicholas said, "Oh, perhaps he was in a hurry." They reached the double doors that led onto the court-yard and went out into the gusty, chilly day. Nicholas glanced up at the sky, where now gray clouds were shutting out the sunshine, and wondered if there would be rain.

"What do you think?" Bruni said.

"My opinion?" Nicholas barely glanced at him. "Such a creature as I has no opinions. I am fit only to run errands and risk my life."

Bruni fluffed up his beard, smiling. "How tender you are today, Nicholas. Tell me your opinion."

"If you think it would be worthy of your honor's hearing."

"Of course I honor your opinions, my dear fellow. But you must admit, to lose fifty crowns would excite anyone to a careless word. It was not your fault, I am aware of that. Now tell me."

"Pope Alexander would hardly suggest that you play cards with him if he intended your downfall."

"Bah. You have a trivial mind."

"Besides, they have just asked a favor of me."

"What favor?"

"I do not know yet."

"Nicholas, you are angering me. What favor?"

"The Pope's niece asked for the loan of my house."

"That!" Bruni flung his arm out, discarding the whole matter. "That strumpet? You pin so much on the whim of a whore?"

The day was definitely turning cold. They walked down toward the river, with the high sloping wall of the Vatican on Nicholas's right. For a dozen strides the wall sheltered them from the cutting edge of the wind, but as they turned to follow the street the breeze took them in the face. Nicholas hunched his shoulders. Ahead, the street divided, with one fork running under an archway toward the Ponte Elio and the other turning back up the slope toward San Pietro. In an open-air taverna at the crossroads, foreigners in foreign clothes leaned over a table, arguing in a foreign tongue. Two Franciscans walked by Nicholas, going up toward the gate into the Vatican.

"I do not believe that she intends to use my house herself," Nicholas said.

"I think you are a fool. Besides, you saw how the French cut us dead."

"Florence is an old ally of France—if they meant to betray us they would smother us with their attentions."

Bruni made another swooping gesture with his arms. "I cannot fathom your reasoning. How can you construct such palaces of inconsequence?"

"What else did His Holiness say?"

"I have told you everything."

"Will he permit us to talk with the Lady of Forli, at least? Give her some comfort?" The dungeons of Sant' Angelo were miniatures of Hell. Perhaps they could induce the woman to yield something of value in return for her freedom, although she had already lost nearly everything she had.

"I tell you, he will not even consider talking about her. This time we have been given an impossible task, Nicholas. Impossible."

They walked under the archway. Ahead of them, the narrow street was packed with monks: another Lenten procession. Until they reached the bridge there was no chance to pass by, and Bruni fumed at having to shorten his stride.

"I do not understand him," Bruni said.

"Who, Excellency?"

"The Pope. He is always the same! Whatever happens, he laughs, he makes jokes, he plays cards, he chases women —he has no sense of the gravity of the world."

They had reached the bridge at last. Nicholas made for the railing, where they could edge past the monks, and stepped short to let Bruni precede him. He smiled at Bruni's back, relishing Bruni's comment on the Borgia Pope.

"Mercury is retrograde," Bruni said over his shoulder. "Mars is in Leo. There is nothing to be done when the stars themselves are our enemies."

"The stars in their courses fight against Florence."

"Indeed."

Nicholas had intended a joke. They were approaching the far bank, crowded with shops and churches. Garbage littered the shore under the bridge, and a line of brown foam marked the edge of the water. The ferry had just passed by on its way to Trastevere and the last little ripples of its wake were breaking on the rivershore.

"You mock the stars," Bruni said. "I tell you, Nicholas— that is folly."

"I see no reason why the movements of a few lights should determine the course of my life."

"Then you do not understand nature." Leaving the bridge, Bruni slowed to let his secretary come even with him and crowded close to him, bent on the argument. "I tell you, all nature is of a piece, and what occurs in one part is reflected in some way in every other part—hence the value of learned study of the stars."

Nicholas rubbed his thumb on the gold handle of his walking stick. Bruni's passion for astrology irritated him beyond reason.

"What shall I tell the Signory?" Bruni said. "That nothing came of the meeting? How tired they must be of hearing that!"

"As you yourself said, they ask the impossible. Nothing will force Valentino to release Caterina Sforza."

"That! Who cares about that any more—Valentino's at our throats!"

"Not really Valentino himself, is it? Only a few of his men."

Bruni snarled at him. "Vitelli! And Oliverotto!"

Valentino's two captains cherished feuds of long incidence with Florence. A sudden thought leapt into Nicholas's head. Among Valentino's captains, none was greater or more in favor than Gianpaolo Baglione. He stopped.

"What are you doing now?" Bruni said, in a voice whining with irritation.

Nicholas leaned on his walking stick, his gaze aimed down the river. "I met a man recently—perhaps—" he drew his lower lip between his teeth.

"What is this now?"

"I must go back. There is someone in the Trastevere who might cast some light on our difficulties."

"When will you come back? My letter to the Signory must go off with the next courier."

"Write it—I shall translate it into the cipher when I get back." Nicholas started away through the city toward the Ponte Sisto.

The Trastevere, as the name said, lay across the river from the rest of Rome, below the Leonine City in an elbow bend of the Tiber. It was a quarter of tavernas, tenement buildings, cow pastures, and fortresses gathered on the stony hillsides above the marshes. Cesare Borgia had a palace there, and the quarter was partial to the Pope's son. Nicholas asked at the first piazza for directions to the Fox and Grapes and was sent off down a twisting lane, behind a haywain lumbering along on screeching wheels.

The lane led him across a shoulder of the hill. Beyond the river a bell tolled, and others joined in, announcing the hour of noon. Soon everyone in Rome would be going home for dinner and the afternoon's rest. Nicholas broke into a trot to pass the haywain and went down the far slope.

In the warren of streets on the flat ground he lost his way, turning here and there among the vineyards and crumbling houses. The streets filled rapidly with people hurrying along, women coming from the baker's with loaves under their arms, and men carrying their hoes and rakes. The street led him into a piazza where an old dry fountain stood, shaped like a scallop shell, and there he asked more directions of the idlers.

The taverna was only three streets distant. Nicholas started off at a brisk walk. There was much yet to do today. The official letter to Florence, the secret letter that must accompany it, of which Bruni would know nothing, were still to be written and encoded. The Signory expected Nicholas to report independently, reviewing every act of Bruni's. Of course Bruni acted very seldom, since the stars were always against him. Nicholas realized that he was yearning toward the Fox and Grapes, not for any good reason, but to see Stefano Baglione again.

He slowed. In the rutted street ahead were children playing with a ball. On either side, the buildings rose in honey-colored stone, echoing the children's voices. When he reached the end of the street, he stopped.

A flight of brisk steps led down to the next street. At the bottom a priest was riding by on a donkey. The Fox and Grapes was in the piazza just beyond. Nicholas flexed his fingers around the knob of his walking stick. He had no business here. Even if Stefano were a cousin of Gianpaolo Baglione's, he could know nothing of the mighty condottiere's thoughts and moves. He had said as much; he knew nothing. Nicholas swallowed. He wondered what he was doing here, when he had so much important work to do. He hurried away up the street, back in the direction he had come.

THE PERMANENT LEGATION from the Republic of Florence to the Court of the Pope rented office rooms in a palace of the Savelli family, in the Banchi quarter of Rome. From the building's second story Nicholas could see across the tiled roofs of the neighborhood to the Tiber, and beyond the strip of water the long, protected corridor that the Pope was having built from the palace of the Vatican to the Fortress of Sant' Angelo. The round building within its crenelated wall had, like other places in Rome, served a variety of purposes, being once the tomb of an early Emperor. During the great plague of a few centuries before Nicholas's time, the angel Gabriel had appeared on the squat peak of the roof to signal God's mercy: hence the current name.

Nicholas walked along the loggia, his face turned outward toward the city, trying to compose himself after the long meaningless walk. At the far end of the loggia he came on Bruni, in his shirt, stooping to pour water from a can into one of the potted plants that grew in the open archways. A trickle of water ran from the bottom of the next pot on in the line.

"What did you find out?" Bruni said.

"Nothing. Have you written the letter?"

"It is on my desk. You may use your judgment, of course —the phrasing might be inelegant. Perhaps too blunt. I'll expect the final draft before five." Bruni set down the can of water. "You'll notice that I've indicated our difference of opinion."

"Thank you," Nicholas said.

"I will be in my chamber if you require me."

Nicholas withdrew into the next room, which was the main workroom of the legation. Usually the scribes were busy at work, bent over the long tables where they wrote out the documents and copies that kept the trash gatherers of the quarter well stocked with paper. The scribes were gone now, until the late afternoon when the workday resumed. Stacks of books and papers crowded the back ledges of the tables. The stools were neatly in place and the pens stuck up from their jars like tail feathers. The sweeper had already been here and the floor was shining, still damp in places from his mop. The smell of ink lingered in the air. Nicholas in his tracks, Bruni went out the doorway that opened on the long corridor beyond, where their offices were.

The ambassador's family was wealthy. The walls of his chambers were draped in carpets from the Low Countries, and the furniture, ornately carved and enlivened with touches of gilt paint, had come from Germany. Along the only wall without a window, rows of shelves held Bruni's books. The windows were all heavily draped, and the room was dim and stuffy and close. Nicholas crossed from the door to the desk. Under a book lay two sheets of paper covered

with Bruni's rakish, disorderly script. Nicholas took them
down to his own chamber, in the back of the building.

In this cubicle there was room only for his desk and chair,
his shelf of books, and the inward opening of the door. When
he moved into this room there had been a second chair also,
but he had removed it, to discourage visitors, and turned
the desk to take up the space. He sat down behind the desk
and read through Bruni's letter.

When he had finished it, he turned his head to look out
the window. One shutter was open; he could see out over
the small courtyard, paved in red brick, dotted with the
white droppings of pigeons and swifts. A trellis was strung
over the top of the courtyard, four or five feet below Nicholas's window, but the vines had not yet begun to put forth
the summer's growth of canes and leaves. Nicholas planted
his elbows on the desk.

Bruni's letter was a masterpiece of ambiguity, its central premise being that Valentino would either attack or
retreat, unless he remained where he was. He advised the
Signory to negotiate with the Borgia prince but conclude
nothing. That was the traditional strategy of the Florentine
Signory anyway: wait and see what happens. Nicholas
could not remember who the chief officers of the Republic
were at the moment. Every two months, elections raised an
entirely new government to power. Since Nicholas had last
seen Florence well more than ten years before, most of these
statesmen were just names to him. In the constant shuffle in
and out of office no one made a decision unless it was forced
on him. Still, they hated indecision in their underlings. If
the Borgia threat cost the Republic dear, someone would
suffer, and Bruni was vulnerable, being out of the city.

Across the courtyard, one of Bruni's young aides appeared on the balcony and began to hang his shirts out to
dry. He saw Nicholas and smiled and waved his hand. Nicholas looked down at the letter on his desk. He worked at keeping the rest of the delegation at a distance, yet some of them

were tireless in distracting him. He turned his mind back to the real problem, which was to make a hero of Ercole Bruni.

He took out his cipher books and translated Bruni's letter into code. As he worked he changed Bruni's ambiguities into his own conviction that Cesare Borgia would not attack Florence, but only hoped to frighten the Signory sufficiently that they would buy him off. From years of doctoring Bruni's reports he had such a skill at it that he needed change only one word in ten, leaving out the temporizing phrase, converting a subordinate clause into a full emphatic sentence. Midway through he stopped to cut another quill. No one in the Signory would heed the letter, but afterward no one would be able to hang Bruni. Unfortunately, because of his surgery the letter was coming out much shorter than Bruni's original; he filled it with a general overview of what he took to be the Borgias' plans for the Romagna.

When he had done that he rewrote Bruni's original in the ornate language the ambassador considered elegant.

While he was taking this draft in to Bruni's chambers, Angela Borgia's little page Piccolo clattered down the corridor on his painted high-heeled shoes. Nicholas made him wait. He left the letter with Bruni, who was reading. Pretending that the key was in his desk, he left the little silken boy outside the door and went in to open and shut a few drawers. There had to be some way to discover why the Borgias wanted a secluded place for one night. He was afraid to spy directly on them; she had warned him, and the Borgias dealt finally with spies. He determined to follow the page back to the Leonine City and see where he took the key. He fingered the key from his purse and went back to give it to the page.

Piccolo did not take the key to the Leonine City.

Nicholas followed him easily; the rose and azure costume was visible for a whole street's length in the quiet afternoon, and the boy's short legs carried him at a pace well under Nicholas's customary walking speed. In their long tandem, they crossed the city away from the Tiber, heading west and south, and passed through a ruined gate in an old broken wall. Halfway down the next little street, Nicholas stopped, his instincts warning him, and watched the little boy go through the gate in a wall.

Nicholas withdrew into the mouth of an alleyway. He knew this wall, that gate: behind it was the chapter house of an order of Spanish monks.

For several moments he watched the gate, until the little pink and blue figure came out again. The boy looked tired. He went on down the street toward Nicholas, but just before he would have passed by, he turned into another lane and went that way down the hillside. He was going straight back to the Leonine City.

Nicholas remained in the alleyway for some time, watching the gate. No one else appeared, going in or out. There were back gates, of course, posterns, easy places to scale the wall. The key could be on its way elsewhere and probably was. Yet it was enough for Nicholas that its route had taken it through a house of monks loyal to the crown of Aragon. The Borgias were Aragonese. The crown of Naples rested at the moment on the head of a prince of Aragon.

The French king disputed that, of course, and the Pope and the Pope's son were supposed to be allied with the French. Nicholas went back down the street toward the embassy.

He had his private letter yet to write. While he was bent over his pen worrying out phrases there was a knock on the door. He ignored it. He was working at the edge of his desk, where the light was brightest; the sun would set within moments behind the building to the west.

After a moment the door behind him creaked.

"Messer Nicholas."

It was Ugo, Bruni's junior aide. Nicholas did not raise his head from his work. "Yes."

"I wonder if I might ask your advice, Messer Nicholas?" Ugo shut the door behind him. He squeezed into the space

between the edge of the desk and the wallshelf overflow-
ing with books. "It's about Giambattista, Messer Nicholas."

Giambattista was Bruni's other junior aide.

"I caught him reading his Excellency's privy daybook."

With Ugo before him and talking, Nicholas finally raised
his head and looked into the broad swarthy face. Ugo's eyes
gleamed with a feral shine.

"Why are you telling me this?" Nicholas said.

"I thought you would want to know."

Nicholas jerked up onto his feet. He was so angry the words
rushed together in his throat and he sputtered like a fool.
Then he shouted, "No! I don't want to know!" He dropped
down into his chair. His cheeks were hot. He swiped with his
hand at Ugo. "Go away."

"Messer Nicholas—"

"Go away!"

The young man fumbled open the door and left. Nicholas
sat with his pen over the paper. They were always trying to
draw him into their petty feuds. He could fritter away his
time as Bruni did, on nothing, if he allowed them to in-
trude on his work. After the interruption he could not
write; he was too distracted even to read the last few words
he had written before Ugo broke in on him. They treated
him as if he had nothing of importance to do. Trying to en-
mesh him in every petty vice of embassies. He forced himself
to read the last sentence he had written. He read it again. His
mind steadied. This was important, this analysis of events,
judgment, and reason. He read the sentence a third time,
reassured, put his pen to paper, and followed out the
thought.

WHEN NICHOLAS ARRIVED at the house of his friend Amadeo,
with whom he was to dine, there were already several other
people there. He gave his walking stick and coat to the servant

and took his place at the table. Another servant brought him a glass of wine.

Amadeo took a deep interest in the relics from the antique world that were to be found all over Rome; it seemed sometimes that hardly a day passed without some laborer, cultivating the earth in a vineyard, digging up an art work of classical times. With his large fortune, got in trade, Amadeo had managed to acquire a number of pieces. His house was filled with them. In this room, where he was accustomed to entertain his friends, chunks of sculpted marble stood in niches in the walls and on pedestals formed like Corinthian columns, and slabs of low-relief hung on the walls. The slabs on the walls were a special collection of Amadeo's, being specimens of the phalluses in low-relief that the old Romans had put up on the gates and outer walls of their houses to ward off evil spirits.

At the table—actually three tables, set up to form a U— Amadeo's friends sat talking in Latin about the historian Livy. Nicholas sipped his wine. It comforted him that Amadeo had no taste for good wine. He bought what was expensive and the wine sellers knew it and loved to cheat him. The men near the head of the table were talking about the decline of virtue from the early Republic to Livy's own time.

"For Livy, of course," one man said, "virtue meant something quite other than for us."

"Another example, my dear friend, of the decline in virtue," said a man across the table, and the others laughed, applauding the neat Latin pun.

Nicholas disagreed with the premise of their conversation but he said nothing. Once he had believed, as they did, that Livy should be read by the letter, but he had realized that the ancient historian had despaired of his fellows and to remind them of their duty he presented an idealized past as an example. People did not change so much from age to age. The uses a state might make of people changed. Nicholas did not expound on these thoughts. His Latin was more Benedictine than Ciceronian and he had no desire to be laughed at.

A few moments later Amadeo came in.

"Nicholas," he said, and came and sat down on Nicholas's right, all smiling. "I was afraid you might not come."

"You must excuse me for being late," Nicholas said. "We are quite overwhelmed with work at the legation."

"But you are here. What else matters? Later—after dinner —there will be some other interesting guests."

"Oh? Who?"

"You will see."

At that Amadeo took his place at the head of the table, and called for the servants to bring in the dinner. After the soup, there was a platter of chickens stuffed with plums; and then, to everyone's amazement, asparagus, which set off a clamoring that Amadeo reveal where he had gotten asparagus before Easter. Amadeo smiled and smiled and would not tell anyone anything.

At any rate the asparagus was woody. Nicholas did not eat very much.

After the fruit and cheese the table was cleared away and talk went to Valentino and the affairs of the states of Italy. Now everyone was speaking in Italian. Nicholas sat cutting thin slices of apple with his knife and putting thin slices of white cheese on top, eating each one before he went on to make the next.

"I say the problem's the French," one man said. "And Valentino is the man to deal with them."

"Valentino and the Pope are under the French heel. No, no, my friends—the hope of Italy does not sit on the Chair of Saint Peter. We must think for ourselves rather than hope someone else can save us."

Nicholas chewed a mouthful of crushed apple and cheese. He reached for his wine. He had remarked this before, that men belonged to either of these two camps, when they spoke of Valentino—in fact he had heard the same arguments, even many of the same phrases, used a dozen times before.

"Italy is the firstborn of Europe. It is for us to take our place, to lead the rest of Christendom back to virtue."

"Ah," Amadeo cried, rising in his place, "and here is Don Pedro himself."

Nicholas startled, his head jerking up and his gaze flying toward the door. Amadeo was striding around the table, his hands outstretched, to meet the two men coming into the room. One was much the older, but their faces were similar, long and dour, their beards trimmed to a point like Amadeo's pointed chin. Amadeo did not have to announce, although he did, that they were gentlemen from Spain.

They were introduced one by one to every man there, and took their places, sitting on the far side of the table from Nicholas. Amadeo went to his seat again.

"Nicholas," he said, as he was seating himself, and his servant was filling up his glass, "you have hardly spoken. What do you think of the problem of the French?"

Nicholas's glass was empty. He leaned back in his chair, sliding his hands into his lap. "The French are no problem to me, since they are allies of Florence."

"Come, come." The man who had spoken out in favor of Valentino leaned across the table, his dark eyes intent. "Surely you must see that this is the very root of our crisis here. Italy is in pieces, in fragments, and each fragment obeys only the blind urge of its own advantage. In such wise does a backward nation like the French find a way to penetrate and destroy us."

"I cannot argue with you over that," Nicholas said. "But the time to lock the door is when the wolf is on the threshold, not when he has come in and sat down at the table. Since 1492 the French have been dining at our table."

"They can be thrust out again," said the man who had argued against Valentino. "By those with strong hearts."

The older of the two Spaniards turned to his son and said,

in Spanish, "Would their Italian hearts were as stout as their tongues," and the son laughed.

"They can be more easily accommodated," Nicholas said.

Several of the other Romans booed and bahed at him like a flock of sheep. At his place, Amadeo smiled and smiled, his devilish chin on his fist and his eyes sliding from one man to the next.

"We cannot fight the French," Nicholas said. "Perhaps we can teach them the arts of civilization, innocent of them as their people are."

"I say we can fight for what is ours! And Valentino is the man to lead us."

The Spaniard turned his head again toward his son and murmured, "As the Devil leads his parade of fools. Do you mark this—how childish!"

Nicholas put out his hand to his glass again. Amadeo had started this; it angered him to see Amadeo gloating over the tempest he had stirred up. His glass was empty. Putting it down, he knocked it over.

"As for you," the man supporting Valentino said, "you are not even of Italian blood!"

"No," Nicholas said, his eyes lowered. "And neither is Valentino, by half at least."

"The better half," the Spaniard said.

"Don Pedro," Amadeo called. "What say you to this argument?"

The Spaniard lifted his head, slick with oil, and said in measured Italian, "This is a matter for Italians—for you men, with your special knowledge and special concern. I can only listen and hope to understand better."

Nicholas lifted his gaze and caught the Spaniard's eye. "Most graciously spoken, señor," he said, in Spanish.

Don Pedro was too dark to blush noticeably, but his head rose, his neck long as a chicken's above his flat Spanish collar, and he coughed. His son fumbled with the napkins.

"You have my apologies," the father said, in Spanish, to

Nicholas only. "But only for speaking what I think. For the thought, I make no apology."

"You do not know the facts," Nicholas said.

"The facts! I know this: while you in Italy waste your wiles on each other, we in Spain have fought the true enemy, now, seven hundred years."

"The true enemy, I surmise, is Islam? That depends on your point of view."

"No," the Spaniard said curtly. "That, sir, depends on God. We are annoying our host, who speaks only Italian." Pointedly he turned his head toward Amadeo, and in Italian said, "Your pardon, my friend. A private matter."

Just after dawn, Nicholas woke suddenly in a strange bed, not knowing where he was. He sat up. He was sweating and his sheets were damp. The air smelled of must and dirt. Above him, the ceiling sloped up steeply to a crossbeam; just under the peak was a little round window. He realized that he was in an attic room in the legation building.

The round window showed a patch of white sky. The rest of the room was still quite dark, the fire having gone out in the grate. Juan slept in a low cot at the foot of Nicholas's bed. He snored like a child, a murmur in the throat.

Nicholas lay back on his pillow. He could not sleep now. He had been dreaming an old dream, familiar as the room was strange. He watched the small round window grow brighter in the wall. In the dream he was lying gripped in a surrounding mass that surged and pushed on him; he could not move, and the tight wall around him, alternately smooth and horribly crinkled, all but shut off his breath.

He let the dream slip away from him and filled the space in his mind with new reveries. The round window held his attention. He had lain beneath such a round window once before, as a child, sleeping with his parents, in another country. He shut his eyes. A light sleep fell on him; he wakened in a few moments, uncomfortable in the warmth of the room, and cast off the sheet. Slept again. Woke.

The boy who slept between his parents never lay abed after dawn. Up with the first light, he went out exploring in the streets of that far-away village. In the stinking alleys and the markets he had enjoyed a fantasy of power and adventure. The town children hated him for a foreigner and took every chance to attack him. He lurked behind trees and walls, waiting until his enemies chanced by, and pelted them with stones or horse dung, and ran. It was the running he loved. The stones and shit were only to incite them to the chase, so that he could lead them here and there at his will, and finally lose them. They seldom caught him.

He pressed his hands over his eyes. When he remembered those times he saw himself as he was now, but smaller: slightly built, with pale brown hair and dark brown eyes, small hands and feet, deep lines around his mouth and on either side of the top of his nose, like little misplaced horns, the marks of one who wrote by poor light. A middle-aged boy.

Above him the round window whitened like a moon. Nicholas dozed again.

IT WAS RAINING BY NOON. Nicholas sat in his chamber making out the duty list for the next week. The rain beat against the shuttered windows and leaked in over the sill until he stuffed an inky rag into the crevice.

Just before noon, Angela Borgia's little page Piccolo came, a cloak over his rosy satin, to return Nicholas's house key. The boy was shivering; his nose dripped. Nicholas sent him out to the corridor to wait while he read the note of thanks Madonna Angela had sent with the key.

She had not written it; a secretary had. The fine chancery hand was almost identical to Nicholas's. Nicholas folded the slip of paper and put it in a drawer of his desk.

He opened the door to send the page away, but Piccolo had already gone, leaving a trail of waterdrops along the brown marble floor.

When the legation closed its doors for the afternoon, Nicholas and Juan walked through the city to the house behind the Colosseo. The wild-growing yard stirred and moved in the rain as if the vines and sprawling shrubs danced to it. Nicholas walked once around the yard, but the rain had blotted away any footprints.

The house was cold. A dead fire lay half-burned on the hearth. The furniture in the main room was slightly rearranged; one of the lyre-backed chairs near the center of the room had been turned to face the other. In the little kitchen, two dirty wine glasses stood on the stone sideboard. Nicholas sniffed at the drying residue in the bottom of one glass. It was not his wine. Whoever had come here last night had brought his own wine.

He went through the main room and opened the door to the bedroom. The bed had been pulled out from the wall, and the blankets tucked under the mattress. He wondered if anyone had actually slept there.

Juan appeared beside him on the threshold of the bedroom. "They were lovers, you see."

"Perhaps." The blankets tucked under the mattress whetted his suspicions. Soldiers did that.

Juan put his head into the room; he turned his head from side to side, birdlike, and let out a chirrup of triumph. Going to the bed, he picked something from the pillow.

"Proof final." The old man held up a long pale hair, blond or gray.

Nicholas turned back toward the sitting room. He did not want to believe that Angela Borgia had slept here with a lover. Something else she had said played on his doubts: *Will you need some place to stay? I can provide one.* Had she not meant that provocatively? He knew her for the kind of woman to whom his preference for his own kind was an irresistible lure. How could she have offered to entertain him elsewhere if she meant to be entertaining someone here? Yet when he considered the words he remembered her speaking, he found nothing really there but mild concern.

He went back to the sitting room. His gaze traveled around the place, the painted walls and spindly furniture. All in a rush he loathed the way the place was appointed. He would have it changed at once, as soon as he collected his salary, to something classic and quiet. Tapestries perhaps. Something more solemn. He crossed the room to the hearth.

Enough remained on the fire to reveal that it had been laid out in a cabin stack. Pleased with this new evidence, he knelt down to examine it. That was certainly a soldier's work. The charred wood looked wet. The rain was soaking coin-sized patches in the deep bed of ash. Nicholas reached into the back of the fireplace. A long thin flake of ash crumbled at his touch. Had it been a piece of paper?

Juan was going into the kitchen. Nicholas took down the heavy-bladed tongs from the rack beside the hearth and propped the half-burned logs up against one another and stuffed kindling from the bucket into the spaces. He lit the fire from his tinderbox. He allowed himself no more conjecture. When the fire was catching well over the logs he pulled the nearest chair over and sat down, his feet to the drying warmth, and waited for his dinner.

WITH VALENTINO'S ARMY eating up the countryside, the Florentines were forced by desperation into offering the Pope's son a contract of employment as the Signory's captain, as the Italian fashion was. In return for maintaining a certain number of armed men at the disposal of the Signory, Valentino would receive an extravagant amount of money.

However, the Florentines carefully left out of the contract when and how the money was to be paid.

BRUNI SENT FOR NICHOLAS one evening, just before the legation's gate would close, and handed a slip of paper to him.

"What think you of this?"

The ambassador's chamber was already dark except for the light of a large lamp on the polished oakwood desk. Nicholas held the paper in the light to read it.

"Per Baccho," he said. "Who sent this?"

"It came from a Florentine merchant trading in Naples. What make you of it? Will the King of Spain respond?"

Nicholas read the note through again. It said in only a few lines that the King of Naples, fearing the French, had asked his kinsman the King of Spain for aid. That single sentence could shake all Europe into a new shape and make a different Italy. He put the note down on the desk beside the lamp.

Bruni was peering at him, expecting some answer. Nicholas cleared his throat. His mind flew to the mysterious use the Borgias had made of his house. "I don't know," he said.

"Find out." Bruni poked his forefinger into Nicholas's chest. "You are supposed to know these things. Everyone always congratulates me on having you—how valuable you must be, knowing everything—" the sharp finger dug into Nicholas's chest again. "How will the Pope receive such interference? If Spain does come to fight the French, which side will the Borgias fall on?"

"I don't know," Nicholas said.

Bruni's voice rose to a bellow. "Why did you not learn of this, Messer Nicholas? Why did I have to learn of it from a trader in salt fish?" He bent forward and shouted into Nicholas's face: "Why have you failed me, Messer Nicholas?"

It was unjust. Bruni never listened to him anyway. Nicholas closed his eyes, his skin burning, as if he were whipped.

"The King of Spain is Aragonese! So is the King of Naples —so is the Pope! Is it so difficult for you to see these correspondences? What do you know of Ferdinand of Aragon? Nothing! What do you know of Gonsalvo da Cordoba? Nothing!"

Which was untrue. Gonsalvo, who had shaped the Spanish army into the most modern in Europe, was even now in Sicily with the Spanish fleet. Nicholas bit his lips together.

."God—God—" Bruni flung up his hands. "I must make such decisions that Florence may stand or fall by, and for your laziness or stupidity I have no information to base them on. You have my leave!"

"Yes, Excellency."

Nicholas's legs were quivering. He went quickly back to his chamber, where a scribe waited with a question about a minor document. Nicholas shut the door in the man's face. Sitting down behind the desk, he raked his fingers through his hair, shaking from head to foot with rage and shame. He longed to go back to Bruni's chamber and there say into his face what follies Bruni himself was guilty of. He wondered who else had heard. Bruni had shouted, at the end—the noise might have carried down the corridor. In the workroom, were the scribes and pages huddling together over this choice humiliation of the hated secretary? He pressed his fingers against his eyes until they hurt.

It was easier to think about Spain. He knew more about Spain, in fact, than Bruni guessed, and that had led him into the error of dismissing the importance of the Spanish fleet to Naples. The war against the Mohammedans meant more to the Spaniards than being Spanish. They had been fighting with the Moors to control Spain for seven hundred years. Only eight or nine years before, united under a Queen of Castile and a King of Aragon, they had thrown out the last of the Moors, and Nicholas, like nearly everyone else, had supposed that by nature the Spanish would follow the Moors into Africa. It was the obvious step on. Sicily, more African than Italian, was the logical point to start from. So he had read it.

He rubbed his hands against his face, wondering how, or even if, he could pay Bruni back. He longed to pay Bruni back.

It was night and his chamber was completely dark. A chill draft crept in under the edge of the shutter. His coat was hanging in the workroom. He shivered in his shirt.

He wondered who had received the key to his house at the Aragonese convent, the afternoon of that meeting in his house. He wondered why he could not stand against Bruni's ranting. For a long hour he sat there in the dark until at last the cold drove him home.

Two weeks later, in the sun of early May, Nicholas and the ambassador were summoned to the Leonine City. Pope Alexander received them in the garden behind the palace, where the old man was overseeing the work of a gardener. After the heavy rains of the winter, the grass and shrubbery were swarming upward in forests of new shoots; huge white and yellow blooms weighted the stems of the exotic plants. In this opulence of nature, framed by the green fountains of the palms, Pope Alexander in his gold brocade and white ermine strolled from flower to flower, directing the gardener which bloom to cut.

Nicholas followed a step behind Bruni, who followed a step behind the Pope; his hands tucked behind his back, Nicholas listened to them argue.

"The agreement was honorably concluded," Alexander said. He looked hot, and slightly out of breath, although he did no more than walk and talk.

Bruni bowed in the elegant Roman fashion, his hands out,

his knee flexed. "Your Holiness, I am devastated that circumstances force me into disagreement with you. Let me bring to the attention of Your Holiness that the contract to which you refer was wrung from Florence by threats and brutality—"

The Pope pointed with one large hand to a magnificent trumpet-shaped bloom; the gardener cut its long stem with his shears. "Are you accusing our dear son, the Gonfalonier of Holy Mother Church, of such base usages? Tread carefully, Monsignor Bruni."

He smiled at Bruni. Alexander enjoyed these dramas. The ermine around his neck was damp with sweat. Bruni, bowing again, missed the smile, which passed instead to Nicholas. The Pope turned back to the flowers.

"Your Holiness, His Excellency the Duke Cesare has led his troops into Florentine territory, threatened to sack a Florentine town—"

The Pope inspected the scentless yellow blossom. "Our dear son needed fresh foraging for his troops. He is a captain of your Republic, is he not, and has a certain right to march in Tuscany."

"Because he has extorted a contract from the Signory."

"Which the Signory now refuses to honor." Alexander glanced around again at Bruni. The coarse skin of his cheek was pocked with large pores like scars, and a pattern of red veins showed on either side of his bold Spanish nose. Jewish nose, said unkind rumor. He held the yellow ruffle of the flower against his cheek again. Its inner surface was flecked lightly with brown.

"Certainly we desire only to serve Your Holiness," Bruni said, in the uncomfortable silence. "However, the cold truth is that we simply cannot—cannot pay so much—not at once."

Alexander gave the bloom to the gardener. "The work of the shepherd is costly and unending, night and day. We are saddened that our errant children of Florence pursue their devilish interests to the detriment of the entire Christian Republic."

"We are utterly committed to the preservation of the honor of Res Publica Cristiana."

Nicholas had heard this all from his childhood on. Next they would summon up the ghastly specter of the Turk. He looked behind them, across the strip of green grass, to the palace. In a second-story window was a woman's face, watching them.

"Yet the Republic of Christendom is sore beset," Alexander said. "From without—from within. Cruel the blows of the pagan, crueler yet the blows of her own children." He nodded to the gardener, half-hidden behind an armful of long-stemmed flowers. "Pack them in snow, if possible."

The gardener murmured, "Yes, Your Holiness."

"She will be pleased," the Pope said. "She will smile again." He sounded wistful. Nicholas wondered which of his mistresses was to be coaxed back to smiles by the dying elegance of the flowers. It amazed him that a man so old and fat still devoted much of his time to sex.

Bruni was saying, "Against the Turk, Your Holiness need only summon us, and Florence will empty her streets of her young manhood in the cause of the Crusade." His voice rang with conviction, louder than before.

The Pope ignored him. He put his fingertips to the flower. Abruptly he was smiling at Nicholas. "From Nepi, can one not see the mountains? Perhaps she can see the snow from her window. The flowers will surprise her—remind her of Rome."

It was his daughter then he missed. Nicholas bowed to him. "Your Holiness knows that the city is not truly Rome in the absence of the Lady Lucrezia."

"Your Holiness," Bruni said, "let me have the pleasure of relating to my state that Your Holiness again bestows on us the warmth of your approval."

"When you pay our dear son the money you promised him," the Pope said, "I will approve. Now go. I have no more to say to you."

Bruni bowed and spoke mellifluous leavetakings. Alexander extended his hand, and Bruni and Nicholas by turn applied their lips to the ring of Peter. As they left the Pope was smiling at the flowers as if he looked again on the face of his beloved exiled daughter.

Bruni said, "Bah. You are a bewilderment to me, Nicholas— He spoke to you directly, and all you could do was prattle about that whore his daughter."

"He spoke to me of his daughter, Excellency."

"Nonetheless, that is why you fail so often in diplomacy. Then you must have turned his mind instantly to Florence and our business with him."

"Yes, Excellency."

"That is the art, Nicholas. To lead men, not to echo them."

"Yes, Excellency."

FROM TUSCANY came daily reports of the ravages of Valentino's troops. Cesare Borgia, demanding the money that the Republic had promised, settled his soldiers in the Tuscan countryside and let them do as they pleased. Nicholas kept lists of the complaints of the Florentines against Valentino's men: so many bushels of grain stolen, so many vines burned, this woman repeatedly raped, that man flogged and castrated. The stories accumulated on his desk. He tried to read them with detachment, but the horrors awakened some ugly response in him, and he found himself reading them over, his eyes jumping back to the beginnings of sentences, dwelling on the evils.

He went daily to the Vatican, trying to gain an audience with the Pope for Bruni, but Alexander refused even to allow the Florentines into his morning gatherings.

When he reported the latest rejection to Bruni, the ambassador threw his hands up over his head. "We are lost," he said. He was sitting behind his desk, a novel open before him; as he took his hands from it, the book's pages turned of themselves. "Venus and Mercury are in opposition, the Sun is in Gemini."

Nicholas said, "Still, Valentino has not attacked Florence—"

Bruni had left his chair. He prowled around the depths of his chamber, past the windows overhung with velvet that shut out the sun. "They say his men are filtering into the city. There is fighting everywhere. You know his tactic—he sends in people to riot and preach riot, so that most of his work is done before he comes within sight of the walls."

"If the Signory would send out a force to confront him—"

"Are you mad? All he requires is the excuse."

"To tie him down," Nicholas said. He knew nothing of military strategies, and he was bad at chess, but this idea seemed obvious to him. "So that he has to keep his men together."

Bruni snorted. His coat was off. His fine lawn shirt, embroidered and frilled with lace, was the brightest surface in the room, standing out against the drapery. "Nicholas, you tire of diplomatics. Do you crave a career as a condottiere?" He smiled unpleasantly and turned away.

"The French king is crossing the Alps," Nicholas said. "He will reach Milan in a matter of days. Valentino will have to withdraw."

"Or attack. With French help."

Nicholas pressed his fingertips to the top of the desk. "Let me go to the French."

"To be humiliated again? You heard how before half the Royal Court Niccolo Machiavelli was forced to listen to a recital of our sins. No." Bruni raised his hands again, shaking his head. "In this we cannot rely on friends—former friends. We stand alone, as once we stood alone against the tyrant Giangaleazzo. I will not see the French."

Nicholas looked down at the leather-bound book on the desk. The title crossed the spine in gold leaf: *Tales of Cathay*. Bruni had turned toward the hidden window and drawn the drape aside a little to look out, his face knotted into a frown. Perhaps he learned such poses from his books. Nicholas said, "Very well, Excellency."

"You may go," Bruni said.

"Thank you, Excellency."

IN THE AFTERNOON, walking home to his house, Nicholas went out of his way to visit a small shop at the very edge of the city. He walked back through the pastures and woods of the Esquiline Hill. As he was moving along the path that curved along the lower slope, he came in sight of some children swinging on ropes hanging in the trees.

He stopped to watch their broad pendulum sweeps across the bare ground beneath the trees. The children did not see him; they shrieked with laughter as they played, their hair flying and the rags of their clothes fluttering.

Here the steep hillside was buttressed with a facing of brick, part of the extensive ruins that covered the hill, and he stood in the lee of the brick wall. His eyes followed the swinging ropes, measuring their motion. The speed did not vary, no matter how the child twisted or pumped. One child's rope broke, and the child fell, then knotting the rope together began to swing again. Now the rope was shorter and swung faster. He watched the child work at his play, how he raised and lowered his body in time with the swing, and so drove the rope farther out and back. That was how the motion worked. The child, pumping his body up and down, changed the length of the pendulum and so enlarged the motion of the rope. Nicholas watched them for some time, enjoying his discovery. He wondered if the child would be able to get the rope swinging at all, if he began pumping with it perfectly still. Usually the children ran a few steps with the rope to start the swing.

If he had asked such questions at the university, the professors would have referred him to Aristotle. He detested Aristotle; the children at their play seemed to have more of a practical sense of the world than the Stagirite philosopher.

It was obvious to Nicholas that a knowledge existed other than Aristotle's idea of knowledge, which was of the essential nature of things. Discussions of essences always dissolved into mere opinion and fashion and had become more decorative than functional. Yet the relations between things could be understood exactly, and expressed exactly, leaving out the nature of the man thinking of them. All nature seemed composed of such simple consequences as the action of the swinging rope. There seemed everywhere in the world an order of a few simple relationships, endlessly repeated.

The idea was an old one. In a previous century Cusanus had proposed that the mind of man, being finite, could know nothing of the infinite; man knew nothing but what was relative to him. Cusanus' liberal and indulgent Church had spared him the heretic's fire, but he had few followers of any importance.

Nicholas had applied that thinking to his own work, but with no success. There seemed no such order in human nature as he saw in the swinging of the rope.

The children sang as they wheeled through the air. Nicholas moved away. He strolled down across the slope, where goats grazed, and the voices of the children faded behind him.

In the narrow street, going toward his house, he came on old Juan, a shawl over his humped shoulders. The servant had two chickens by the feet and a braid of onions in the other hand. The chickens were plucked from the necks down. Their full-feathered heads were ruffled.

"Old Caterina looked so sad today," Juan said, just as if

he and Nicholas had been in the midst of conversation. "Maybe her husband has left her again. He wasn't in the butcher's stall." He shook his head and gathering the lacy spittle in his mouth spat it out onto the dust in front of them.

Nicholas walked short to keep from leaving the old man behind. Juan chattered on, full of imagined gossip. After twenty years in Rome he spoke no Italian; he made up lives for all the people around him whose true lives he could not penetrate. There was a parallel between that and the way Bruni made up actions for the stars to suit the caprices of fortune in the affairs of Italy. Ahead was the gate to Nicholas's house. He slipped his fingers into his wallet for his key.

NICHOLAS BROUGHT HOME a friend to spend the night with him. As usual Juan slept in the kitchen. Past midnight, when Nicholas's friend was asleep and Nicholas was dozing, Juan slipped in through the bedroom door.

Nicholas sat up. The nightlight was burning a deep saffron flame on the window sill. His friend curled up in the bed beside him, his head on his folded arms. Juan put one finger to his lips and drew the door shut.

"Someone is trying to force open the pantry window."

Nicholas lowered his feet to the floor and reached for his dressing gown. His friend stirred.

"What is it?"

"A burglar," Nicholas said. He opened the drawer in the chest by his bed and groped for the candle he kept there. His friend, immediately awake, sprang out of bed.

"Where is my sword? Where is this burglar?"

"Be careful," Nicholas said. He lit the candle from the nightlight, took Juan by the arm, and started him out of the bedroom. "We'll make a lot of noise—maybe he will run away." The candle fluttered and he let go of Juan to cup his hand around it.

"Nicholas," his friend said. "Don't be a fool. Where is he?"

"We aren't certain there is only one."

"In the pantry," Juan said past him to his friend. He spoke Spanish, but the words were close enough.

"Then he must come through the kitchen, and the kitchen has no windows. Let's see if we can trap him." Nicholas's friend threw open the window and plunged out, knocking over the nightlight as he went.

Nicholas gave Juan a narrow look, which the old man ignored. He marched ahead of Nicholas out to the main room of the house. Only the three candles on the table by the front door were lit. The painted mountains and clouds on the walls had faded into an intense gloom. Nicholas pushed Juan along ahead of him toward the kitchen; the servant's impudence annoyed him and made him rough.

As they were crossing the room a huge shape came silently out of the kitchen. Nicholas stopped dead, his scalp tingling with alarm. He clutched Juan's arm. The gross monster glided forward, and the candlelight resolved it into a man wearing a floppy hat and carrying a sack over his shoulder.

It was Stefano Baglione. He saw Nicholas; he wheeled to face him, and Nicholas saw the club in his hand.

Juan shouted and lunged at the thief, his arms flailing. Nicholas dragged him back by the sleeve to his side. He dropped his candle and thrust out his open hand to show that he was harmless.

"Don't hurt us. I've sent for the watch."

Stefano grunted at him. Juan twisted and struggled in his master's grip and gave out a string of Spanish oaths. Stefano thrust his club under his belt. Leisurely, he went to the chest and took the silver plates and loaded them into his sack. He opened drawers and found the box of money and that also clinked into the sack. He was swift. Nicholas seemed hardly to have drawn two breaths between the time the thief entered the room and the time he turned back toward the kitchen. The door swung closed at his back.

"Hah!" Juan cried. Nicholas let him go, and the old man

pitched himself against the door, barring it with his body. Nicholas dragged a chair and a case over to hold the entrance.

Inside the kitchen, there was a hoarse cry of surprise.

Nicholas and Juan struggled with the weight of the oak table against the wall and hauled it up far enough to stop the edge of the door just as the heavy panel shook under a blow from the far side. The chair blocking it jumped at the impact but the table caught the edge of the door and held it closed. Juan screamed a curse. He and Nicholas heaved again at the table and got it across the doorway. The door shivered again, trembling under several blows, but the table held it firmly in the frame.

Nicholas stepped back. He wondered if Juan had recognized Stefano.

"He won't starve," he said, and Juan laughed. Nicholas cuffed him.

"I will not have you speaking directly to my guests."

Juan bowed, awkward, a parody of a courtier. "You are a cowardly man. Someone must protect the house."

"I am rational, not cowardly."

The banging on the kitchen door ceased. Nicholas went through the bedroom to the window and looked out.

His friend trotted toward him through the shrubbery. His face was round with pleasure. The dry herb scent he wore could not mask the smell of his sweat. He brandished his sword grandly in one hand.

"I threw the storm shutters up. He won't be out of there for a while. Have you summoned the watch?"

"Wait until morning," Nicholas said. "If the watch sees you here the gossips will plague you all around Rome." He did not want to give Stefano Baglione to the watch. Surely an accomplished thief would find his way out by morning.

They went to bed again. Juan slept at the foot of the bed on the floor. In the morning, Stefano was still fast in the kitchen.

"Call the watch," his friend said. "I'll say I was just passing and happened in."

"No," Nicholas said.

"Oh, Nicholas. I helped you catch him—can't I be here for the kill?"

Nicholas coughed into his rounded hand. "Yes, you did catch him. Thank you very much, I had no idea you were so resourceful. But you must consider your family, and your career. The Church frowns on such as we did last night. Trust me now. Go before someone sees you."

His friend left, disgruntled, holding the scabbard of his sword with one hand to keep it free of his legs. Nicholas had always supposed that he carried the sword for show. It was certainly out of place on a churchman's belt.

Juan was scraping candle wax off the floor in the sitting room. Nicholas went around the outside of the house to the pantry window.

The shutters were heavily barred with stakes from the garden. He pulled them down and lifted the shutters from the hooks above the window, tilting them up against the wall beneath it. Within the window the pantry was dark and quiet.

"Stefano," Nicholas said.

For a moment there was silence; then footsteps grated on the stone floor. Nicholas backed up, out of reach. Stefano appeared in the window, bare-headed, his coat open down the front. He looked quickly out the window from one side to the other and swung agilely through the narrow opening.

He was bigger than Nicholas remembered. His red-blond hair hung disorderly around his ears and over his shoulders.

"You didn't call the watch," he said.

Nicholas started off through the garden, going toward the front door. "Get out," he said, over his shoulder.

"Wait," Stefano called. "Let me talk to you."

Nicholas wheeled, angry, his skin prickly and warm inside his clothes. "You did not want to talk to me last night."

As soon as those words left his mouth he regretted revealing so much interest.

Stefano was standing beside a fat oak tree, the shadows of leaves on his face and shoulders. He said, "You told me that you would come to my place. Was that just to get rid of me?"

Nicholas walked away again, stiff with unreasoning temper. The big man came after him.

"I don't like being played with lightly."

At that Nicholas laughed, and he stopped and faced Stefano again. "Revenge? Is that why you came to rob me?"

"Yes."

"I paid you in good coin."

"There was more to it than that. I'm no whore."

"Really? You bargain like one."

"Why didn't you call the watch?"

"It could be embarrassing, if you decided to talk about me—and I was with someone else."

They were standing at the corner of the house; as Nicholas spoke, the front door opened, and old Juan came out on the walk to shake his broom. He saw Stefano and his jaw dropped. Nicholas turned back to Stefano.

"I've been busy. The times are very difficult."

"Who was he? The man you were with last night?"

Nicholas shook his head, dismissing the question. Juan was staring at them, the broom cocked back in his hand. With someone watching, the talk between Nicholas and Stefano turned into low comedy; Nicholas pulled on his sleeve, embarrassed and amused. He nodded to Stefano, but he could not meet his eyes.

"Very well. Either you come in the front door or the back, is that it?"

Stefano said nothing, but his weight shifted, and the leaves crunched under his boots; he put out his hand. Nicholas had no idea what this gesture meant. He shook the extended hand and that seemed to serve.

"Tomorrow?" he said.

"Yes." Stefano smiled at him and walked off through the garden toward the gate.

Juan watched him go. When the gate slammed, the servant hurried over to Nicholas.

"That was—he was here, once."

Nicholas said, "Hunh." He started around the corner again, going to the back of the house, to put away the shutters.

"What sort of fellows do you bring into your house?" Juan came after him like a harpy.

"Thieves and rogues."

He stowed away the shutters in the little shed against the back wall of the house. Juan followed his every step.

"And now you have invited him back again!"

"He amuses me," Nicholas said. He backed out of the shed, brushing the dirt from his sleeves. "Go in and make me a breakfast."

The old man scowled at him, turned away, and went around the house to the door, muttering of Nicholas's sins. Nicholas shut the door of the shed and fastened it with a bit of wood.

WHEN HE WALKED into the workroom of the legation, where the scribes were bent over their tables, all work and talk stopped. That warned him; without hanging up his coat he passed through a hush to the corridor leading to his chamber. At top speed he ran down the corridor and threw open his door.

Beyond his desk the young aide Ugo snapped upright, his cheeks ashen. His hands were still in the drawer he was rifling.

"Shall I help you look?" Nicholas said.

"I can explain," Ugo said, at the same time, so that the words intermingled.

"Explain!" Nicholas started around the desk, and Ugo jumped back, as if Nicholas might attack him. Pressing himself to the wall, he shot forward again like a freed spring, jumped across the desk, and dashed out the door.

Nicholas slammed the open drawers. He pulled on the bottommost of them, which was shut, and found the lock still closed. Relieved, he straightened. Ugo's footsteps reached him from the hall, going fast away. He went at a leisurely pace around the desk and down the corridor after Ugo.

As he walked into the workroom, Ugo was just leaving by the rear stair. Nicholas went onto the landing. Down the flight of narrow steps the top of Ugo's head raced away around the corner.

"I will see you when you return, Messer Ugo," Nicholas called.

In the workroom the scribes and pages all wore grins like painted puppet faces; they were poised over their work, but no one worked; no one moved. Nicholas looked slowly around the room. They avoided his eyes. The grins were less in his favor than against Ugo, whom everyone hated. Probably they all hated Nicholas as well. He went calmly along behind the stools of the scribes, examining each man's work over his shoulder.

The last of the scribes murmured, "I told him not to do it, Messer Nicholas."

Nicholas said, "You write an excessively vulgar hand. I suggest you practice from a copybook."

A page hooted. Nicholas turned on his heel, sweeping his gaze around the room. The four boys stirred and pulled their faces straight. Nicholas began, "Perhaps you young gentlemen have not—"

Bruni walked through the main door, his hat in his hand and his cloak over his arm; he looked sleepy or half-drunk. At the sight of him Nicholas broke off his pompous little speech, the pages came to attention, and the scribes left their stools and stood up straight. Bruni looked around him, his eyebrows lifting. One page came forward to take his cloak.

"Is something wrong?" Bruni asked.

Nicholas said, "Good morning, Excellency. The morning dispatches have not yet arrived, I'm afraid."

Bruni's eyebrows lowered again. "What is wrong?" He shook his head at Nicholas. "Come into my chamber."

"Yes, Your Excellency."

Bruni walked heavily toward the corridor. Nicholas hurried around ahead of him to hold the door; just as they were going into the corridor there was a shout in the workroom.

"The dispatches!" Ugo burst in from the back stairs. "The courier came—Valentino is retreating! Florence is saved!" Ugo wrung his hands together over his head and danced a jig in the center of the room. "He is leaving Tuscany!"

The scribes and pages screamed, cheering, bouncing off their stools. Bruni's face cracked into a broad smile.

"I knew it. Mars is retrograde at last."

Nicholas walked away down the corridor.

PRETENDING TO READ, Nicholas waited three hours for Stefano Baglione to come. At last, well after the watch had gone by on their ten o'clock round, there was a knock.

Juan opened the door. A low sound escaped him; Nicholas, waiting tensely over his book, shot up onto his feet. Stefano crossed the threshold. His face was swollen out of shape, and mottled with patches of drying blood.

"Good God," Nicholas said.

"Close the door," Stefano said.

The old servant shut and latched the door. Without waiting to be told, he went out to the kitchen. Stefano forced his lumpy cheeks into a smile at Nicholas.

"Am I late?"

"Very." Nicholas sat down.

Stefano took the chair opposite him. He sighed as his weight left his feet. His fingers pressed his side through his gaudy green coat. His hands were bloody.

"I won a lot of money at cards," he said. He arranged himself gingerly in the chair, his legs stretched out, and his broad shoulders pressed to the chair back. "Those I won it from tried to take it back."

"Tried," Nicholas said.

The kitchen door shrilled on its hinges; Juan brought a basin of warm water and vinegar across the room. He set the basin down on the chair beside Stefano and stood back, a piece of clean linen folded over his arm. His face was screwed up in distaste. Stefano picked the basin up and setting it on his knees plunged his hands into it. He groaned with pleasure. Water slopped onto his coat and onto the floor. He splashed handfuls of water over his face. The vinegar penetrated the room with its acid smell. Nicholas laid his book aside. In the big man's thick damp hair he saw an oozing lump, and his stomach twisted. He looked away, at the walls, at Juan.

"Wine," he said.

Juan went away on the new errand.

"I did not know you played cards," Nicholas said.

"Yes. Tarocco." Stefano blotted his streaming face on his sleeve. "That's my chief work. I only steal when I run short of money to gamble with." Juan brought him a glass of the strongest wine, and he gulped it, like a horse drinking.

"That's too good a wine to drink so fast," Nicholas said.

Stefano smiled at him again. There was a kind of triumph in his looks, a buoyant elation, as if the wounds were awards.

"I knew them," he said. He flicked one bruised hand at Juan. "Give me the towel." His attention snapped back to Nicholas again. "I knew they would try something, so I was ready. I left a few more lumps with them than they left with me." Scooping up the vinegary water in his hands, he bathed his face again.

"Don't order my servant about," Nicholas said. He spoke to Juan in Spanish. "Give him the linen. And see if there is lotion of aloes." Juan left.

"What tongue is that?" Stefano asked. "You are not Italian, are you?"

Nicholas shook his head. He watched Stefano daub and rub at his battered face and hands; Juan returned and stood there with the towel and the white jar of lotion. The water and the towels were bloody. Nicholas looked away, down, off across the room, turning his mind to other subjects, but his gaze and his mind turned constantly back toward the bloody man before him. The dirt and the blood disgusted him, and yet the sight of the work of violence quickened a hateful interest in him, which he could not restrain or fathom, some lust.

Stefano patted lotion at the deep oozing cut on his head. He winced. Nicholas's face contorted in mimicry. He pulled his cheeks and mouth straight again, forced his eyes away. His was the superior life. He crossed one leg over the other, staring at the wall, his armpits damp with sweat.

WITH THE FRENCH KING and his army marching south toward Rome on their way to Naples, Valentino withdrew his troops out of Tuscany; as a vassal of the crown of France, he was required to join his suzerain in the war against Naples. The spring's bullying of Florence had won him little. He had forced a contract of employment for himself and his troops, but the Signory had never paid him any of the money.

Now the attention of everyone who mattered turned toward Naples. The ancient city in the south was the head and heart of a kingdom embracing all southern Italy. The King of France had an old claim to its throne, and once be-

fore, in 1494, he had marched through Italy to enforce that
claim. In 1494 the French had taken Naples, but as soon as
the king went home to France the kingdom fell back into the
hands of the Spanish dynasty that had ruled it since the
days of the Sicilian Vespers.

The Borgias had fattened on that campaign, and no one
doubted that they would feed their ambitions again in the
course of this one. There was also the matter of the King of
Spain, who was sending an army under Gonsalvo da Cordoba, his greatest captain, to the support of the King of
Naples.

NICHOLAS SAID, "An agent of the Borgias used my house in
the spring to meet someone connected with the Aragonese.
Whatever the Spanish intend in Naples, the Pope surely is
informed of it."

He and Bruni were walking down a path in the garden of
Cardinal Barbieri, whose Sunday gathering as usual had
attracted hundreds of Romans, diplomats and hangers-on,
pretty women by the dozen, churchmen, nobles, and philosophers. The garden extended along three sides of the palace; hedges divided the walkways from green, sun-bathed
meadows where the Cardinal's assemblage of antique statuary was arranged in groups. The orange trees were flowering
and the warm opulent scent filled the air. Inside a laurel
bower at the middle of the garden a consort of lutes and
pipes played French music. Nicholas had been told that in
France one heard only Italian music.

Nicholas went on with what he was saying. "Yet Valentino
will march south with a French army. The only solution to
this puzzle is that the French and the Spanish do not mean
to fight."

Bruni sighed dramatically.

Nicholas said, "I suggest that they have already reached
some agreement over Naples. It cannot be that the French

king will come all this way merely to surrender his rights. Therefore the King of Spain must have betrayed Naples to the French. The only question is what Spain receives in return."

Bruni was shaking his head. His hair curled back from his ears in the latest fashion to display a dark pearl shining in one earlobe. "You have supplied me with no evidence for this."

"The evidence," Nicholas said, "is the logic."

"Ferdinand of Aragon, the King of Spain whom you credit with—or discredit with—such base intentions, is a great soldier, and a most strictly pious man. I cannot believe he would betray his kinsman."

"He is also a worldly prince, and therefore must act according to the laws of the world, and not the precepts of Heaven."

"What does that mean? What are you suggesting?"

"That whatever the King of Spain chooses to do will be justified or not by its outcome. And rightly so, for what other real measure have we?"

"The will of God."

"Is obscure to me, and I imagine, to most men, especially when I consider the example of Pope Alexander, who does all evil in his office, but who can be seen to prosper even beyond his ambitions."

"What a dance you lead me, and all for nothing!" Bruni cried. "I think you are seriously demented, Nicholas—perhaps you require time alone, to meditate and pray."

Bruni would listen to no more. Nicholas stopped his arguments. They walked side by side along the gravel, came to an opening in the hedge, and went through it onto a little lawn, polished by the sun and studded with pieces of antique marble.

Amadeo was there, Nicholas's merchant friend. Nicholas paused in his steps. He had not seen Amadeo since the evening his friend had thrown the Spaniards at him. Bruni went away to admire the statuary, and Nicholas strolled across the green grass toward Amadeo's side.

The taller man jumped, seeing him, and a shadow passed across his smile. He burnished it again and put out his hand.

"Nicholas, my dear—I have not seen you these past two weeks."

Nicholas took his hand in a flaccid grip. "No—I have been much at my work. You must have heard."

"Oh, yes, of course." Amadeo would not let go his hand, but shook it up and down, and fastened his other hand to Nicholas's forearm. "Tell me—how have you been doing? You look well."

"Oh, very well," Nicholas said. He was determined not to speak of the Spaniards. Amadeo's eyes shone, and his smile creased his cheeks. His voice was strained with excess of fellowship.

"And your old man, there—Pedro?"

"Juan," Nicholas said. "He is well, very well." His hand was going up and down between them like a pump.

"Such a splendid house you have—I must come by—you must invite me by one of these days, to enjoy it again. Such a marvelous house."

"Do," Nicholas said. "Whenever you have an afternoon free."

"Such a marvelous house!"

"I must go now," Nicholas said. "I see my superior, there, looking for me."

"But we must find time to talk," Amadeo said. He let go of Nicholas's hand and took one step back, away from him.

Nicholas gave him a vague smile and a wave and sauntered off across the lawn. He did not look back all the way across the clipped grass, until he came to the edge of the lawn, where several men and women were standing before the newest of the Cardinal's antiques; there, taking shelter among them, Nicholas did glance back. Amadeo stood rooted where he had been, staring after him. Jerking his eyes away, Nicholas went through the hedge to the gravel path.

THE KING OF FRANCE entered Rome in a magnificent procession, with seventy gentlemen personally attending him, all in scarlet coats embroidered with the royal emblems in silver, and riding chargers whose harness glistened with silver; all along the way of the procession, the Roman people greeted the French with drums and flutes, staged scenes from history, and masses of girls carrying flowers and singing. The procession wound through the Arch of Titus and the Arch of Constantine and through several more arches made of wood and plaster especially for the occasion, and circled below the Campidoglio twice before it headed up the wide straight street called the Corso. All the palaces along the way were hung with tapestries. Most of the nobles had hired folk to stand and cheer before their houses; the French king distributed gold and sweets. Nicholas did not go to watch this triumph.

Juan did, and reported everything to him in more detail than he wanted to hear.

With Duke Valentino at his side, Pope Alexander welcomed the King of France to Rome at the gates of the Vatican. This public ceremony Nicholas did attend. He stood behind Bruni in the dignified crowd as the Pope spoke of the love and faith that unified the Holy See and the King of France. Valentino waited behind his father, his hands clasped behind his back. Beside the Pope in his stiff gold robes and the cardinals in their princely red, Valentino was dressed all in black, like a stranger. Nicholas was too far away to make out his face.

Bruni said, "Is he in mourning, do you suppose?" and laughed.

At that moment Valentino stepped forward to kneel before the French king as his liege lord. The crowd murmured in a diffused excitement; the young Borgia had the gift of action that every gesture drew all eyes to him.

Bruni said, "Mummery. When does the General Council meet?"

"Tomorrow."

The men around them were pushing to the right, where a line was forming; someone trod on Nicholas's foot. Bruni strode toward the line. His hands patted over his brushed velvet coat, his gold chains and medals, and his fine hat trimmed with braid. He drew his beard down into a cone with his curled hand. Nicholas went along in his shadow. They joined the line, already moving past the Pope, whose shoe each man knelt to kiss, and the French king, before whom they bowed. A herald spoke their names and offices. When Bruni and Nicholas were presented, the herald confused them and gave Bruni's name to Nicholas and Nicholas's name, garbled, to the ambassador. As he bowed before the French king's vacant smile, Nicholas imagined that it was a doll inside the rich clothes, a wooden man that wore the crown.

IN THE TWILIGHT of that evening Bruni went off to a formal dinner for the king. Nicholas went to a gathering at Valentino's rambling palace in the Trastevere.

All along the east and south walls of the palace, second-story balconies overhung the street. Through their open doors several strains of music spilled out, muffled in laughter and voices. Here and there in the street the local people had gathered in little knots; they stood on their toes, striving to look in, and the scattered light from inside the palace gleamed on their eyes and now and again shone on half a face.

Nicholas loitered a moment outside the gate. A steady

stream of frivolously dressed people rushed by him into the courtyard beyond, as if something were there they could not wait for. One or two arrived in chairs, like merchants of Cathay. The torches in their iron stanchions rippled and made ghastly shadows against the walls of the palace. Inside, a shout went up from many throats, a horn blared, and a kettledrum began to pound. Nicholas went in.

In the courtyard a large plaster fountain gushed streams of wine. The horn and the kettledrum were playing tunelessly just beyond in a recess in the wall. Nicholas went through the crowd there toward the nearest door.

Inside the palace building the crowd thickened, the noise grew louder, and the air warmer. Nicholas went from room to room, remarking to himself which folk were here. He saw no one important—hangers-on and flunkies. In a long room set with tables he found himself a glass of wine.

He took up a post near a window covered with an iron grille and watched the passing faces.

There were fewer women by far than men. No one seemed to talk very long to any one person; even while they exchanged a spirited chatter they were looking off around the room for someone else. Nicholas held a sip of the wine on his tongue. It was a fine wine, superior, which surprised him, that Valentino would throw his doors open to the herd and treat them with good wine as well. It amused him to see that the glass itself was cheap.

Gradually a strain of low music reached him through the general babble. At first he heard it only inattentively, but then he recognized it; he straightened, alert.

The music came from a doorway down the wall. Nicholas followed the song into a small room hung with wine-colored draperies. Before a hearth where a fire crackled sat a man playing the guitar. Nicholas paused.

It was Miguelito da Corella—the Italians called him Michelotto—one close to Valentino. He did not seem to notice

Nicholas. His black hair, slick with oil, hung in curls to the shoulders of his velvet coat. His fingers arched delicately over the strings of the guitar. For Cesare Borgia, he used other instruments: the sword, and the Spanish garrotte.

Abruptly the music stopped; his head turned toward Nicholas. "Yes?"

"I was listening," Nicholas said, "to the melody. Did I disturb you?"

Miguelito's fingers plucked three or four more notes from the guitar. He slapped the box with his palm. "Who are you?" A jewel studded the left nostril of his long nose.

"My name is Nicholas Dawson. The song's from Navarre, is it not?"

"Dawson."

Miguelito's eyes opened wider; Nicholas expected the obvious question, but the heavy eyelids drooped again, and the man turned his head away; picking up the guitar, he began to play once more, another song, another ballad of Navarre.

Nicholas listened a while longer from the middle of the room, but Miguelito did not look up again. Nicholas went away.

He wandered up to the second story of the palace. Here, in a room whose walls were lined with huge paintings of princes and condottieri, were tables stacked with roast meats and piles of steaming bread. Masses of folk gorged themselves at this feast. Many of them were Frenchmen, dressed in clothes of plainer cut and coarser cloth than the Italians'. Nicholas strolled the length of the room, coddling his half-empty glass in his hand and holding his walking stick under his arm. Every time he paused near a knot of talking people, the name of Valentino fell on his ears. He raised his eyes to the carved woodwork on the walls.

Behind him, satin rustled. He turned to see Madonna Lucrezia Borgia come into the room.

Nicholas bowed, and still bent over he hurried back out of

the way. In waves down the room, the other revelers turned to stare at her. She laid one hand on the arm of the young man who escorted her. She laughed, and in the sudden hush her laughter carried down the room. A band of filigree gold held her blond hair back from her forehead; long filigree earrings hung from her ears and a filigree necklace covered the fields of white skin lying between her throat and the top of her dress, cut low over the breast.

Nicholas watched her pass. This was her first appearance at a public gathering since her second husband's death almost a year before. Rumor said that it was Miguelito da Corella who had widowed her, on her brother's orders. Of course anyone who died in Rome was generally reckoned a victim of the Borgias. Still, he knew it to be true that the Pope had sent her off in exile to the country when she mourned her husband too loudly. Now she laughed, a sweet high laugh, and flung herself forward into the bright loud crowded room.

He watched her go, his interest rubbed. She had the Pope's ear. Things impossible to attain before might be available to him, if he courted her.

The French king's lackeys surrounded her now. Nicholas watched them fight over the opportunity to kiss her hand and bow and praise her beauties. A stream of Lucrezia's attendants and friends flowed through the doorway on Nicholas's left toward the swelling crowd on his right. The air grew warm, and the laughter and the talk mingled.

A page pulled on Nicholas's sleeve. "Come with me, Messer."

"I ask your pardon."

The page tipped his face up. Nicholas had taken him for a boy at first, but the broad meaty face belonged to a man in middle age; he was a dwarf.

"My master wants to see you, Messer."

Nicholas raised his arm away from the crooked fingers.

"Who is your master?"

The dwarf's head bobbed. "Valentino."

"I will go," Nicholas said.

The dwarf spread his lips in a broad leer. He made a mocking little bow. "At your convenience, Messer." He led Nicholas away through the crowd, going along the edge of the room, past the roast pigs and chickens.

Nicholas made himself walk calmly, his expression bland, as if Valentino summoned him every hour. There was no use in wondering why this was happening. The dwarf led him out a side door and up a flight of steps. It was Bruni who had suggested Nicholas come here tonight. Had the suggestion come from someone beyond the ambassador? The dwarf led him into a place where there was no party.

Nicholas followed the little man through a succession of empty rooms, half-furnished, with a chair in one room, a table in another, candles in sconces on the walls, and a smell of must in the air. The windows were open over the courtyard. The sound of the horn and the drum drifted in from below. The dwarf let Nicholas into a corner room.

Miguelito da Corella was there, alone, with no guitar. Disappointed, Nicholas let his shoulders down an inch. He said, "Your Excellency, I am at your service." The dwarf was gone, shutting the door behind him.

"Sit," Miguelito said.

Besides a carved chest reaching to the ceiling, there were two chairs in the room, of which Miguelito was using one. Nicholas sat down in the other. There was dust on the arms of the chair and the cushion under him gave off a scent of mildew.

"You approached me before," Miguelito said. "Why?"

"I was curious. I heard you playing music from Navarre."

Through the open window came a roar of merry drunken noise. Miguelito bolted up out of his chair and pushed the window shut. Nicholas was still mastering his disappointment; he chided himself that he had seriously expected to find Valentino here waiting for him. He propped his chin on his hand, his elbow on the arm of the chair.

"Italians," Miguelito said. With his thumb he tripped the latch. "Light-minded pigs."

Nicholas said nothing. He cast a quick look around the room. One wall was hung with a heavy old-fashioned tapestry of northern workmanship. Only one lamp burned, on the wall by the door, but with the window shut the room heated rapidly.

Miguelito pulled his coat off. He walked aimlessly around the room, tugging on the neckband of his shirt. Without his coat he seemed smaller; slender and dark, with high narrow shoulders and long hands, he reminded Nicholas of the garrotting wire. There was a rip in the sleeve of his white shirt. He faced Nicholas, belligerent, hands on hips.

"What is your interest in Navarre?"

"I was born in Pamplona," Nicholas said.

The other man's face grew round with surprise. He fingered the tear in his shirt. Suddenly he was speaking Spanish. "In Pamplona? Your name is not Navarrese."

"My parents were exiles."

"I do not believe you. Where is the Church of the Holy Spirit?"

"Facing the marketplace. On the south side. The portico's a favorite place of wool traders. The graveyard behind is supposed to be haunted by a nun and her lover." The room was swelteringly hot. Nicholas longed for the courage to remove his coat. He wished he could stop thinking of the garrotte so much connected with the name of Miguelito.

"Perhaps you do know Pamplona," Miguelito said. "That proves nothing, of course. What are you doing here? Among these dogs?"

"The Italians?" Nicholas shrugged his shoulders; his coat encumbered him; he felt laden down and trapped between the arms of the chair. "I am not Navarrese, either."

"Or Spanish?"

The voice behind him brought him to his feet like the touch of a hot coal. He wheeled, putting his back to Miguelito, and faced Cesare Borgia, the Duke of Valentinois.

"Magnifico." Nicholas flexed his knee and bowed his deepest courtly bow.

"Messer Nicholas Dawson." Valentino walked around to the chair Nicholas had just left and disposed himself on it. He was smiling. Like his sister, he was fair, with fine pale skin and bright hair, although his hair was darker than hers. He wore black, unrelieved even by rings or medals, so that there was nothing to look at save his handsome leonine head. He let Nicholas stare at him a long moment before he spoke. Like his lackey, he used Spanish.

"You and I have never met, have we? Yet of course all Rome knows you—the shrewd secretary of the vainglorious Florentine ambassador, forever rescuing his master and his arrogant little state."

Nicholas felt Miguelito's silent presence behind him like a weight against his back. A stream of sweat coursed from his armpit down his side. He did not answer Valentino; all the customary flatteries and modesties sounded false to his inner ear. He searched the splendid young face of the prince before him for some sign of what Valentino intended.

Valentino smiled at him. "Dawson. That name is hardly Navarrese."

"My parents were English-born," Nicholas said tonelessly.

"Oh? Why came they to Pamplona?"

"I do not know. I only know their names—they died when I was still very young. I was raised in a monastery—" he twisted to speak over his shoulder—"by the monks of Saint Dominic, hard by that haunted graveyard."

"Where were you educated?" Valentino said. "Your Spanish has no trace of accent."

"When they found some aptitude in me the monks sent me to Salamanca to study law."

"And you never went back?"

"There was nothing in Pamplona for me."

For a moment there hung before his eyes the image of the loved old monk who had tutored him, who had died in Nicholas's first year away from Pamplona.

"Oh? What is there for you in Florence?"

"Magnifico, I have not seen Florence in fourteen years."

He was gripping his moist fingers together behind his back. Miguelito could see that, yet Nicholas could not keep his sweating hands still. His walking stick lay under the chair. He could not remember when he had dropped it.

"Yet you serve Florence," Valentino said, comfortably. He seemed cool and at ease, older than his twenty-odd years. "As do I, now, of course—we are comrades of sorts, you and I, are we not? Of course our talents widely differ."

Nicholas murmured a conventional compliment. Valentino waved it off impatiently.

"It's said you know Rome better than any Roman."

"I have some small knowledge of the ways of the city."

"You are modest, Messer Secretary." Valentino smiled at him, smiled and smiled, the lamplight glistening on his hair, on his unreadable eyes. "Yet you must endure my curiosity. When I meet a man who interests me, I cannot rest until I understand him. Tell me why you serve the Signory of Florence."

"I enjoy it," Nicholas said.

"Enjoy. What? Giving your talents to a pack of petty scribblers whose doings have no more significance than the meanderings of ants? Florence is nothing! A cipher, a pawn!"

With each epithet his hand struck down on his thigh. "Certainly you owe them no loyalty."

"Not at all," Nicholas said.

"Perhaps you would be willing to give your loyalty to me?"

Nicholas clamped his fingers together. He half-turned his head toward Miguelito. Valentino sat smiling, smiling, in the chair before him.

"I have no loyalty, Magnifico," Nicholas said.

"Wise. Why burden your life with such a falsehood?"

"I strive against it," Nicholas said.

Valentino's hands turned in the air, palms up. "Think on all the people who devote their lives to the pursuit of such lies—truth, beauty, good, evil. All illusions—there is only *what is*. They spend their time sorting out the high moral good and never really act." He struck the air with his fist, his eyes shining.

Nicholas's mouth curled into a smile; Valentino was a young man, after all, with a young man's pleasure in rhetoric.

"For example," Valentino said, "here is a fact from which much might be abstracted—you falsify the reports of your chief."

Nicholas's lips stiffened; he lost his sense of amusement.

"I require your service, Messer Secretary. What I have said must have made you aware that I will use whatever means necessary to secure it."

"I would be of no service to you, if I lost my position," Nicholas said.

Valentino leaned forward toward him. "Would you not? The scandal would reach from here to Tuscany. Your Republic is already wobbling. Perhaps this blow might send the Signory down." His smile widened across his face. "Then as captain of the Florentine army, I of course would have to restore order."

"There is the matter of Naples to deal with first."

A wave of Valentino's hand dismissed the matter of Naples. "That is disposed of. You may depend on it."

Nicholas touched his lips with his tongue. He wanted a graceful way to yield to necessity; he said, "Yes, but how long do you think the Spanish and the French will lie down together? They will be in one another's teeth soon. Well. There might be something to be made of it. I will serve you."

Valentino had stopped smiling; his pale eyes were sharp with attention. "Whatever do you mean?" he said softly.

"I, Excellency?"

"How did you know that? About Spain and France lying down together, as you put it, over Naples."

Nicholas had said too much. The backs of his hands tingled unpleasantly with fear. Sliding his eyes into their corners he tried to catch some glimpse of Miguelito behind him.

"That was as tight-kept a secret as the Philosopher's Stone," Valentino said. "How did you know it?"

"It seemed obvious, to me—" Nicholas babbled out the words, hot with fear. He wondered whether to mention the Lenten meeting at his house and plunged recklessly on. "I knew someone had met a Spaniard at my house—someone of your family—"

"Ah." Valentino's head rose, and his shoulders flexed; he smiled again. "You did find that out. You have my father fooled, he thought you too dull to question it. I see they judge you rightly who say you are dull by your art. Very well. There's no real harm done."

"Excellency." Nicholas bowed his head down.

"You may trust me," Valentino went on. "I shall use your service better than any other master. I am the only man in Italy who recognizes exactly what this crossroads is we have come to, and I have the craft to take us down the proper turning. You have made the correct choice."

He left the chair and went to the door in three long strides. With one hand on the latch, he looked back. "Miguelito likes boys also. Did you know that? You two ought to be friends." He let himself out of the room.

For the first time in many minutes Nicholas became aware of the stultifying heat. He turned slowly around, wondering if he were alone, but Miguelito was still there, sitting now in the other chair, his arms folded over his chest.

"Whatever did he mean?" Nicholas said. "Does he find fellowship with every other man who sleeps with women?"

Miguelito stirred all over, like an animal awakening. "He is less free-minded than he imagines. But he is the greatest man in Italy. You must see that."

"Let us hope so," Nicholas said. "Have I leave to go?"

"From me?" Miguelito rose from the chair; his damp shirt clung to his ribs and stomach; the back of the chair had left a black smudge across it. "Leave me when the whim takes you—I am unimportant." He looked away, presenting the back of his head to Nicholas. Nicholas left.

"IT STEALS MY WITS," Bruni said, "even though, of course, we suspected that this would indeed be the outcome. Yet how a king like Ferdinand of Aragon, renowned the world around for his piety, should sacrifice his honor and the respect of all right-thinking men far eludes my understanding."

The Venetian ambassador touched his perfumed beard with the backs of his fingers. "What I fail to understand is why the French king should give the Spanish half of Naples, without even a trial at arms. For in doing so, perceive, he replaces a weak enemy with a far stronger one." He nodded to Bruni. "Did you say that you had some foreknowledge of this infamous contract?"

Bruni smiled mechanically. He and the Venetian sat side by side, both facing the same direction, so that they spoke to one another out of the sides of their mouths. Along the two sides of the table the dozen other men seated down to dine were chattering away on the same subject. Their opinions were all the same, or were all rapidly becoming the same, as they all sought to be the first to say the shrewd thing in a repeatable epigram. Nicholas was sitting behind Bruni, going over his notes of the Grand Council, and did not speak.

The cardinals had sat only a few moments. The French king and the Spanish ambassador presented the Curia with their pact: that Naples should be divided between France and Spain. Immediately Pope Alexander announced his agreement, and his control of his Court revealed itself in the cardinals' haste to support him.

"Infamous," Bruni was saying to the ambassador of the Estensi, on his left. "I thought so when we first had wind of it."

Nicholas filled out the abbreviations he had made, writing down the Pope's speech. He kept his head lowered. Valentino, with his army outside the city, had not appeared before the Curia.

Valentino obviously had a spy in the Florentine legation, who had told him of Nicholas's tampering with Bruni's dispatches, and who had to be ferreted out. Through a sleepless night Nicholas had nagged uselessly at that. The scribes disliked him but were too low placed to have such information as Valentino was getting. Ugo and Giambattista, the junior aides, ranked higher, and they hated him; yet he could not see how even they would know what he wrote in place of Bruni's letters, since he composed the dispatches directly into cipher and kept no copies.

The servants were bringing around the first wine and the fruit soup, and Nicholas had to draw his feet in under his stool to keep from tripping them in their bustle around the table. The diplomats were all tilted to one side or the other, passing comments up and down. Someone laughed; a glass clinked on silver, and the perfume of the spring soup reached out through the room. Nicholas took the pen in his left hand and worked his cramped fingers up and down. Bruni's back was directly before him, the brushed red velvet topped with lace; on either side were other well-groomed backs, all splendidly covered, all the same. Nicholas lowered his eyes to the page but he did not write.

None of them had known. He had known. None of them had bothered with his opinion.

Bruni said, "You may be sure that we have not seen the

final settlement of the issue of Naples," and the others rumbled in agreement.

Until Nicholas caught the spy in his legation, he belonged to Valentino, since he could do nothing without Valentino's knowledge. He felt as if Valentino's eyes might be on him even now.

Valentino valued his opinion.

"You say you knew of this pact beforehand?" The Venetian ambassador was saying to Bruni.

"I surmised," Bruni said. "The signs were there. For a man of sensibility to read."

VALENTINO AND THE French army marched off to Capua, where the betrayed King of Naples hoped to defy his enemies. Nicholas sat in his chamber at the legation writing out a copy of his notes of the Grand Council for the Signory. As he worked he fretted over the issue of the spy, searching out some way to trap him.

There was a knock. He said, "Come in," and Stefano Baglione entered the room.

"What are you doing here?" Nicholas said, peeved. He pushed his chair away from the desk.

"I need a hundred crowns," Stefano said, taking off his floppy hat.

"One hundred crowns!"

"I lost at cards. They want it now—today. Or they'll throw me into the river."

"One hundred crowns." Nicholas glared at the younger man. The temper he had checked so long broke forth in a flood of words. "How dare you come here asking me for money!"

"I will pay you back—all of it." Stefano leaned over the desk, his face taut; he looked much older, harried. "These people are dangerous. There is no one else I can ask, Nicholas!"

"One hundred crowns!"

There was another knock.

For a moment neither Nicholas nor Stefano spoke; they stared at one another across the desk, Stefano's face full of pleading and Nicholas resisting. He said, "One moment," loudly, and went around the desk and Stefano to open the door.

It was Ugo, with a document to be read. While Nicholas stared at him, forcing his temper down, Ugo turned to Stefano and introduced himself, holding out his hand.

Gracelessly, Stefano said his name and shook the other young man's hand. At the sound of the name Baglione, Ugo bloomed into a brilliant smile.

"Oh, really! How long have you been in Rome? Are you attached to Gianpaolo's staff?"

"No," Stefano said. He slouched against the wall, one hand on his hip.

"Here," Nicholas said. He poked the document into Ugo's face. "This needs His Excellency's approval, not mine. But you were right to bring it to me first."

"I assure you, Messer Dawson, I have every respect for your prerogatives in this office—"

Nicholas ushered him, still talking, out to the corridor, and pulled the door shut between them. He turned to Stefano. "You have the courtesies of a peasant."

"Oh Christ," Stefano said.

Nicholas stared at him, thinking that he was wrong: Stefano had the true manner of an aristocrat, the only people who could be wholly free with their feelings. There was that in Stefano, nothing so respectable as honor, really, but a kind of honesty. After all, he was a Baglione.

"How much do you want?" Nicholas asked.

Stefano wheeled, all his attention intensely fixed on Nicholas. "One hundred crowns. I'll pay you back every carlini—you may be sure of it."

Nicholas was not sure. He doubted Stefano's honesty extended that far. Yet it was worth a hundred crowns to have him, a Baglione. Nicholas went to his desk to write out a bank draft.

"I WARN YOU," Angela Borgia said, "my cousin does not care for those who try to reach her father through her. She has turned away far greater men than you, turned away magnificent gifts. She is very likely to listen to you and send you away."

"Even that would be more than I have been able to achieve elsewhere," Nicholas said.

Angela gave him a quizzical look. They were walking up and down on the loggia of the palace of the Pope's daughter, in and out of the sunlight; Angela had taken Nicholas's arm and tucked it firmly around her own. She smelled heavily of Egyptian perfume. Nicholas turned his nose out of the mainstream.

"What are you trying to achieve, anyway?" Angela asked.

"A trifle."

"You can tell me."

"I would not bore your beautiful ears."

A page appeared at the end of the loggia, at the doorway. Nicholas let go of Angela's arm. Angela did not let go of him; she clung to him like an anchor.

"Your secret's safe with me, love. You can tell me."

"Madonna, you have done enough in procuring me the introduction."

She glowered at him. The page rescued him, coming to his side, and without a bow demanding, "Messer Niccolo Dawson?"

Nicholas followed him out through the doorway to the waiting room beyond.

Away from the sunlight, his eyes struggled to adjust to the darkness; he followed the page more by instinct than sight—by the sound of his feet on the marble floor. A door opened ahead of him and he was let into another room. Still half-blind, he bowed toward the hazy group of people before him. The page said his name.

"Messer Dawson," Lucrezia Borgia said coolly. "My cousin tells me that you desire some few moments' speech with me?"

He blinked; now he could make her out, seated before him, with a woman behind her arranging her fine-spun golden hair. The room was full of mirrors. What he had taken for a group were her repetitions in the glass wall behind her.

"Madonna," he said. "I know that men come before you as suppliants with precious gifts of fur and jewels to purchase your kindness, but I have no gifts, only an entreaty. Please hear me out in spite of my poverty."

"Go on," she said. "I have little time."

"I come here to ask you to intercede for a prisoner in your dungeons, a woman like you yourself, a fabled beauty who has lost her beauty in the cellars of Sant' Angelo, a woman like you yourself, of noble mind and courage, whose only court now are the rats and lice."

She was watching him intently now. She seemed paler than before. She said, "Who is this luckless creature?"

"The Lady Caterina Sforza."

She jerked her head away. The hairdresser murmured, plucking at the smooth curls of hair on the crown of the Pope's daughter. "My brother's prisoner," Lucrezia Borgia said. "I have nothing to do with that."

"Your brother's victim, Madonna."

"Her cities belonged to us. We were right to take them back from her." Still she would not look at him. He went down on one knee before her.

"Forli and Imola are yours, as they have ever been the Pope's cities. She cannot take them back. Even her children have deserted her cause—signed their patrimony over to your brother Valentino and sworn never to help her. Madonna, she has nothing left, nor beauty, nor wealth, nor even the privacy of her body. Valentino has taken everything."

Her blue eyes flashed; she faced him again, leaning forward. The hairdresser caught at the mass of sliding uncurling hair and Lucrezia struck over her shoulder at her.

"No—leave it! You, Messer whatever-your-name is—you insinuate that my brother violated—had her by force? That whore! How many lovers has she had?"

"Madonna," Nicholas said, "surely a woman may give herself endlessly without consenting to a rape."

"I do not believe it. Not my brother."

"Madonna, let me ask only this—that you visit her in her dungeon. See for yourself what has become of her, and remind yourself that once she was a woman much like you."

The princess stared at him, her cheeks patched with red and her hands clenched in her lap. The hairdresser was standing behind her, arms folded. In the mirrors Nicholas saw their backs, their profiles, all sides of them at once.

She took her eyes away from his. The masses of her hair were spilling down over her shoulders and her breast and throat.

"Well," she said, "you are right, Messer whoever-you-are. Someday I may need mercy too." She lifted her hand, palm out, a gesture much like the Pope's in blessing. "But that changes nothing—I cannot help you. You may go."

"Madonna." Nicholas left.

YET A FEW DAYS LATER he received a summons from the Madonna Lucrezia to attend her at Castel Sant' Angelo. Surprised, he hurried there—the message commanded him *immediately*—and found the Pope's daughter already in the courtyard of the fortress.

Her cheeks were sucked hollow, and her eyes looked damp. She wore a gown whose heavy satin skirt was picked out with tails of ermine and rows of seed pearls. Two or three handsome men in her livery attended her; she had brought no women.

"Madonna," Nicholas said, kneeling. "I dare hope that you have called on me to mediate at an interview between you and Madonna Caterina Sforza."

He reached for her hand, expecting to be given it to kiss, but she recoiled at his touch. She backed away from him.

"I have seen her just now," she said, her voice sibilant. "I have no will to talk to her. Men say she was beautiful! Oh, I could not face her."

Nicholas got up off his knees. Dust clung to the knees of his hose. He held his hat in his two hands before him.

"I shall—" her voice was low. "You may tell your principals that I shall—Oh God, here is Cesare."

Nicholas startled. She was looking beyond him, into the courtyard by the gate, and he jerked his gaze around over his shoulder.

Valentino was dismounting from his horse, only a dozen feet away. He strode down on Nicholas and his sister, coming fast at them; Nicholas he brushed aside, without noticing him, and his sister he caught by the wrist.

"What are you doing here? This is no place for you."

Lucrezia pulled her hand back from his grasp, as she had from Nicholas's, but Valentino would not let her go. She said, between her teeth, "I have just seen your victim for myself."

Valentino laughed. He lifted her hand to his cheek. "Which one?" Her fingers cradled in his hand, he stroked his cheek over her palm.

"Madonna Caterina," Lucrezia said. "Please, my brother, let me go—see how many are watching us."

He pressed his lips to her hand. "The virago—my victim? I assure you, dearest one, she fought more staunchly for her city than for her virtue, such as it was."

He let go of her hand. "Go. You will need the afternoon to bathe away the stink of the dungeon."

"With your permission," Lucrezia said; her eyes flashed at him. She lifted her skirts in one hand and swept off across the courtyard.

Nicholas backed away, hoping to escape without more attention falling on him, but Valentino wheeled toward him. "Where are you going?"

"Nowhere, Magnificence." Nicholas bowed.

"Why did you bring her here?"

"Magnificence, I assure you—"

"Tut tut tut, my dear Nicholas, let me assure you that I will let nothing taint my sister's happiness. Nothing. You brought her here to make her unhappy for your own ends. What a cur you are for that."

Valentino's voice was soft enough that no one but Nicholas heard him. Nicholas's scalp crawled; the dungeons were only minutes away. He plunged his hand into his wallet.

"Magnificence, I would cut off my arm before I would suffer the princess Lucrezia one moment's unhappiness—she summoned me here, my lord—" he found her message and held it out, folded in quarters, toward her brother.

Valentino blinked at him. He plucked the folded paper out of Nicholas's hand and held it a moment, unread, unopened, his eyes still on Nicholas's face. Suddenly he tossed the letter into the dirt and walked away.

Nicholas stooped to retrieve the letter. His head whirled with relief and he remained down squatting on his heels a moment, until Valentino had left the courtyard. With the letter in his hand he hurried out of the castle.

VALENTINO AND HIS ARMY marched away with the French to Naples. A few days later, the Lady of Forli, Caterina Sforza, rode out of Sant' Angelo prison. Bruni escorted her, since his negotiations had freed her. Some curious folk waited on the street to watch her pass by, but when she did they did not look at her. They expected a great lady of beauty and station, not the ruined woman who went by them, wincing from the sun, her clothes in rags and her hair turned white as ash.

"SOME SAY THE CARDS can tell the future," Stefano said. Shuffling through the deck, he came on another of the major trumps and laid it on the table.

"Do you?" Nicholas said.

The other man laughed. His eyes were lowered to the cards and his fingers stroked the edges of the deck; he loved the cards.

"Do you believe in that—in such things, astrology and the like?" Nicholas asked.

"I believe in luck," Stefano said. "If the future is determined, I don't want to know it."

He swept the cards up again and the carnival faces of the trumps disappeared inside the block of the deck. He and Nicholas were sitting opposite one another at a table in the center of the room. The walls were draped with cloth and scaffolding; the workmen had begun plastering over the old scenes only two days before and the entire house stank of lime. Even so Stefano had managed to eat two platefuls of the soup Juan had made them and a loaf of bread. Nicholas had eaten nothing. The smell and the disorder upset his stomach.

"I could love a game," Stefano said.

"I suppose you could teach me," Nicholas said, "but I am witless at games."

"Tarocco needs time to learn. Months. Years." Stefano braced his elbows wide-spread on the table. "Come down to my den, and I'll play and you can have a decent supper."

"Go where? To that taverna? I assure you, I am not hungry enough to eat in a taverna."

"Not the regular food. One of my girls cooks my dinner for me—she'll have something there, you can eat of that."

Nicholas snorted. Stefano's hands were laying out the major trumps again, the Fool, the Hanged Man, the World, painted in blue and red, and hedged around with Hebrew and Greek letters.

"I would not care to put her to any trouble."

"No trouble for her. She'll be under some soldier, if she's doing her job, and if she isn't, I'll know why."

"Do you mean she's a whore? Your girl?"

"I have three of them." Stefano's hands herded up the cards again.

"Whores? You're a pimp, among your other interests. Per Baccho, what a diverse creature." Nicholas sat back, his arm draped over the back of the chair. "Shouldn't you be there, collecting the money and arranging customers?"

Stefano made an indefinite sound in his chest. His head was tipped down but Nicholas caught the glitter of his eyes in a single, quick, resentful upward look.

Neither of them spoke for a moment. In the kitchen Juan shuffled about humming an old song.

Finally, to open the conversation again, Nicholas said, "The cards have meanings? What does this one mean?" He picked up the card called the Hanged Man.

"Reversal of fortunes," Stefano said, brusque.

"Would you like to go to the Leonine City?"

"What—to hear Mass?" Rapidly the cards slapped together, interleafing, and the Hanged Man disappeared.

"His Holiness spends the evenings rather more boisterously than that. You'll find a game of tarocco there."

"With a lot of clerks." Stefano rubbed his nose. His mouth still curled down a little at the corners, sulking.

Nicholas thought, crossly, What do I mean to him, anyway? He watched the painted faces of the cards flash together between the gambler's long arched hands. If his undignified pursuits embarrassed Stefano, he could have left Nicholas ignorant.

"I assure you," he said, "however you care to live, it's all the same to me."

"Thank you," Stefano said. "Let's go to the Vatican—if you can get us in."

"No problem there," Nicholas said. He called for Juan to fetch his coat.

The sun had just set. The stifling summer heat still hung over the streets. They walked down past the Colosseo and along the southern flank of the Campidoglio. The cats were mating in the ruins; their witchy cries and moans rose singly and in chorus from the tumbled walls. Stefano swore under his breath.

"Like voices from Hell."

Nicholas hid his smile.

The night deepened. The sky was clear and the brightest stars were already shining. The hill they were skirting turned steeper and higher. In ancient times the center of the city, it faced west, looking down the gentler slope toward the broad swampy lowland where the Colosseo was now, and the markets and gathering places and temples of the antique Romans had grown up on that side; but since the Church had put its roots in the Vatican, the city's heart now lay to the east of the hill. The main approach to the Campidoglio had shifted to the opposite side from the Forum, to the difficult slope below the Church of the Aracoeli. Nicholas and Stefano walked into the piazza there and had to swerve to avoid two files of monks just beginning their climb up the steep steps to the church.

"Clerks," Stefano said, and made a sign against the evil eye.

Nicholas put his walking stick into the other hand. He turned to watch the procession mount the harsh slope. There was something in that toiling climb, something of a symbol:

most of his Roman friends insisted that the antique world lived on in Rome, and yet the Forum lay in ruins and the living city struggled up to the ancient Capitol by this cliff of steps. He turned back to Stefano.

"Are there no clerks in Perugia?"

"My family did not live in Perugia, actually—we lived outside, in San Marco. You've never heard of it?"

"There are a dozen San Marcos."

"It was very small, this one. Smaller still, since the plague came by."

"Is that why you came to Rome?"

They were crossing the piazza toward the Corso, where the Barbary horses ran at Carnival. The pavement began where the street met the piazza. Lanterns shone on the broad front of the Venetian palace on the left.

"I went to Perugia first," said Stefano. "But there are Baglioni there by the score, I mattered for nothing."

"Your family?"

"No, they are all dead. All save my father and I."

In Rome, what did he matter? He kept three women busy, and spread money from hand to hand over the gambling table; he kept the provisioners busy. It was a city of foreigners.

Nicholas and Stefano walked along the front of the palace of the Venetian Pope, the ground floor let out to shops and dealers. Through one window came the ranting voice of a woman arguing with someone who never answered.

"So I came here," Stefano said loudly. "And I've done well enough for myself."

"Very well," Nicholas said. "When may I expect my one hundred crowns returned?"

"As soon as I have them."

"How often in the past have you had one hundred crowns all at one time?"

Stefano thrust out his lower lip. He walked with a swinging countryman's stride. "I've had more than one thousand pass through my hands at a single night's gaming."

"Did any of it stick?"

Stefano gave him a sideways angry look. Nicholas swiveled his head away. He felt safely above Stefano.

They turned off the Corso and followed the dark crooked streets toward the bridge over the Tiber. It was the hour of Vespers and every church they passed gave forth the singing of monks.

After they had gone a little way, Stefano said, "Besides, you seem to have enough money now. I thought you said the plasterers would not work in your house until you paid them?"

Nicholas flexed his shoulders under his light coat. "My fortunes come and go, like everyone else's." In truth, he had spent his last savings on the work to be done; the plasterers would do no more than cover up the old work.

There were lovers meeting at the bridge. The Tiber swept by, carrying patches of dirty foam in its current. Nicholas and Stefano, no longer speaking, crossed over the bridge and followed the curving street toward the palace of the Vatican.

The watch was changing; at the gate were two sets of guards with pikes. Nicholas gave his name to each officer in turn and each in turn solemnly referred to lists and waved him in. With Stefano a half-step behind him he went through the courtyard and passed beneath an arch into the garden.

They stopped. The garden was hung around with lanterns that bobbed in the fitful summer wind; the light confused more than it revealed. At first Nicholas could not separate the people from the shadows, dancing over the grass. Musicians played at the far end of the garden, out where the flowers were blooming, but the wind toyed with the music too, so that now it was clear and bright, and then the sound faded to a tuneless mutter.

Stefano said, "It's too dark here to play cards."

Nicholas started off again across the grass. He skirted a dozen girls forming a line to dance in. Ahead, lights in the windows picked out the stone wall of the palace, two stories high. Someone was lowering a basket from one of the upper-story windows, while a man in black and white livery waited on the walk below with a bottle of wine in each hand. Nicholas and Stefano passed him and went on down a gravel walk.

They walked under a trellis overhung with grapevines. A door stood open, midway through, and Nicholas went in.

"You do know the place well," Stefano said.

"I've been coming here for twenty years."

He did not add that he had seen more of the Vatican in the past three months than in all those twenty years. For those three months, although nothing important yet had come of it, he had served Cesare Borgia. But now Valentino was away in Naples, and Rome was a very dull place.

They went through a darkened audience room to a stair and climbed into a swelling clamor of voices and laughter. There was no one in the room at the top of the stairs save a drunken man snoring in a chair, but the next room was crowded with people cheering and passing a cup from hand to hand. In the corner, directly under the lamp, three men were hunched over a table, playing tarocco. Stefano left Nicholas at once to go watch.

Nicholas strolled off through the crowded rooms. Nearly all these folk were young, friends of Valentino and his sister. They were all drunken. No one seemed to mind the breathless heat. Nicholas passed among them without drawing a glance or a word.

In the central room of the suite he found Pope Alexander himself, with his mistress Giulia on his knee. Before he saw the Pope, he heard the old man's hearty laugh. Alexander had both arms around his lady's waist, and she was feeding him bits of cheese on a fork. Nicholas watched from the threshold, loath to go nearer and force the old man to recognize him. He knew Alexander saw him. The Pope's embroidered red gown was open down the breast, the skirt tucked up over his widespread knees; he looked like nothing more than a well-off Spanish peasant doing his best to live out the heat.

"Nicholas."

He turned. Angela Borgia slithered around to his side and twined her arm through his. Beneath her painted smile her lips curved in a true one.

"You are exactly the man we want to see. Come with me."

"We, Madonna?"

"My cousin. Come along, Nicholas."

He followed her off through the maze of little rooms behind the audience chamber; most of these rooms were dark, and there seemed to be no people in them, but he did not look closely into the shadows. Angela pressed herself against Nicholas's side and stroked his ribs with her fingers. In the dark once she breathed hotly in his ear.

"Madonna," he said, "are you ill? Let me send for your physician."

She grunted and her grip on his arm loosened.

"Lucrezia," she called, "see whom I have brought. He will solve our problem."

They went into a sitting room, set around with pieces of statuary on pedestals and on their own feet. At the far end of the room, Lucrezia Borgia put down a book and rose from her chair.

"Messer Dawson."

Nicholas performed his most elaborate bow. "Madonna, I am your lifelong servant."

Angela whispered something into Lucrezia's ear. Nicholas stood back, admiring the contrast of the two heads set together, one black-haired and the other fair. They both began to laugh, and Lucrezia tossed her head back.

"I don't believe you." She put out her hand to Nicholas. "Here, Messer Dawson, before she turns me giddy—"

She led him to a statue against the wall, which was draped in heavy red velvet to set off the piece of marble. The figure, half-lifesize, was a copy of an antique Hercules.

"Who is this?" Lucrezia asked him.

Nicholas cleared his throat. "That is Hercules, Madonna."

Lucrezia was smiling at him, pleased. Angela pushed against his other side. Her perfume did not cover the volatile female odor of her body. "Are you sure?" she said. "It has no inscription."

"The club, Madonna. The lion skin." Nicholas circled the statue, drawn to it. "It's a fine piece of work, too."

"Yes," Lucrezia said. "I love it. He seems about to move. So natural."

"How old is it?" Angela asked. "Is it antique?"

Nicholas shook his head. Lucrezia was still beside him, following him around the statue. He pointed out to her how the workman had shaped the statue's side in heavy ridges of muscle. "See how he has suggested a man of middle years? A young man's muscles are more flexible than this, smoother."

Angela giggled. "You would know."

"You are right," Lucrezia said, and smiled at him again.

"In your service, Madonna."

Angela came at him again, her arm snaking through the crook of his own arm. Nicholas paid no attention. Moving around the statue had brought him within view of an open door on the far side of the room and through it he saw Miguelito da Corella, slumped in a great chair.

"Why don't you think it's old, love?" Angela touched his chest.

Nicholas was watching Miguelito. All summer Valentino had been with the French in Naples; but Miguelito never left his master's side. Therefore Valentino was in Rome again.

"Tell us, Nicholas," Lucrezia was saying; a peevish whine harshened her voice. Perhaps she had smiled and he had not noticed.

"Madonna." He searched back for the subject of the talk.

Turning his gaze on the statue again, he touched the figure's hip, where the marble was stained brown. "Oh, it seems old—it's been cleverly forged, there are dozens such sold every year. But the marble is wrong, and the antiquing is rather exaggerated, you see—" he touched the figure's shoulder, overdarkened where the edge of the lion skin sheltered it. He looked again through the open door to Miguelito. All summer he had found himself explaining the obvious to the ignorant, while the great work he had thought he might have a hand in went on elsewhere, without him.

"It's only my opinion, Madonna. Perhaps it is old, and I am wrong. Has my lord Cesare been in Rome for many days?"

"Just this morning," Angela said.

"He and my father are hard at work deciding whom I am to be sold to next," Lucrezia said. "More giving and taking, you see." She nodded to him with emphasis over the words.

"Hush," Angela said.

"Although if I were a bachelor," Lucrezia said, fondling the statue, "I would think twice before I bound myself to me, in view of the fate of my two previous husbands. Oh, be quiet, Angela. He knows. Everybody in Rome knows everything I do and a hundred things I've never dared to do."

"No," Nicholas said, "nor anyone else, Madonna."

"Bah." Angela pushed at him; her lower lip protruded, striped with lip paint. "He is more interested in that butcher Miguelito than in us." She minced away, her shoes clacking on the floor.

"I'm sorry," Lucrezia said. "We use your time—it's from selfish ignorance, Messer Dawson—nothing worse."

Surprised, he looked her in the face and saw she meant that. He wanted her to smile again, and he cast about for a witticism, but she was turning away. She called, "Angela," and her cousin trailed after her through the gallery of statues. Nicholas went to the open doorway.

Miguelito looked asleep. His head was tipped forward on his chest. He wore riding clothes; his boots were scuffed. Nicholas stood there a moment, drawn to his aloneness. Everyone hated Miguelito, just as everyone ignored Nicholas.

He was about to go when Miguelito raised his head. Their eyes met. Nicholas went into the room.

"Hello, Messer Mouse," Miguelito said, in a drowsy voice. "Were you looking for me?"

A small round table stood beside his chair, and on the far side, another chair; Nicholas sat down in it. He was uncertain what to say. Miguelito's head dropped backward onto the padded shoulder of the chair.

"What do you want to know? How we fared in Naples?"

"That's common knowledge," Nicholas said. "From the moment Capua fell, there was no doubt anyway, was there?"

"None at all, even before," Miguelito said dreamily. "Mene Tekel Upharsin. Except that this kingdom was divided between the French and the Spanish."

"Did you fight at Capua?"

"That farce?"

"The stories were rather more colorful than believable. Is it true that Valentino sorted through the female prisoners and kept the forty most beautiful for himself?"

Miguelito laughed, an unpleasant growling in his throat. "There are not forty beautiful women in Capua." He raised his head again, facing Nicholas. "It was bloody, boring work, Messer Mouse. Be thankful you are no soldier."

"Who has given me the unappealing name?"

"My master. 'The little mouse, who nibbles all the cheese.' He says you know everything that happens in Rome."

"Would that I did."

"I overheard you adding to your knowledge, in there with the ladies. What if he had taken the women? Would that offend you?"

"Rome feeds on scandals. It's an offense not to provide them."

Miguelito was leaning toward him over the arm of his chair. The lamp on the far wall threw his shadow over the little table top.

"All creatures are bound in the chains of nature. All save man. So says my master. Only man may choose what he will be. Therefore it behooves a man to live beyond all limits, however reasonable or natural they seem." Miguelito's black eyes gleamed. "Do you understand?"

"I try," Nicholas said. "Do you customarily indulge in Italian philosophies? I thought you disliked Italians."

"I obey my master." Miguelito let his head fall back onto the chair. "Go away, mouse. I am very tired."

Nicholas sat still, watching the other man compose himself and shut his eyes. Miguelito like all actors needed his audience. After a long silence Nicholas rose and went out to the room full of statues.

"Nicholas! There you are."

In the gallery Angela swooped at him. She had Stefano by the hand.

"I found this lovely fellow looking for you. You should not leave him alone, love, really, not here."

Stefano put out his free hand. "I need some money. Not much. I left my purse at your house."

Nicholas slid his hand into his wallet. Angela leaned against Stefano's side, her fingers pressing and pulling on his arm. He paid no heed to her at all. Nicholas gave him the wallet.

"Come watch," Stefano said.

"I will," Nicholas said. "Madonna, you will join us?"

He glanced back through the open door. Miguelito's eyes were open, watching. Nicholas went away amused.

STEFANO SAT DOWN to play cards with the men in the sala grande. Angela was devoting herself to him, playing with his hair and simpering into his ears; Nicholas went off to the nearest window to breathe cool air. The room was full of drunken dancers, swaying to the sound of laughter, since there was no music. A page brought Nicholas a glass of wine. He watched Stefano play cards. The lamplight shone on his face and the faces of the four men he was gaming with; only Stefano was smiling.

After a few turns of the cards, Stefano swept half the money stacked before him into Nicholas's purse and gave it to Angela. She brought it to him, glowing.

"What a beauty," she said, and stuck her tongue out.

He took the purse, turning away from her, disgusted.

The dancers swayed and bobbed in the center of the room, like weeds under the ocean, their feet hardly moving. In the darker corners men and women were joined in lascivious embraces. There was wine spilled on the floor. Nicholas kept his nose turned to the fresh air coming through the window beside him; he laid his hand on the sill. The wine he was drinking was very strong and he resolved to have no more of it. The light fooled his eyes. He thought he saw winking eyes watching all around him but when he looked straight he saw only the reflection of the lamplight on the shining surfaces of the room, the golden cups, the jewels, the puddled wine on the floor. He strangled down a yawn.

A leopard stalked into the room.

Sluggish from the wine, he needed a moment even to become alarmed. A woman gasped. It was real; it was huge. It paced slowly forward through the room, its broad head turning from side to side. The lamplight struck a gleam from its golden collar.

No one moved. The dancers, suspended in their drunken rhythm, stood goggling at the leopard as it passed among them. Its long body hung supply from the frames of its shoulders and hips; it seemed about to move in every direction at once. Nicholas put his other hand on the windowsill and without moving his head looked quickly out. The drop was too far, he could not escape that way. The beast passed him, and its long tail flicked and the fur grazed his knee.

With a scream a woman wheeled and bolted for the door. The cat recoiled at the sound; its head like an arrowhead swung to point at the running figure in her billows of skirts, and everyone else in the room broke and fled. Nicholas alone did not move, having nowhere to go. Stefano shot up from his chair, gripped Angela Borgia's arm, and swung her around behind him into a corner. In the two doorways the screaming dancers fought to get through and clogged the way out with their bodies. The leopard crouched and leapt on them.

Nicholas cried out. The cat landed in the midst of the people; Nicholas saw the broad paws stroke down a puffed sleeve and slash it into fifths, the white padding gushing out like guts. The shrieks hurt his ears. The people fled back into the room and the leopard turned and sprang again.

"Nicholas!"

The animal brought down a woman, rolling on the floor.

"Nicholas!" Stefano shouted into his ear, and pulled him.

He could not move. Through the door a tall man came, laughing, and whistled.

The cat, straddling the woman on the floor, lifted its head and looked around. Behind him, the tall man advanced a few steps and stopped; a leash dangled coiled in his hand. It was Valentino. The screaming stopped. In the sudden calm everyone heard Valentino say, "That's enough, now. Sit."

Nicholas let out his breath in a sigh. Valentino could deal with it. Indeed, the cat was moving away from the sobbing woman, its long tail trailing over her, and it went up by Valentino's side and tucked its hindlegs under it and sat. The big man fondled it. Nicholas thought he saw the cat lick the man's hand.

Stefano still clutched his arm; Nicholas moved a little, and Stefano let him go. Nicholas looked around at him. "Are you saving me?" His sleeve was rumpled and he stroked it smooth

again. Valentino with the leopard was gone. All the tension
left the room with him, and the frozen folk along the walls
sighed and slumped and went over to inspect the woman
crying in the middle of the floor.

"Did he do that on purpose?" Stefano asked. "Turn the cat
on us?"

Nicholas had the same suspicion, and he turned away,
back to the window, to the darkness and the cool air. Down
below him a door opened in a wedge of light and let out
the golden-haired Valentino and his golden hunting cat.
The beast sprang forward across the grass and the man ran
lightly after it.

Stefano had gone back to his card game; Nicholas turned
his head enough to watch him. Like everyone else, the other
players were moving restlessly around the room and talking
over the incident. Angela Borgia, in the corner, was staring
at Stefano with eyes that glowed unpleasantly. Nicholas
looked out the window again. Far out there in the darkness
the man running and the beast were two shadows in passage over the grass.

On the windowsill by his hand a half-full glass of wine
still stood. He reached for it with an untoward haste and
poured the liquor down his throat.

The racket of talk behind him swelled to a cacophony. The
woman was unhurt; the others were jabbering about the
leopard, mostly nonsense, foolish things they repeated over
and over. "Did you see that? Did you see that?" The smell
still lingered in the room of the excitement, a taint of sweat,
souring all the perfumes. Stefano and Angela Borgia were
gone.

Nicholas took his glass off in search of more wine; he
found it in a carafe on the table across the room, under the
lamp. His hands were trembling. Nothing like this had ever
happened to him before.

Of course it had not really happened to him at all. He had
watched, only. He was that sort of man. His life was one

thing observed after another; he lived at a window, looking in. He drank a full glass of the wine in a few swallows, unable to take his mind from the memory of the man and the leopard racing across the grass.

Stefano came in again, through the far door; his coat was open and his eyelids drooped. He pulled out his chair at the gaming table and sat in it and picked the cards up.

Nicholas filled his glass once more. He walked back across the room to the window where the air was markedly cooler and sweeter. The woman whom the cat had struck was propped up on the couch among three or four courtiers who plied her with wine and draughts.

At the gaming table the other players were one by one taking their places. Stefano shuffled the cards.

Angela had returned, her hair mussed, looking angry. She crossed the room to Nicholas's side. Her teeth were set together like a cage over her tongue, and she spoke through them.

"You should have warned me."

"Warned you about what, Madonna?"

She jerked her head around and with one hand raked back her heavy shining hair. A huge gold earring dangled from one ear but the other was bare.

Nicholas laughed; he was too drunk with the wine to stop himself, or even to want to, and he shook his head at her. "Someone will give you another pair."

"They are a gift from a very important man," she said. She tossed her head violently so that her hair covered her ears again. "Get it back for me, Nicholas."

Behind him he heard the slap of the cards on the table. He said, "What will that win me?"

He saw her hand move but in his wine-haze he was too slow to dodge. Her palm cracked across his cheek. She marched away from him across the room to the door. The door slammed behind her. Everyone turned to look.

Nicholas's cheek burned and he laid his hand over it. He

glanced across his shoulder at Stefano. His lover's gaze was turned on him, and when their eyes met, Stefano smiled, broad and merry. Nicholas grunted. He reached for his glass of wine again.

"THE BORGIAS' NEXT AMBITION," Nicholas wrote, "is to marry off the Pope's daughter, the princess Lucrezia, to her third husband. Although any sensible man would abhor such an offer, it is believed here that His Holiness and Duke Valentino have settled on the heir of the Duke of Ferrara to warm the bed of the notorious princess."

Actually Bruni did not believe that; Bruni as usual refused to commit himself until the choice was obvious to everybody.

"Why the Borgias should desire an alliance with the Estensi, no one can misguess, since the duchy of Ferrara borders on the Romagna; and Alfonso d'Este, the proposed spouse, is an expert in the forging and handling in the field of the new artillery; the mystery in the scheme derives from the question of why the Duke of Ferrara, whose house is accustomed to marry only into the purest and most noble lineages, should agree to bestow his eldest son and heir in marriage on a lady who, while not yet twenty years of age, has been quit of two husbands already, under the most unsavory circumstances, and who has, if gossip may be believed, filled the interstices with countless lovers."

Nicholas dipped his pen into the ink. He was proud of that sentence; no one familiar with Bruni's style would believe anyone else had written it. In spite of its length, its meaning was rather too clear, but that Nicholas could not help, since unlike Bruni he intended to be understood.

"It has been remarked, indeed, that since the negotiations with Ferrara began, the princess and her court have observed an utter propriety, which ought to surprise no one, since the past summer witnessed such extraordinary and shocking events in the Vatican that as far away as Germany the pamphleteers have been moved to righteous indignation that such behavior should take place in the residence of the Vicar of Christ."

He sat back, chewing his lip, while he hunted through his mind for some choice libel. Ever since he had found out that the Borgias kept a spy in the Florentine offices, he had been trying one way and then another to discover him. Nothing so far had served. Of late he had been salting his dispatches with scurrilous remarks and gossip about Valentino's family. Alexander laughed at slander but Valentino heated violently at it. Every time Nicholas saw the Borgia prince, he watched him keenly for any sign that Valentino knew of the backbiting in the dispatches; if he did, then his spy had to be in the chancery offices in Florence herself.

He went on, "In spite of this, I—"

There was a sharp rap on his door. "Messer Nicholas, the courier is here."

He left his desk and the letter and went down to the workroom.

THROUGHOUT THE END of the summer, when the heat was at its worst and the damp unhealthy air of Rome hummed with insects, Nicholas was overwhelmed with work. Besides his usual duties at the legation, Bruni piled him up with other matters: the Signory required certain information, or wished a summary of old knowledge; everything had to be done at once. The Papal datary was still trying to force someone to pay a fee for the Pope's kindness in releasing Caterina Sforza, and Nicholas met with him every few weeks to discuss and deny any responsibility for Florence. The Borgias also insisted on his time, dragging him here and there over Rome on errands of no real importance, except to show him who led him.

They paid him better than the Signory; more promptly, too.

He could not rely on the other members of the delegation, even Bruni, to perform the ordinary tasks of day-to-day work. Without him constantly at their backs the scribes left out whole pages of documents, the aides spent their time at public gatherings flirting with pretty women rather than attending the great, and Bruni submerged himself in a book of poetry or a novel rather than read bad news. There was nothing Nicholas could do about Bruni. The others he harassed and scolded until even to him his voice sounded shrill as a witch's, and then, as if in revenge, his voice disappeared altogether.

He came in to the legation offices in the morning, just after six o'clock, and found Bruni's junior aide Ugo loitering in the courtyard. Nicholas crossed the flagstone yard toward the door into the building. Ugo moved to intercept him.

"Good morning, Messer Nicholas—may I ask how your throat is this morning?"

Nicholas frowned at him. He whispered, "No better," and pushed by him to the stairs.

"Have you tried lemon and honey?" Ugo bounded after him into the building, still cool from the night's relief. "An old remedy of my nurse's. It always works for me."

Nicholas croaked, "A pox on your nurse." He climbed the narrow turning stair to the workroom. Here already the sun penetrated. The place smelled of stale sweat. A hundred flies clung to the white rims of the windows. Nicholas hung up his coat and walking stick. There was no one else here but him and Ugo, who was following after him faithfully.

"I want you to know, Messer Nicholas," the young man said, "that I, if no one else—" he pressed his hand to his breast—"understand how intolerable you must find your present situation."

Nicholas swiveled his head around to fix Ugo with a stare, amazed at such innocence. It was as if the young man had said simply, "I am the spy." As soon as that thought entered his mind, he held it off, doubting; everything had two mean-ings. Perhaps the remark was innocent. He said something in a painful whisper and turned away.

Still Ugo nagged after him. "If there is anything I can do—"

At the threshold to the corridor, Nicholas wheeled around, one hand out to fend Ugo off. "Yes—you can stop making me talk and get to work on the Spanish dispatches." He walked into the corridor.

"Messer Nicholas—I was hoping—"

He stopped and turned again, his voice echoing in his throat.

"I was hoping to take leave, until the next week."

"No!"

"I have not—"

"No!" Nicholas stamped away down the corridor. This time Ugo let him go.

IN THE LATE AFTERNOON, when Nicholas returned to the delegation, Bruni was on the loggia watering the palms. Nicholas stood in the archway. Bruni called, "Oh, inciden-tally, young Ugo will be gone the rest of the week."

Nicholas stiffened.

"He has some family business to attend to," Bruni said.

His back to Nicholas, he was bending over a pot with his pitcher of water; Nicholas could see only his legs and back-side. A murderous desire came over him to knock Bruni's head into the palm and kick his backside. At the same time he would say, "I am leaving." The urge like another man inside him yearned and yearned but was a coward. At length Nicholas went back into the workroom and down the corri-dor to his chamber.

His desk was heaped with work. He thrust it all aside and sat down and buried his head in his folded arms. It was absurd; he was near tears, and over nothing more than an order reversed by a superior. That happened to him every day.

He sucked in his breath, sitting up, lightheaded, with an evil in his stomach. He laughed at himself. When the Borgias had blackmailed him into their service he had imagined his life would change somehow. Like the rest of humankind he sweated his days out in routine and detail, all held together by the foolish hope that someday everything would change, something would happen; and he had supposed that Valentino's magic would transform him, too, into a creature of power.

He stroked his sweating hands together. The awful heat filled him with gloom. He felt sick. He laughed again. He was prey; men like him were born to be prey; just because Valentino preyed on him, would he become a predator too? His thoughts whirled. It was the heat that made him sick. The heat and work made him brain-sick.

Yet it was true that in Valentino he had a chance to change his fortunes. It would not happen if he waited for the Borgia prince to come to him asking for his help.

He pressed his hands to his cheeks. Within a few weeks the heat would break, and the delicious autumn would make Rome livable again. Gradually he became aware of something climbing on his ankle.

He sprang out of his chair like an Indian dancer. Landing on the threshold, he shook his leg madly in the air, his heart racing, until he saw the spider lying on its back on the floor a few feet away, wiggling its hairy black legs in the air. He put his foot down. The spider's fangs were like tusks. He took off one shoe and hammered the spider into a puddle on the tile.

"Nicholas," Bruni said, behind him, "whatever are you doing?"

"Tarantula," Nicholas said. His voice wheezed.

The spider's remains stank. He went around the mess to

open the window as wide as he could. Bruni watched him from just outside the door, smiling.

"See how your hands shake."

Nicholas said nothing, his voice exhausted.

He raked the papers off his desk into a drawer and locked it. "I'm going home."

"Oh, now, Nicholas, no need for panic," Bruni said sharply. "It's hours yet before the end of the day."

"I'm going home." Nicholas brushed by his chief and went on down the corridor.

HE DID NOT GO HOME. Instead he walked across the city to the Ponte Sisto, the bridge that led to the Trastevere, where there was a mapmaker.

The shop was in a crowded lane in the shadow of Santa Cecilia. When Nicholas entered, someone else was occupying the mapmaker's attention. Nicholas went to the side of the narrow room, whose walls were built up with shelves from floor to ceiling, each shelf holding a roll of paper.

The smell of ink reminded him of the scriptorium in the monastery where he had grown up, where old Brother Leo had taught him to write the monk's hand. Once, coming cheaply on a fine edition of the gospels, Nicholas had sent it anonymously to the monks for their library. Of course Leo had been dead then for years. He wondered if the book had ever reached them. Strange, the power of the senses; the mere smell of ink opened so many old rooms. He wondered if they might guess, somehow, that the book had come from him.

On a shelf he found a map tagged *Donation of Constantine*. When he opened it out he saw the outlines of the states of central Italy. He rolled it up again and waited for the shopkeeper to finish his business with the other man.

Leaving the shop, he started home again, the map tucked like a loaf of bread under his arm. Evening had come. The sky was dark blue, still luminous, but here and there picked out with stars. The rims of the horizon, still pink and orange with the sunset, were made ragged with trees, the spikes of cypress, the flat umbrellas of the pines, and the ragged puffs of palms. In the east, swollen and yellow, the moon was rising like an alien face.

Nicholas hurried back toward the bridge. He did not like walking after dark in this quarter. The twilight confused his eyes. He passed a boy with a long stick, herding home a cow with a bell jangling around her neck. The sound followed him, fading slowly. He smelled cow dung. Small hope he would reach home with his shoes clean. On his left the moonlight glittered on pools of still water in a marshy meadow.

On the bridge, he came face to face with Stefano.

"What are you doing here?" Stefano said. "Were you looking for me?"

Nicholas did not deny it. They stood by the railing and exchanged the usual remarks. Finally Nicholas said, "Will you walk me home? You know this area swarms with thieves."

Stefano put his head back and laughed. He leaned on his elbow on the railing of the bridge. "Yes, if you want. Of course."

A passer-by called, "Eh, Bello!" Stefano waved his hand languidly in answer.

Nicholas set off across the bridge. It was not below this bridge, but nearby, that he and Stefano had first met.

"What are you doing here, anyway?" Stefano asked, falling in beside him as he walked. "I thought you stayed at your work until nine or so."

"Usually," Nicholas said.

"Your voice seems better, at least."

"Not much better."

He told his lover of the tarantula. That led him backward

to Bruni's remarks and to Bruni's letting Ugo take leave and to the amount of work Nicholas was expected to accomplish.

"They would not drive you if you were not the only one who could manage it all," Stefano said, and later, "This Bruni seems a perfect ass."

"He is," Nicholas said.

They were walking by the Colosseo. The night was deepening around them, and the smoke of cooking fires and the sound of voices came from the hovels that were crowded along the lower wall of the ruin. There had been several cases of plague in the wretched huts; Nicholas swerved wide around the place and held his head turned to keep from breathing the poisonous air.

"What is that?" Stefano asked.

"Oh—this? A map."

"A map? Are you sailing somewhere?"

Nicholas prepared a lie, but Stefano waved one hand at him and said, "If it is work, don't tell me."

They walked up the dark lane toward Nicholas's gate and passed through the garden. Juan opened the door of the house for them.

Nicholas put the map on the table by the door and shed his coat. Stefano was already across the room, at the sideboard. The sound reached Nicholas of wine splashing into a glass. That irritated him, as it always did, Stefano doing here whatever pleased him, Stefano acting master of the house. His gaze fell to the map again.

"Bring me a glass," he said, and unrolled the map.

The chart was done in a patchwork of blues and greens and yellows, with the names of the states in heavy black letters. Nicholas, who left Rome as seldom as possible, found the Romagna with some difficulty; he had imagined it much nearer Rome. He saw at once why the Borgias were hot to ally with Ferrara, which stood between the heart of the Papal States and Venice, the Pope's old enemy.

"I should have looked at this much sooner." He sat down in his chair with the map on his knees. Stefano brought him the wine; Nicholas did not look up.

He ticked off the cities that Valentino had already taken. There was art to his campaigning; he had concentrated his attack so far on the cities along the Via Emilia. From his readings in Xenophon Nicholas knew the importance of lines of communication in warfare. The Borgias had been systematic in their attack on the Romagna. Yet several cities and strongholds remained outside their control.

To Nicholas, Urbino stood out; it was closer to Rome than the others and controlled the approaches to the heart of the Romagna. He wondered why it had gone untaken.

Juan was shuffling his feet behind Nicholas's chair. He wanted to bring in the meal. Nicholas shook his head.

"Not now. I'm not hungry."

"I am," Stefano called.

Juan coughed; Nicholas waggled his hand to him to go away. He circled Urbino with his forefinger. That was the city of Federigo da Montefeltro, the great condottiere of the previous generation, who had built a huge palace there. Federigo's son ruled it now. Guidobaldo. Scraps of information about Guidobaldo jumped up from his memory. Married to a sister of the Marquis of Mantua, they had no children, and a nephew of tender age was his heir. A quiet man, Guidobaldo kept a court of scholars and philosophers, where his wife shone like a jewel.

"No, no," Stefano was saying. "Here. On the table."

Nicholas glanced up. With his hand Stefano guided old Juan about. The old man put down a platter on the table Stefano indicated. He was serving Stefano with Nicholas's dish, with Nicholas's dinner. They were putting hot dishes down on the olivewood table, whose beeswax finish would be ruined.

Stefano pulled his chair up to the table, sat, rubbed his hands together, his face alight with appetite. Juan waited beside his chair. Juan loved having someone to wait on. Stefano shook out the white napkin and laid it on his knees.

"Nicholas." He looked over at Nicholas. "What is it?"

Nicholas cleared his throat. After all, he had sent Juan away.

He said, "Have you ever been to Urbino?"

"Never."

Nicholas turned back to the map.

UGO CAME BACK the following Monday to his duties at the legation. Nicholas watched him narrowly for two days after that. He was sure now that Ugo was the spy who had betrayed him to the Borgias. Only a few days before, Valentino had sent Nicholas a fat purse and a letter full of fair words thanking him for the trivial work he had done; therefore Valentino could not know the calumnies with which Nicholas packed his dispatches to the Signory. Whoever the spy was, then, he knew only that the dispatches were forged over Bruni's signature. Ugo could know that.

Nicholas gave twenty carlini to Ugo's manservant. "Where did your master spend his leave-time?"

The manservant slid his hand with the money into his purse and did not remove it. "I shall tell him that you asked, Ser Niccolo."

"Do."

"He has a light o' love," the manservant said.

"Boy or girl?"

Without humor the servant laughed in his face. "A girl." He walked away across the paving stones of the courtyard.

"I HAVE READ YOUR REPORT on the Romagna," Bruni said. "Only a summary, of course, nothing new, but shrewdly said, Nicholas."

"Thank you," Nicholas replied. He was proud of the report.

"I saw a map. Somehow in that I saw the entire problem in a new way."

"Fairly obvious, you must understand." Bruni rubbed his nose. They were in his private chamber, the ambassador, his coat off, sitting behind his desk and Nicholas standing before it. The ambassador stroked his finger briskly up and down his nose.

"Now, young Ugo has come to me with stories that you are harassing him."

So that occasioned the praise. Nicholas lost his pride. He met Bruni's eyes exactly, wanting to appear truthful. He said, "I, Excellency?"

"He says that you have had him followed at night, that you heap him with trivial work and complain about everything he does."

"Excellency," Nicholas said, "I have done nothing with the intent of harassing him. He has been slack of late. We are all overworked."

"I understand that. To be candid, I cannot imagine it of you. Then Ugo is slacking, you think?"

"He is a lazy daydreamer," Nicholas said.

"You are too harsh with him. As you said, we are all heavily worked these days. I don't take his complaints seriously. It's the quarter phase of the moon, many men are garrulous now."

Nicholas raised his head, startled. "Excellency, the moon is full."

"In quarter phase."

"Excellency, I remarked it especially, last night, walking home."

"We shall see." Bruni reached for a leather-bound book on the left-hand side of his desk. He flipped through the pages and laid the book down open before him. "No, you are wrong, it is the third quarter phase."

"Excellency, I saw it last night myself."

"You see here." Unruffled, Bruni stressed a line in the book with his fingernail. He shut the book firmly and laid it where it had been on the corner of his desk. "I do not lose track of such things."

"Yes, Excellency," Nicholas said.

"As for young Ugo, perhaps we should send him back to Florence for a few months."

"Excellency, we need someone of his rank for so many things."

"Oh, we can bring in someone else." Bruni laced his fingers together. "The new elections in Florence will make quite the difference."

"Yes, Excellency," Nicholas said, pleased.

IN THE FIRST COLD WEATHER of the fall, part of the Colosseo collapsed. Several people were buried in their huts under the rubble. Nicholas went down to stand in the crowd that watched and prayed and moaned while other folk dug away the moldering limestone and rock.

Beside him old Juan wrapped himself in his shawl against the chill. The lowering gray skies made everyone shiver. Nicholas hunched his shoulders under his coat and thrust his hands into his sleeves.

"It was the weather that caused it," he said, speaking to Juan in Spanish. "They lit their fires too high, and the sharp heat on one side and the cold on the other burst the stones."

Juan was praying to his favorite manifestations of the Virgin. He shifted from foot to foot, mumbling into his knotted shawl.

Just before dark, the diggers uncovered several bodies. The crowd screamed in pity. Nicholas shook his head, turning, ready to go, but Juan was poised on his toes, intent. The diggers lifted the bodies of a woman, an old woman, and two small children out of the debris and stretched them out in the street.

Juan began to weep. He went down on his knees and sobbed and prayed, lost in emotion. Nicholas hovered near him, uncertain. The old man's grief confused him. It was distasteful to him. The wailing of the crowd struck his ears like the discordant sounds of animals. Many of them knelt around Juan and prayed for the dead. Above them the huge ruined ampitheater's wall stood against the evening sky. Vines and shrubs festooned it. Gaping holes pierced it. Who knew when more of the ruin might free itself from that web of green vines and roots and ancient mortar? Nicholas pulled on the old servant's shoulder. Juan was beyond his reach, deep in a half-hysterical prayer. Nicholas went home.

"THEY ARE SO LITTLE INCLINED to the match," the Pope said, "that I am minded to let the matter drop."

"Let the matter drop!" On the far side of the room Valentino wheeled to face his father. The sunlit window behind him framed his golden head. His voice was strident with high feeling. "Before I let drop such an insult to my sister, I will take an army to Ferrara and make him marry her on his knees."

"And so doing secure her perfect married happiness," the Pope said.

Nicholas was watching from a place near the door; he knew they saw him, although they went on as if they were alone. Valentino had summoned him here; they would find some use for him in time.

Alexander said, "I will not send my daughter to a family that despises her." He was sitting on a little chair, which he overlapped on either side. His feet in embroidered shoes were set primly together and he clasped his hands on his lap.

Valentino stalked across the room again. "I will not allow them to refuse her. She who is as kind and sweet and full of loving life—"

It was early in the day for him to be about; he was inclined to sleep the day through and conduct his business at night. He was making sleepwalkers of half the diplomats in Rome.

Alexander was saying, "What sort of life will she have in an alien city, with people who detest her?" Alexander raised his hands a little from his lap. "I could force them to accept her, but when I am dead, what reason will they have to treat her well?"

"I will protect her," Valentino cried. He walked around in front of his father, face to face with him. "I will keep them well in hand!"

He thrust out his arm to point at Nicholas. "Messer Mouse —we wish—*I* wish my sister to marry Alfonso d'Este. Tell me how I may have my will of that family."

Called suddenly to answer, Nicholas lost his wits; his jaw fell open. He could remember nothing of the Estensi of Ferrara. The Borgias were staring at him. Their eyes were extraordinarily alike, father's and son's, although the son's were pale and the father's black.

"Well?" Alexander said.

"They need money," Nicholas said.

"Sweet Jesus!" Valentino exploded, and he strode away across the room again. "Who in Italy does not?" At the window he spun around to stare back across the room at Nicholas.

Alexander's mouth curled down, pensive, and he put his head to one side.

"Every man has his secret weakness," Valentino said, walking back toward Nicholas. His voice was crisp. "Tell me Ferrara's."

Nicholas said again, "Money."

"Bah." Valentino dismissed him with a sharp gesture of his hand and walked away again in his ceaseless pacing.

"By your leave," Nicholas muttered.

Alexander said mildly, "Ah, well, perhaps I am only a poor old father who wants an excuse to keep his only daughter by him. Go, Nicholas."

While Nicholas was crossing the empty hall toward the stairs, the little page Piccolo who served Angela Borgia met him and took him away across the palace to a balcony, where Lucrezia Borgia and her cousin were playing tarocco in the golden October sunlight. When Nicholas appeared, the Pope's daughter put her cards down on the table between the women.

"Angela," she said, "I am hungry. Go see if they are bringing us our supper yet."

Angela shrieked. "And leave you here alone with this notorious rake?"

Nicholas shook his head once, annoyed. He aimed his gaze away from Angela, looking over the railing of the balcony. South-facing, it was sheltered from the wind, and the sunlight made it balmy. Angela, with another piercing, mocking scream, took herself out of the room, her page at her heels.

Lucrezia pushed the table away. Her shoes lay on the floor, and her legs were curled up under her as she sat in the cushioned chair, but while she talked to Nicholas she put her bare feet down and groped with her toes for the shoes. She said, "My brother sent for you over this courtship?"

"Madonna," Nicholas said.

"What do you think of it, Nicholas? Will I go to Ferrara?"

Nicholas went nearer the open edge of the balcony. The keen air cooled his face. "Madonna, I cannot say. If His Holiness presses the suit warmly enough, certainly the duke will accept."

One of her narrow white feet slid into a satin slipper. Her feet looked soft as her hands, as if she never walked on them.

"Ferrara," she said. The other foot stroked lightly over the floor, hunting its shoe. "What is it like, the city?"

"I have never been there, Madonna. I am told it is a fair city. But it is not Rome."

She tossed her head, giving out a burst of brittle laughter. "That tells it all, doesn't it? To a Roman." For an instant her eyes met Nicholas's; her eyes were bright as if with fever. She looked unhappy. Swiftly she lowered her head again, away from Nicholas's scrutiny.

"And my husband to be? What does rumor say of him?"

"He is a soldier, Madonna." Nicholas looked down at her foot, still groping over the floor for the shoe, which was some inches away under the table. He knelt and took the shoe and slipped it onto her foot. "He is much enamored of the new light field artillery." He stood up, putting his hands behind his back.

"Really," she said. "Iron rivals." She laughed again, her eyes lowered. "Thank you, Nicholas."

"Madonna?"

"For putting my shoe on. Greetings, Cesare!"

Nicholas twitched his gaze around to the doorway, where Valentino was crossing the threshold. He put out his hands to his sister, and she rose to embrace him; their hands met and then their mouths. Nicholas, withdrawing as fast as he could, saw them kiss and thought he saw their lips part and Valentino's tongue slip into her mouth. He bent down in a bow, to avert his eyes from that, and left them alone there.

IN THE LATE AUTUMN came news of the betrothal of the Pope's daughter to Alfonso d'Este of Ferrara. Nicholas was a witness to the leavetaking of the princess to her father, when Lucrezia left Rome to journey north for her wedding. The Pope led his daughter by the hand to her horse. Both shed tears. They kissed each other many times, and the old man spread his arms around her and held her fast a moment. She mounted her horse, a trumpet played a flourish, and she rode away. A swarm of courtiers accompanied her, Angela Borgia among them.

Behind them in the square of Saint Peter they left a small

horseshoe of observers around the aging Pope. Alexander spread his arms again and pressed his hands again to his chest, embracing the air where she had been. The gold of his robe was spangled with tears; he turned back to the entrance to his palace, and his back seemed bowed; his feet shuffled heavily over the pavement.

IT WAS WINTER. For three days a steady rain had been battering at the streets and roofs of Rome. Wrapped in two coats, Nicholas still shivered, standing on the icy marble floor in the public room of the Torre Borgia, far from the fire. The hearth of the fire was the only place where it was possible to stay warm, and greater men than Nicholas had taken possession of it. Nicholas paced up and down the cold floor at the other side of the room, his hands tucked under his arms.

Outside in the rain a bell began to toll. "It's late," said one of the men by the fire. The other men grunted. No one spoke more.

Nicholas pulled his coat higher on his neck. He watched the three men by the fire through the sides of his eyes. He knew them by looks and by repute, although he had never spoken to any of them. They were three of Valentino's condottieri, each one a lord in his own right: Oliverotto, the short squat man who had remarked on Valentino's lateness, was tyrant of the tiny city of Fermi, and the other two men were both of the great Roman family of the Orsini.

Lean and pale, dressed in the newest fad of Roman fashion, their sleeves dagged and hooped and trimmed with gold braid, the two Orsini stood as far from Oliverotto as they could without leaving the warmth of the hearth. Nicholas had seen the tyrant of Fermi walk in, shambling along on wide-spread feet, his gait as much as his poxy face a sign of the French disease that rotted him alive. While Nicholas watched, Paolo Orsini took a gold comb from his purse and stroked his perfumed hair into place.

The outer door opened. Circled by hurrying pages and servants, Valentino strode into the room.

The three men by the fire wheeled like swifts to face him. He greeted them, not pausing in his stride; he did not notice Nicholas. He went on through the public room to the small chamber in the back, and the door shut behind him. A moment later a page came out again and summoned Oliverotto and the Orsini into Valentino's presence.

Left alone in the public room, Nicholas made for the hearth. He opened his coats and spread them to let the warmth in. A puffing servant brought in a hod of wood and built the fire higher. Nicholas rubbed the stinging rims of his ears.

Again the outer door swung open, and another man came in, trailed by followers. Nicholas backed away from the fire. The newcomer, who was Gianpaolo Baglione, went up into the glow of the hearth.

He and Nicholas had met. The tyrant of Perugia nodded and Nicholas bowed. Nicholas pulled his coats around him again. He began to pace up and down, trying to keep warm.

Gianpaolo gave his coat to a lackey. He stood taller than his men. His face was shaped like Stefano's, the wide setting of the eyes and the flaring battler's jaw, or perhaps Nicholas only wanted to see a resemblance. The hair was the same color. Gianpaolo noticed him watching. Nicholas bowed; the prince turned his back.

A page looked into the public room from the chamber where Valentino was holding his court, saw Gianpaolo, and withdrew. A moment later he reappeared to summon the condottiere into the council. All Gianpaolo's men went in with him. Alone again in the antechamber, Nicholas hurried back to the fire.

He began to go over his scheme in his mind; he had half-memorized a little speech wherein he would present the idea to Valentino. He burned to know what they were saying in the next chamber. Urbino seemed such an obvious target. Surely someone else would propose it. Yet it was said to be invulnerable to attack, and for two years' campaigning, now, Valentino had passed it by; the habit would be set and hard to break. Nicholas turned his back to the fire and held up his coat to let the heat reach him. The wind was driving the rain against the shuttered windows.

Urbino stood on a precipitous mountain. The great cannon of Federigo da Montefeltro looked out from the walls. A condottiere had built it, with an eye to discouraging other condottieri. Nicholas hoped Federigo's work would keep its magic. He set his teeth together and endured the wait.

Oliverotto left first, grumbling, stamping through the public room in his awkward bearish walk. A few moments later the two Orsini came out of Valentino's chamber, putting their hats on as they passed by Nicholas. He heard them burst forth into talk just beyond the door into the corridor.

The page looked out and saw Nicholas and shut the inner door again. Nicholas reworked his arguments in his mind. His legs ached from standing so long, hours now. His left ear began to hurt. That was the cold; every winter he suffered pain in that ear from excess of cold. Gianpaolo's hangers-on came out of the private chamber and crowded around the hearth with him, talking. Although they buffeted him and nudged him, he did not give way to these menials.

A candle guttered in its brass wall sconce and went out.

The time stretched unbearably long. Nicholas could not stay still; he began to pace again along the hearth, dodging Gianpaolo's chattering familiars. He polished his arguments for the fiftieth time. It was so obvious, so simple a plan; perhaps they had thought of it. Perhaps there was some flaw, something a military man would see at once, invisible to a diplomat.

The page looked in. "Messer Dawson, come in, please."

His mind numb, he went through the doorway into Valentino's chamber.

Only one candle burned. The little room was almost completely dark. The roaring of the wind and the rain outside sounded dimly through the walls. Valentino sat so that the light of the candle shone on his face, his gleaming feral eyes, and his hands. He wore black, unrelieved by ornament, and his face and hands seemed to float unbodied in the darkness. He said, "What is it, Nicholas?"

This room was warm. Nicholas coughed, already beginning to sweat. He became aware of Gianpaolo Baglione sitting to his left, slightly behind him. Valentino was watching him intently. He looked irritated. It was the wrong moment. He would only anger Valentino.

All his wit had flown; he could not gather the words he had memorized. He blurted out, "I have a plan for you, Excellency. For the spring's campaigning in the Romagna."

Valentino's mouth worked behind the masking beard. His gaze shifted toward Gianpaolo. "Who does not?"

Gianpaolo said, "Do you fancy yourself a tactician, Messer Secretary?"

"My lord," Nicholas said. "It seems so obvious to me—you must have considered it—I am a fool to suggest it, perhaps—"

"What?" Valentino said.

"Urbino."

Gianpaolo made a rude sound with his lips. Above Valentino's luminous eyes, the pale brows flattened.

"You've never seen Urbino, little mouse. It's beyond reach."

"I know all that." Nicholas took a step forward, his hands out. "The guns, the walls—everything. I tell you, Urbino can be taken. With that city under your command, only think how strong—"

Valentino smiled at Gianpaolo. "How may Urbino be taken?"

"The walls and the cannon were Federigo's," Nicholas

said, "but he is dead. Guidobaldo, his son, is another sort of man entirely. He trusts in honor and justice."

"On with it, mouse."

"Make him your ally," Nicholas said. He was talking at a racing speed, trying to reach the end of his argument before they sent him away. "Plan an attack together on some other city—beyond Urbino. I thought Camerino perhaps. He will put his troops and cannon at your disposal. You will seek permission to march through his territory on the way to Camerino. Then you swerve, at the last moment you march on Urbino herself while her defenses are gone. He will have no choice save to surrender."

"Sweet Cross of Jesus!" Gianpaolo exploded. "The Devil's mouthpiece."

Valentino's glowing eyes were rapt on Nicholas. "Messer Mouse, there are certain expectations of a man, even in war."

"Is it more acceptable to slaughter hundreds of people— lose your own men by the hundreds?" Nicholas said. "This way Urbino can be had without the shedding of a drop of blood."

Gianpaolo swore again in a voice harsh with outrage.

"You see," Valentino said. "My own men will not accept it. It is too extreme. Unworthy of a soldier."

"Urbino is property of the Church," Nicholas said. "You are the standardbearer of the Church. You may recover your property efficiently, without wanton slaughter—I cannot see why any reasonable man would refuse."

Valentino laughed. He shook his head at Nicholas. "War is not the game of reasonable men, my mouse. Go home. I will send for you again, before I leave Rome—there is some intelligence I require of other matters."

"Yes, Excellency."

"Leave the tactics henceforth to such as have some real knowledge of the practice of war."

"Yes, Excellency."

Nicholas bowed himself out of the dark room. He was relieved that it was over. Now he himself saw how rash his plan was. In fact he had forgotten that, like Urbino, Gianpaolo's city Perugia was nominally a Papal fief, and so the Baglione prince's reaction was utterly predictable. He had overlooked too much. Wrapped in his coats, he hurried home through the driving rain.

"Is Stebano coming tonight?" Juan asked.

"No," Nicholas said. Juan's half-Spanished name for Stefano galled him. The old man set a dish of soup before him and sprinkled rubbed cheese over the dark surface.

"Bread?"

"Yes." Nicholas picked up his spoon.

"Butter?"

"I always have butter on my bread." He dipped the spoon into the soup and raised it to his lips. Juan was cutting slices from the loaf.

"Per Baccho." Nicholas put the spoon down beside the soup bowl. "The soup is cold."

Juan goggled at him. "Really?" He reached for the spoon, to taste it himself.

"You may take my word for it." Nicholas thrust the dish away. The spoon clattered to the floor.

"I will put it on the fire," Juan said, and slid his hands under the dish.

"Don't bother. I will eat somewhere else."

"It will be hot in a moment."

Nicholas left his chair. He toed off his fur-lined house shoes and kicked them aside. "Bring me my shoes and my coat."

Juan left the soup on the table and went away to the bedchamber. Nicholas strode across the room to the rack by the door where his walking stick was hanging. The old man returned, and kneeling put the shoes on Nicholas's feet, then rising helped him into his coat. Nicholas shifted his stick from hand to hand.

"Keep the door. I shall be late, probably."

Juan gave him an instant's pointed look but said nothing. He opened the door for his master.

Nicholas went across the city, past the Colosseo and the gloomy walls of the basilica by the Forum, and turned into the warren of alleys and lanes across the Piazza San Marco from the Campidoglio. The rain had stopped but the street was slippery and smelled of mud and refuse. There were no lights. He went along slowly through the narrow way, listening for voices. Sometimes bands of men prowled the streets at night looking for easy theft. Pope Alexander kept better order in Rome than most Popes but at night the city was still unsafe for unarmed people. The street ended against a hillside where goats grazed and Nicholas found and climbed the footpath up to the top.

On the far slope was a taverna; two sputtering torches lit up the doorway, and along the front wall a dozen young men were ranged. Most of them leaned up against the wall; they all wore their coats and shirts open to the waist, in spite of the cold. It was their uniform, their invitation. On the far side of the street was a myrtle tree, where Nicholas waited in the shadow while a few people entered the taverna.

When the street was empty and he had made his choice among the young men, he crossed the open way to the third boy from the door, whose broad shoulders and fair hair attracted him.

"Good evening," Nicholas said. "It's a raw night."

The young man smiled at him. He had excellent white teeth. "Yes, but at least it isn't raining."

"A cup of wine would warm us both. Will you join me?"

"I'm not thirsty," the boy said. His lips performed the smile even while he talked. "I'll sit with you, if you wish. While you drink."

"The wine here is inferior in any case. Perhaps you'd take a stroll with me?"

"Forty carlini," the young man said, through his smile.

"Very well."

They went around behind the taverna. In the darkness by the wall, between two tall wine casks, Nicholas accomplished his pleasure. He gave the boy a crown.

"Go buy yourself some wine. Elsewhere than here."

The boy laughed. He pulled his clothes together and walked away down the alley without another word. When Nicholas came out to the street again, the boy had taken up his former station along the front wall of the taverna.

Nicholas went down the hillside to another taverna, where he knew the wine was good, although all the whores were women.

He stopped in the doorway, surprised at the crowd that filled every bench and overflowed across the floor. A knot of men diced on a table under the lamp. Nicholas slipped by them to the rear of the common room, where the wine was sold, and bought a glass from a drunken slattern.

He drew away to one side. The wine was pleasantly sharp. The sex had left him clean and exhilarated. Stefano had told him once that he pitied any man who had to buy sex. Yet it was so orderly that way. Already he had forgotten the young man's face. The act was pure; nothing remained after the fire was out.

With a start he let himself hear what his ears had attended to for many moments. Guitar music sounded on the other side of the room. He did not know the song but he recognized the style of play. He walked through the press of drinkers and gamesters.

Miguelito da Corella sat in the corner, playing the guitar. Nicholas paused. He thought of going away. The slender hands on the instrument gripped his attention. At their last meeting, Miguelito had told him in gestures as clear as words not to bother him.

The music stopped abruptly. Miguelito said, in Spanish, "Well, hail, Nicholas."

"Hello," Nicholas said.

He took a step nearer the other man, who was sitting on a stool against the wall.

"What are you doing out so late?" Miguelito played an idle chord and broke it into separate notes.

"What's done in the dark." Nicholas raised his glass and drank. "And looking for my supper. Come share bread with me."

Miguelito shook his head. "I am not free."

With his chin he pointed across the room.

Nicholas's head turned. There, in the middle of the gamblers, was Valentino. He wore a black velvet mask that covered his face from hair to chin, yet there was no doubt that it was Valentino.

As Nicholas watched, the prince won his cast, and with a roar he clapped the men beside him across the shoulders; he snatched up the dice and brandished them. The men who flanked him swung around him like puppets, their eyes fixed on him.

Miguelito was playing music again. Nicholas turned back to him.

"Does he do this often?"

The other man shrugged. His coat hung over the edge of his stool, and his shirt was open at the throat; his oiled hair hung dankly beside his ears and over his shoulder. He plucked quick dance music from his guitar.

"Well," Nicholas said, "one learns. I'm off to find my supper."

"Stay here." Miguelito silenced the guitar strings with a slap. "He's seen you—he'll want to talk to you."

"I'm hungry."

"Wait."

Miguelito returned to his music. Nicholas hung at his

elbow, uncertain. If he left, what might Valentino do? Nothing. He turned his gaze toward the dicers again, and saw the Borgia prince standing with his hands on his hips, looking down at the gaming table; he had lost the dice. His hat was off. The strings of his mask dented his lustrous redbrown hair. Even idle, he seemed full of force and coiled strength, ready for any challenge. Nicholas drank the last of his wine. He knew he would wait on Valentino's whim.

Much later Miguelito stood up suddenly and put his guitar against the wall. "Come with me," he said to Nicholas, and went away across the room.

Nicholas followed him through the mob. The hour was very late: past midnight. Valentino was still presiding over the game of dice, now with a fat whore giggling on his arm.

Following Miguelito, Nicholas went up the rickety wooden stairs to the taverna's second story, divided into a honeycomb of little rooms. In one room was a table, laid with a white cloth, a plate, a selection of forks and knives, and a wine glass. When the two men entered the room it was quite dark, and Miguelito struck a light in his tinderbox and lit the candle in the middle of the table.

A moment later Valentino came into the room. The whore still clung to his arm, shrieking with drunken laughter. Nicholas withdrew into a corner. He loathed drunkenness. The woman's hennaed hair and face smeared with rouge horrified him. Valentino tucked money into the front of the whore's dress and pushed her away.

"Oh, honey, let me stay. I'll give you service—" she burst into uncontrollable giggles, her hand across her mouth, and lunged at Valentino and fell into his arms.

He shoved her savagely away from him. Without a word or signal, Miguelito jumped on her. She had fallen to her knees; when she began to rise, Miguelito gripped her hair and dragged her to the door. She screamed once. Miguelito put his foot on her backside and kicked her out of the room.

Nicholas watched from the corner. He thought, That might befall me, if I am careless.

Valentino sat at his table. He reached behind his head to unfasten his mask and laid it beside his plate. Miguelito left, shutting the door behind him; Valentino smiled at Nicholas.

"Well, my darling mouse, what brought you here?" He spoke in Spanish.

"The wine," Nicholas said.

"You were not seeking me?"

"Excellency, I had no notion you were here."

Miguelito returned. After him came two serving girls with platters, who put food on Valentino's plate and poured his wine. Miguelito paid them, and they left.

The Pope's son said, "Fate brought you here, then, mouse, because you have been much in my mind."

"Magnificence, I live to serve."

Miguelito tasted of the prince's meat and bread; he drank of the wine. Nicholas looked hungrily at the white veal flesh, smelling of the herbs with which it had been spread before roasting.

"You should not have told me your plan for Urbino in front of Gianpaolo Baglione," Valentino said. He began to eat. He spoke between bites. "He is too conventional a man not to be shocked."

"I am devastated that I embarrassed you, Magnificence."

"All my condottieri are such men as that. They are not thinking men. They obey, which is what makes them useful." Valentino reached for the wine glass. The candlelight caught glints on the gold thread in the sleeves of his coat. Miguelito, standing behind him, was all but invisible in the dark.

"As for the embarrassment, Nicholas, it was none. I have talked of your plan to some others. We are agreed. There is merit in it—great merit. Of course it needs some changes, but on the whole we are inclined to use it."

A shock like an electric pulse ran through Nicholas from head to foot. He grew warm all over.

Valentino went on, "I shall need more intelligence of Guidobaldo. First, you say he will surrender. How do you know?"

"He is no soldier, Magnificence. And he is impotent. Thus he is predisposed to—"

"Impotent! I did not know that."

Nicholas moved his shoulders up and down. "I know a physician who treated him, Magnificence."

Valentino chewed a moment and swallowed. He glanced at Miguelito. To Nicholas, he said, "You are thorough."

"It is not secret knowledge, Magnificence. One need only ask."

"Ask. Yes. He is married to—" Valentino snapped his fingers.

"Elisabetta Gonzaga," Nicholas said. "She is his strength, in fact. But she is gone from Urbino for the winter; she followed your sister to her wedding in Ferrara."

"What about her relatives? Can they help him?"

"They are too far from Urbino to help him defend against you. The whole power of the plan is that he will know only a few hours before you reach his doorstep what you mean to do."

Without marking it, Nicholas had come up to the table.

"Yes," Valentino said; he touched his mouth with the napkin. "I am aware of the military advantages, mouse. What concerns me are Guidobaldo's family connections, for instance the Estensi, my new kinsmen."

"His wife's brother is married to Beatrice d'Este," Nicholas said, "whose only concern is her collections of statuary and painting. You might let her acquire a few of the prizes of Guidobaldo's collection. I understand he has a piece by Michelangelo that she once tried to purchase from you."

"She offered much too low." Valentino leaned back, his hand on his stomach. He looked off across the room, past

Nicholas, his pale brow furrowing. "I do not like your Republic, Nicholas."

"Yes," Nicholas said, startled at the sudden shift.

"Better than giving me Urbino would be a plan to bring Florence to her knees before me."

"Yes, Magnificence."

Valentino frowned, his face still turned so that his eyes were directly past Nicholas; he spoke much louder than before. His hand had clenched against his stomach.

"They have insulted me, abused my faith, betrayed a contract signed and sealed—yet I hardly even know their names!" The prince hammered with his fist at the table. "They reach power, they humiliate me and my father, and then before I can retaliate, those men are down and another set are up, claiming no knowledge of what went before."

Nicholas's mouth was dry. He said, "It is a government intended to be ineffectual, Magnificence."

"It effects my shame." Now Valentino raised his stony gaze to Nicholas's face. "You will tell me how to remove it."

Nicholas's eyes burned; he wanted to look away, sure that Valentino would read his mind through his eyes. He said, "Magnificence, you need only threaten Florence, and the Republic will fall."

He did not say that any government that followed would certainly be more adamantly against Valentino than the existing state. He pressed his sweating hands to the table linen, wondering how the conversation had led him to this precipice.

"So easily?" Valentino asked.

"Oh, yes," Nicholas said. He forced himself to go on meeting the prince's gleaming feral eyes. "You need only send your armies into Tuscany to put this Republic in its grave."

Valentino twisted to look at Miguelito behind him and straightened again in his chair. "It will serve as a diversion, too—while we take Urbino."

Nicholas said, "Yes—and the King of France cannot accuse you of disobeying his order against attacking Florence directly."

Valentino frowned again; his gaze slid away from Nicholas and he stirred in his chair and rubbed his throat with his hand. "The French king," he said, loudly again. "The French king may dance as he wills. Now that the Spanish have an army in Italy—"

Then the French had in fact guaranteed Florence against the Borgias. This was fresh news. Nicholas did not look away from Valentino now. He had the sensation of rushing into the slack jaws of a crocodile, picking at the morsels between the teeth.

"There are a number of cities in Tuscany who hate the dominance of Florence," Nicholas said. He lowered his voice. He wanted to seem diffident. "You need only convince one city to open her gates to your army—"

"Which?"

"I shall study the problem." One more succulent tidbit between the crocodile's back teeth. "You know that Pisa has defied Florence, now, for so many years—if it could be revealed to the Florentines that Pisa has offered herself to you—"

Valentino tipped his head back. "Will Pisa come to me?"

No, then. Nicholas smiled at the prince before him. "Whether she will or no, the rumor will be enough."

Valentino laughed and slapped his hand on his broad thigh. "My darling mouse. To think your talent might have withered and died, there in the Florentine legation."

"He is hungry," Miguelito said.

The Borgia pushed his chair back and stood. "Eat," he said to Nicholas. "Send for more, if you wish." From his full height he smiled down on Nicholas, his leonine beauty vivid with good humor. He took his mask from the table and went out.

Miguelito followed him to the door, where he turned again toward Nicholas; sober-faced, he bowed his head and made a little flourish with his hands. The door closed silently behind him.

Nicholas took his place in Valentino's chair. He fell upon the feast that Valentino had left to him.

CARNIVAL BEGAN. White as skulls, the painted faces of the celebrants swarmed along the Corso and through the web of crooked streets beside the river; every piazza resounded with dancing music and the racket of fights. Nicholas kept his purse tucked safely away under his coat. He avoided the thick of the crowds, going always down the side of the street, along the edge of the piazza, until he came to the bullring near the river.

There the sausage vendors and the sweetmeat vendors were hawking their delights in voices hoarse from overuse. Nicholas loitered near the wall of new lumber that kept the bulls in. He watched a young sprig of the Cattanei, mounted on a gaudy chestnut horse, chase a black bull around and around the ring. None of the Italians knew how to fight bulls. Nicholas bought a drink of wine from a vendor wearing a red and white mask and a false beard. Down the street to his left came a chain of people, singing and dancing, each with his hands on the shoulders of the one before him.

The young nobleman at last succeeded in turning his bull, and the bull in one charge drove him out of the ring. The crowd hooted. Bits of bread and small stones showered him as he rode away.

"Well met, Nicholas," a voice boomed, "and what do you today?"

It was Amadeo, splendidly dressed, his face half-concealed behind a jeweled mask; he wore jeweled gloves also.

Half a dozen of his familiars were standing in the street behind him.

Nicholas turned his walking stick up under his folded arm.
"Well, Amadeo, I am looking for an honest man."

"During the daylight, Nicholas, how decadent!"

Nicholas laughed unconvincingly; Amadeo always pushed
him into these half-witted duels, grasping for witticisms.
"Only in Rome is honesty a matter for the dark," he said.
Beyond the ring, the crowd's voice swelled to a thunder:
someone was riding to the bull.

"When you find him, will you do me the favor of joining
me?"

"Really, Amadeo. In the daylight?"

Now Amadeo laughed. He ran his fingers over the bottom
edge of his mask, adjusting it on his nose, so that all the
jewels glittered. "Feeble, my dear Nicholas. I see you've
been drinking, it affects your wit."

At that moment Stefano came up to them. Already more
than half-drunk, he was not wearing a mask, only the great
floppy hat pulled low over his eyes. He said to Nicholas,
"Am I late?" and looked curiously at Amadeo.

Nicholas said, "This is Amadeo Risi, Stefano."

"Oh," Amadeo said, smiling. "Is he honest?"

"What?" Stefano asked blankly.

Amadeo was grinning at him like a fox. "An old continu-
ing joke between me and my friend Nicholas here. We haven't
met, have we? I thought I knew everyone in Rome. Nicholas
is coming with us to a little party at my house—do come too."

"I haven't seen much of the Carnival yet," Nicholas said
quickly, before Stefano could agree.

Without a word, Stefano brushed between them to reach
the wall of the bullring. Amadeo's avid stare tracked him
faithfully.

"Oh, come," Amadeo said, "what's to see? Carnival is tame,
now—a hundred years ago, only think, we'd have enjoyed

the spectacle of a hundred pigs dashed to pieces on the rocks below Testaccio. Come to my house. I have a keg of Perugian—we'll broach both ends before the night's over."

Stefano said, "Isn't that Valentino?"

Nicholas reached the wall in a single step. It was Valentino; the man riding to the bull was indeed Valentino. He should have guessed it by the racket of the crowd, still roaring and waving their arms and hats.

Valentino rode a black horse against a black bull; he turned it at the far side of the ring from Nicholas and the bull charged. Its horns were longer than the horns of a Spanish bull. Valentino bent his horse neatly around a circle, avoiding the bull's rush, and when it wheeled, he raced past its heels. Confused, the bull stopped and shook its head and snorted.

The crowd whistled and cheered its approval. Valentino raised his hand to them; he made his horse dance sideways, its legs crossing one over the other, for another shout of applause. Word that he was riding had spread and more and more people were moving in around the ring, shoving for a place near the wall. They pressed against Nicholas, uncomfortably close.

Valentino took a lance from someone at the gate and played the bull from side to side, leading its charge with the lance. They turned in circles in the middle of the ring, the bull around the horse and man, like the sun around the world. Suddenly, with no warning, the bull veered from the lance and struck the horse in the shoulder.

The horse fell and Valentino leapt to the ground; he slipped and went to one knee in the dust. The screams of those around Nicholas made him catch his breath. Stefano pushed into him from one side, pushed himself by the people behind him. Nicholas was pressed against the rough boards of the wall. Across the sand from him Valentino surged up onto his feet and pulled his sword from its scabbard.

The bull dropped its horns and charged him. Valentino stood like a stone before the sweeping horns until the bull was one stride from him; he pivoted to one side, and the black beast shot by him. With both hands Valentino brought his sword down across the bull's neck.

The bull went down so suddenly that it tumbled head over heels. Blood sprayed in a broad sweep over the dust; one horn had broken off against the ground. While it thrashed its legs Valentino ran in behind it and struck it again, and the bull's kicks gradually ceased. Valentino backed away.

Nicholas sighed. The wall shook and rocked under the impact of the cheering people around it. He turned toward Stefano, who gave him a shocked frown.

"I think you are in love with him."

"Bah," Nicholas said, which was not denying it.

Amadeo had taken off his mask, and held it in his hand, while he smiled at Stefano. Abruptly he turned to Nicholas and said, "What does he have?"

Nicholas gave him a pointed look, embarrassed; he hoped that Stefano would not judge him by this friend. "What he needs," he said.

"Really, Nicholas. Jealousy is a woman's trait." Amadeo fit his mask smoothly back over his head. "Well, we're off. Are you coming? I promise you we shall enjoy every pleasure this evening."

Nicholas glanced at Stefano, who had turned back to watch the bullring, where some men with a cart were butchering the dead bull. Valentino was leading his crippled horse out of the ring at the far end. Nicholas faced Amadeo again.

"Another time, perhaps."

"I'll join you," Stefano said.

Amadeo beamed all over. "Oh, wonderful!" he cried, and looped his arm through Stefano's. "Nicholas," he said, "how sad you can't come too. But we will see you—another time?"

Stefano's face was carefully bland. He glanced at Nicholas,

but his eyes focused somewhere beyond him. Amadeo hurried away down the street. Nicholas stared after them, sour.

OLD JUAN WAS USED TO planting a kitchen garden by the back fence of Nicholas's house. As soon as the winter rains broke, not long after the beginning of Lent, he searched out the shovel and the rake and lugged them off into the weeds.

"I cannot fathom you," Nicholas said. "You are too old for such exercises."

He was washing his hands in the stone basin in the kitchen. On the table to his left, Juan was opening a pouch of seed he had traded for in the marketplace. The old man inserted his nose into the pouch and took a loud sniff.

"You might easily purchase all you need," Nicholas said, shaking water from his hands. Juan put down the pouch of seeds and brought him linen.

"Nothing tastes as fine as fresh herbs," Juan said. "And it reminds me of Navarre."

"You live in memories."

"It is pleasant to me—the work."

"When you strain yourself, that will not be entirely pleasing, I am sure."

The old man brought him his coat and he put it on. The coat was new; the stiffened lining under the fur collar bit his neck.

"Is Stebano coming tonight?"

"Yes."

"There are some apples left. I shall bake an apple cake."

"Why do you bother with him so much? Per Baccho, perhaps I ought to be jealous."

"He appreciates such things."

"And I do not?"

The old man was sniffing at his seeds again. Wisps of colorless hair floated here and there over the dome of his bald head. He poured seed out onto the palm of his hand.

"I think he must have belonged to a large family, wher-
ever he came from. He longs for them, and so he lives in a
family with us."

Surprised, Nicholas searched the old man's face, pacific
with age. Juan was always making up tales about people he
did not know, yet this one, this was very close to truth.

"His family is dead," he said slowly. "Died of plague, all
save him and his father."

Juan crossed himself. "Holy Mother gather them to Thee."

The gold hooks of the coat were cool under Nicholas's
fingers. He slipped the prongs into the loops, pulled his
sleeves straight, and ran one finger around the scratchy inside of the neck. The old man was right: this house was home
to Stefano, living in a taverna, dining on whore's leavings,
over a rented table. It irritated him that this simple explana-
tion had eluded him but not Juan.

"I will make the apple cake." Juan went into the pantry.

"HERE, OLD MAN, bring me another glass of wine." Stefano
made pouring gestures with his hand over his empty glass.

Nicholas came out of his room to the sight of Stefano,
already lounging in the chair now recognized as his favorite,
and ordering Juan about. Annoyed, Nicholas paused. Stefano
turned his beaming smile on him, and his eyes widened.

"Sweet Jesus." Stefano got up out of his chair. "You look
like a prince. Where did you have your coat made?"

"In the Lily-Row Street."

"It looks expensive."

Juan brought in the wine jar and filled Stefano's glass;
Stefano ignored it. He moved around Nicholas, fingering
the coat and murmuring in appreciation.

"But you should have done it in some color other than
brown. Or at least you could wear a gold chain. Maybe
two."

Warm inside the coat Nicholas lowered his gaze to the

floor. Under Stefano's scrutiny he felt like a piece of merchandise. Yet had he not worn it so that Stefano would admire it? He walked away from Stefano's humiliating touch.

"Juan, will you light the rest of the candles? And I shall have the Spanish wine."

Stefano was behind him, still watching him; Nicholas kept his back to Stefano.

"You are early."

"I was losing," Stefano said, "so I left the game."

He sounded amused. Nicholas turned the lyre-backed chair around and sat in it, now facing Stefano again, and saw with rising anger that Stefano was smiling at him. He pulled at the lavish fur cuffs of his sleeves.

"I'm pleased you've learned to stop when you must."

"It isn't hard. When I have somewhere to go."

Juan brought Nicholas his glass and went off to light the candles.

"How much did you lose?"

"Two hundred carlini. How much did that coat cost?"

"Rather more than that," Nicholas said.

"Where are you getting all this money? It seems to me when I first met you that you were always poor. Haggled with me over a penny."

"I have made some wise investments."

Stefano took his favorite chair by the back and brought it across the room toward Nicholas.

"May I sit by you?"

Nicholas grunted. The gleam of amusement still danced in Stefano's eyes, in his smile, his whole expression. "Yes, of course," Nicholas said. He felt suddenly that Stefano knew him too well.

"When are you going to have the walls finished?" Stefano nodded around the room.

"When I have decided what to put there."

"It seemed right the other way."

"I was bored with it."

"It made the room seem . . ." Stefano stirred up the air with his hand, "it was like being in the country."

"Yes. It seemed very empty and bland. I loathe the country."

A banging on the door jumped him up out of his chair, startled, like some animal. He took three steps toward the door before he thought to let Juan open it. He touched his palms to the fur on the front of his coat. Juan hurried by him to the door.

"Yes?"

The old man spoke out through a crack of an opening. The voice that answered was muffled and Nicholas could not hear the words. Juan turned his head.

"He speaks Spanish. He wishes to see you privily."

Nicholas went up to the threshold; one hand on the old man's shoulder sent him away. On the walk outside the door stood Miguelito da Corella.

"Are you alone?" Miguelito said. He was wrapped to the ears in a cloak. Nicholas wondered how he had come past the gate. "May I come in?"

Stefano must have left the gate open. "There is one here," Nicholas said. "He speaks no Spanish."

Miguelito nodded, and Nicholas let him into the room. Stefano was fifteen feet away, watching them curiously. Nicholas took Miguelito by the elbow and turned him so that his back was to the room.

"My master ordered you to determine where in Tuscany to strike."

"Arezzo," Nicholas said, low. "Tell him that the people are so sore from the taxes and abuses of Florence that they will probably welcome in any army he sends."

Miguelito's mouth quirked. His thin black moustache hid the corners of his lips but the smile gave his face a kinder look. He said, "I thought it would be Arezzo. Or Piombino."

"It's obvious."

"You will tell them of the matter of Pisa?"

Nicholas nodded his head. "Will you take wine?"

"No. We are leaving now for Cesena in the Romagna." Miguelito's smile broadened. "I will see you again, after Urbino."

"Oh?"

"Yes—if it fails, he will want you notified appropriately." Miguelito nudged him, as if that were a joke they could share. He brushed by Nicholas and went out the door.

Nicholas pushed the door shut. When he turned, Stefano said, "Who was that?—Sweet Jesus, you are white as a ghost!"

"It's nothing." Nicholas went across the room to his chair; his legs were wobbling, although he could not tell if Miguelito's threat had made him coltish, or only that his plans were at last to come to bloom. He sat down. Juan stood in the kitchen threshold, unsmiling, his eyes sharp. Nicholas raised his head.

"You may serve us now."

"Who was that man?" Stefano asked. "On my life, Nicholas, you are still pale as death. What did he say to you?"

"Just a messenger."

"What did he say?"

Nicholas put his hand up to his face, shielding himself from Stefano's eyes. "Nothing—it was the cold wind in the doorway. That's all. Why I paled." He raised his voice. "Juan! Serve me!"

Unsettled, he spoke in Italian. Stefano cleared his throat. His gaze never left Nicholas. Not his interest so much as his right to an interest annoyed Nicholas and made him uneasy. He had no self any more that was safe from the man. Juan brought their meal on a tray painted with red poppies. Besides the soup, made of onions and dusted with a fine Italian cheese, he had brought them bread, a thick yellow butter, and a cake filled with slices of apple.

"Magnificent," Stefano said. He leaned forward eagerly over the soup.

Nicholas could barely eat. He stirred his soup with his spoon, his eyes lowered. Everything in his plan against Urbino depended on speed and surprise. The roads were good, but a sudden rain, an accident, a landslide in a mountain pass, any unforeseeable freak would bring Miguelito back to his door with his looped bowstring in his hand.

Stefano leaned back. "Old one!" He snapped his fingers at Juan. "Come take this dish."

"Damn you!" Nicholas flung his spoon down. "Stop ordering my servant about!"

Stefano goggled at him in round surprise. Juan came up and removed the empty soup dish.

"I will not have you ordering my servant around," Nicholas cried.

"Calm yourself," Stefano said.

"Per Baccho, I shall not listen to you speak so to me! I am not to be patronized, my man! Get out of my house!"

Stefano looked up at Juan, and returned his gaze to Nicholas; his expression was abstracted and pensive. Swollen with his feelings. Nicholas could not keep still; he cried again, "Get out!" and Stefano rose from his chair and left.

Juan stood in the kitchen doorway, watching, the soup bowl in his hands. Nicholas could not meet the old man's eyes. He pushed his chair back and went away to his bedchamber.

THE SURPRISE ATTACK against Urbino would not come until well into the spring's campaign. Valentino spent the first months of the warming year raising his army. He had no trouble there; soldiers grew in the Romagna as if the stones were dragon's teeth. Nicholas read every report, talked to every traveler he could find from the north, and heard of turmoil and excitement but no real action.

Bruni hired a new scribe, who could barely write three words without a gross error. At first Nicholas corrected him patiently; then he kept the boy in the workroom during the afternoon to practice; finally he lost his temper and beat the boy with his walking stick.

The youth's screams set the other scribes roaring with laughter; Bruni came down the corridor from his chamber to see what was happening.

Nicholas's walking stick cracked its length. He let the sobbing boy go. Taking the stick into the sunlight by the archway that opened on the loggia, he inspected the split in the wood. Behind him, the other scribes screeched jibes at the beaten boy.

"Now, Messer Nicholas," Bruni said.

Heavy feet sounded on the stair and a dusty man rushed into the room. "Arezzo!" he cried. "Arezzo!"

All the others hushed. The courier was pulling his dispatch case off over his head. Nicholas's fingers curled. He saw Bruni standing as if he grew up out of the marble floor.

"Excellency."

Bruni started forward. "Give me the dispatches," he said in a commanding voice.

"Arezzo," the messenger said. He thrust the case into Bruni's hands. "The most horrible rumors—"

"Shut up," Nicholas called. "Whatever's happened, keep it to yourself." He dropped his broken stick and went around the room herding the scribes and the pages back to their tasks. To the beaten boy, he said, "Take this courier downstairs and give him some wine and help him get his boots off." For that the boy need not know infinitives.

Bruni was disappearing down the corridor. His face grimy with tears, the boy shambled across the room to the courier. Nicholas cast a sharp look around him, to see that everyone else was occupied, and went down after the ambassador to his chamber.

Bruni settled himself behind his desk and slit the seal on the dispatch case with a knife. He spilled the letter packets onto the desk. There were many, but most of them were marked for some other destination than this office; only three were actually addressed to the legation, and only one was marked with the red wax that announced a special, secret message.

Nicholas stood on the far side of the office. He locked his fingers together behind his back.

"Arezzo," Bruni said. "I knew there was a disaster coming, the sky's most ominous." He slit the red wax seals.

Nicholas said nothing.

The ambassador opened out the folded letter. A moment later he pushed it across the sleek surface of the desk toward Nicholas.

"Make of that what you will." Bruni rubbed his palm over his eyes.

The message was short; wild rumors were traveling the roads from Arezzo, no direct word had reached Florence from the subject city in many days, and the Signory feared that something evil had taken place there. Bruni was to learn all necessary to an understanding of the situation. Nicholas glanced at the signature: the city's Gonfalonier. He felt nothing, not even relief, only a cool distance from all this.

"Where do we begin?" Bruni was saying. "What can we do? Arezzo is much closer to Florence than to us. Why do they not simply send a messenger there to look? What do they consider me—a crystal-gazer?"

Amazed, Nicholas watched him take up the novel lying to one side of his desk and open its pages. Bruni seemed to shrink down into his chair, settling himself to read. The little silence grew. Finally the ambassador looked up.

"You do it, Nicholas. This is your sort of work. Report to me when you have satisfied the request."

"Yes, Excellency."

Bruni was already deep into his novel. Nicholas gathered up the dispatches, stuffed them back into the case, and returned to the workroom.

WHEN HE HAD ARRANGED to have the various messages delivered, he went off across the Tiber to the Leonine City.

As he walked, the thought of Stefano forced its way into his mind. He had not seen Stefano since the night he had ordered him to go. Of course Stefano would not come back, and Nicholas did not intend to go to him. It was not what Stefano had done but what Nicholas had done that prevented it: he would not admit to being a frightened fool. The only way to save his dignity was to act as if he regretted nothing. Still he could not help thinking of Stefano every day, nearly every hour.

Where the street narrowed down to enter the lane of the bridge, the traffic crowded together, wagons and folk on foot and on mules, and Nicholas had to shorten his steps. Without his walking stick his hands seemed awkward no matter what he tried to do with them. The ripe smell of the river reached his nose. He passed a large orange cat sitting on the stone railing of the bridge. The cat turned its head to look at him; one eye was a brilliant luminous green, but the other had been gouged out and nothing remained but the oozing socket. Nicholas's stomach heaved. He hurried on across the bridge.

With a crowd of monks and foreigners he walked up the street at the foot of the Vatican wall. Near the gate of the palace were wine sellers and orange sellers hawking their wares in several tongues. Everyone seemed to be shouting. Nicholas thought again of the cat. It was like an omen, somehow, like a messenger waiting there on the bridge for him, although what its message might have been he could not sieve from his confused imagination. The pavement under his feet, here and there marked with the Papal seal, was slippery with spilled wine and peelings of fruit. Near the palace entrance a man in foreign clothes was calmly pissing into the street in full view of every passer-by. Nicholas went up the street and into the palace. He told himself that his current height of feeling gave everything he saw a false reality; none of this meant anything, not even the cat.

The palace was crowded, although the Pope was receiving no one. Nicholas wandered from one room to the next. With Angela Borgia gone off to Ferrara he had lost his prime source of information and one of his chief means of gaining entry to the inner circles of the Borgias. Of course he was a hireling of the prince now, but he could not trade too openly on that, lest the Signory learn of it.

He did not consider that he had betrayed the Signory. They had made mistakes, and he was only making use of that; they had betrayed themselves. Nothing would come of it all anyway, in the end, nothing ever did.

In a long narrow room, among other familiars of the Borgia court, he found Valentino's secretary.

"I need some information," Nicholas said.

The secretary was eating a peach. In his free hand was a napkin poised to catch the dripping juices. Calmly he bit into the fruit, swallowed, and said, "Of what sort?"

"The campaign against Arezzo. My emp—the Signory of Florence is hot to know what is happening there."

The secretary laughed, holding his lips tightly closed to keep in the juice of the peach. He touched his lips with the napkin. "What can I tell you of that, who planned the whole of it? Except possibly this: Piero de' Medici is coming to Arezzo."

"Possibly you could tell me that," Nicholas said.

It was a decorative addition to the plan that he had not considered, to bring the exiled prince into the rebellion.

"And the rest of the campaign goes well?"

"Excellently well," the secretary said, having nothing left in his fingers save the pit of the peach; he looked around him for some way to discard it. Nicholas took it from him.

"Allow me the honor." He bowed, and the secretary, his smile more natural, gave him an elegant courtesy in reply. Nicholas left. As he passed over the bridge below Sant' Angelo, he flung the peach pit into the Tiber.

"WHAT CAN I TELL THEM?" Bruni said. "There is no hope to give them."

Nicholas went back to the door into the ambassador's chamber and opened it, so that he could see down the corridor and make sure that no one spied. His eyes directed there, he said, "They do not need hope, only facts. Arezzo is in the hands of Valentino, and I have heard that the citizens of Pisa are offering him their city—"

"Holy Mary, Mother of Mercy."

"But the forces that protected Florence last year have not changed. The French are committed to keeping the Republic independent of the Pope. The presence of the Spanish army in Naples will only strengthen their resolve to help us."

Bruni was shaking his head, his face long with gloom, and his arms folded over his breast. "You have misread the thing—the Spanish are the Borgias' protectors, and the protectors of the de' Medici, and they, not the French, possess the main force in Italy. Close the door! Do you want the entire quarter to hear us?"

Nicholas toed the door shut; no one seemed interested in spying. As usual the drapery was closed over Bruni's windows and the chamber was gloomy as a crypt. Nicholas took out his tinderbox to light the two candles on the wall behind Bruni's desk. At the blooming of the light Bruni jerked his head away.

"Excellency, we must have light to compose the letter."

"I cannot write the letter," Bruni said.

"Surely Valentino is trying to frighten the Signory into negotiating. We must help them—"

He stopped. Bruni was opening a drawer of his desk; he was removing from it a leather-bound novel, the same one he had been reading when Nicholas left that morning for the Leonine City.

"I cannot write the letter," Bruni said. "You write it, Nicholas. You always change everything I say anyway."

"Excellency."

Bruni spread the novel open on his desk. "This is a fine story, Nicholas. The knight's true-love puts him to every test, and yet he remains pure of heart and ever-faithful."

Nicholas's mouth hung open; he stood like a day-scholar, gaping, while Bruni spoke. Not Ugo, then, but Bruni himself must have made Nicholas's work known to Valentino. Bruni had known all the while what Nicholas was doing in the letters. Bruni, who now lowered himself into his novel and read himself away. Nicholas went out of the office.

NICHOLAS WORKED over the letter until long after the rest of the legation had gone; by the time he shut up the offices and went away to his home and his supper, night had fallen.

The sky was moonless, sprinkled with stars sparkling in their subtle colors, and the air was humid and warm. To-morrow would be a hot day, the first hot day of the summer. Nicholas enjoyed the walk, only wishing that he had his walking stick. He had seldom needed its support but the feel of the knob and the sound tapping in the road had added something to the walk. Also he thought that it made him look more interesting. He was crossing the piazza below the Campidoglio when he noticed several men following him.

He stopped at once. From here the way was narrow and dark, and he knew better than to lead a pack into such a place. Immediately the men surrounded him.

"Don't be foolish," Nicholas said. "The watch will come by at any moment."

There were four of them, all standing very close to him. He opened his hands and closed them again.

"I have no money."

Something hard struck his arm from behind, numbing it to the elbow. "Get your hands up!"

He put up his hands. They could see he had no weapon, nothing but his tongue, which ran out of control.

"I have no money. You're wasting your time. The watch will come by any moment now."

A blow on the side of the head knocked him to the street. He knew they would kill him. He had come so happily, so innocently to this.

"Wait," a rough voice said, "that's Il Bello's honey man."

"He's rich! Get his purse."

"Il Bello is a bad man to run against."

"He says he has no money anyway."

They were going. They were leaving him alone there. Disbelieving, he lifted his head, and the last to go cast him an angry look and swung his foot at him, which Nicholas dodged by rolling over. Now that man too was hurrying away across the empty piazza.

In the tower of the Aracoeli, up on the hill, a bell began to toll.

Nicholas stood up, his coat filthy with grit and his left arm still a lump without feeling. Il Bello: Stefano. He tugged at his clothes. His hose was torn on one knee and he had lost a shoe. All the bells in Rome were beginning to toll around him and he could hear the monks assembling on the stairs of the Aracoeli, behind him, but he did not turn.

Stefano: Il Bello. He began to walk painfully toward his home. It didn't matter, really. Stefano did not matter, and it was a weakness to long for him, especially now, when at last Nicholas's own influence and work were of weight in

Rome. That was important, not Stefano. He lifted his head up; he was walking along under the trees that lined the street toward the Colosseo, and the dusty air pent under their broad canopies brushed over his face. His arm was tingling to life again, throbbing. His life he owed to Stefano, whom he had cast out. He dragged himself painfully back to his house, where Juan would care for him.

FIXED AS USUAL on the recovery of Pisa, the Florentine Signory paid little heed to the rebellion in Arezzo, although Nicholas wrote two letters describing the situation there as needing quick action. Then in the height of the summer, Piero de' Medici, head of the exiled house, entered Arezzo with Vitellozzo Vitelli, a captain of Valentino's who owed the Signory a blood debt for the killing of his brother; the Aretines packed the streets to cheer them all the way to the palace. The Signory panicked. A courier rushed orders to the Florentine ambassador with the French king to plead for help, and duly enough King Louis sent orders to his troops in Milan to support the city against Valentino.

Talk of this dominated every gathering in Italy through the summer. No one marked it especially when Duke Valentino, with the cannon borrowed from his new ally Guidobaldo da Urbino, marched away across Guidobaldo's territory to attack Camerino.

IN THE HEAT of the summer night Nicholas slept in snatches, tormented by dreams. He woke once before midnight and went out to the kitchen for a cool glass of wine to settle his sleep. Juan slept on his cot in the narrow space between the wall and the wooden table. Nicholas slipped past him; the old man turned and broke into a hollow snore. Nicholas drank his wine and returned to his bed.

Yet he did not sleep. He lay on his back, thinking of Stefano.

Somewhere nearby a dog began to bark. Nicholas rolled over; the sound penetrated his ears like thorns. He rolled over again, trying to stop his ears with the pillow. The light sheet slid off his body and he clutched at it and pulled it up over his shoulders.

Under the racket of the dog another sound reached him, much nearer. He sat up in his bed, his ears stretching. Someone was walking about in the garden outside his house. He remembered the time that Stefano had broken into the house, but then he had not been alone. Perhaps it was Stefano. He pulled on his dressing gown and stuffed his feet into house shoes. If it were Stefano—if it were not Stefano—he opened the door enough to put his head out and scan the main room.

It was as he had left it; one candle burned in the iron bracket by the front door. Nicholas went across the room to make certain that the door was locked.

Just as he reached it the door swung open. He stopped. Miguelito stood there on the step.

Nicholas said, "What do you want with me?"

Miguelito came by him into the room. He wore a long black traveling coat; his muddy boots left a trail on the floor. He flung his hat off across the room.

"I have come from Urbino," Miguelito said.

"Ah," Nicholas said, and was out of breath.

"It worked," Miguelito said. "Guidobaldo fled, Urbino belongs to Cesare Borgia. Who sends you this, with his respects."

He gave Nicholas a ring.

"It worked," Nicholas said.

He closed his fingers over the heavy jewel. A hot delirium welled up in his mind, a triumph almost like sex. He smiled, and Miguelito smiled too, a sudden bright unexpected flash of teeth.

"Have a glass of wine with me," Nicholas said. "We shall drink to the victory."

Juan was in the kitchen doorway, blinking at them. Nicholas waved him away again. Miguelito was smothering down a yawn; he glanced around the darkened room and smiled sleepily at Nicholas again.

"Aren't you going to look at the bauble?" He unfastened the front of his coat and shrugged it off; it fell to the floor.

Nicholas opened his hand and looked down at the ring. In the light of the candle he could not make out the color of the stone, which looked black. The massive setting was carved of gold.

"Very fine," he said.

Miguelito went to the nearest chair. "He is right. There is something mad about you—who can trust a man who cares nothing of a ruby? My horse is outside. Someone must tend him." He sank into the chair, swung one filthy boot at a time up onto the plush cushion of the chair opposite, put his head back, and shut his eyes. Within the space of two heartbeats he was asleep.

Juan had come back into this room from the kitchen, a ragged gray shawl over his shoulders. Nicholas stood irresolutely. He was frightened of horses. He opened his hand again to look down at the ring. Now he saw that the stone was red, indeed a ruby.

"Go to bed," he said to Juan. He went out to the garden, caught Miguelito's exhausted horse, and led it by the bridle down the street to the nearest inn with a stable.

By morning the news of the fall of Urbino was general talk in Rome. Nicholas reached the Florentine legation half an hour later than usual; the rest of the staff was already in their places, buzzing, not a one of them at work. When Nicholas came in, every scribe and page rushed at him jabbering.

He went through the midst of them to the coat rack and hung up his coat. All in one voice, they were shouting at him, repeating over and over again the names of Urbino and Duke Valentino.

"Be quiet!" Nicholas shouted.

They all fell into a rapt attentive silence.

"Go back to your work. Whatever has happened in Urbino, our work must be done."

"Messer Nicholas!" a scribe cried. He flung up a cocked fist. "Is it not evil—is it not such an infamy—"

"Whatever it is," Nicholas said, "we shall not know for some time. In the meanwhile, we have a schedule of work to be met. If it is not met, I shall take steps."

He nodded at them, all silenced, their faces long and furrowed with new doubts. He wondered what they would think if they knew who had conceived the infamy. They turned back to their desks, and Nicholas went down to Bruni's office, where he was trying to order the ambassador's daybooks.

Everywhere he went that day, people talked only of Urbino. When he met the Venetian ambassador during the noon hour to exchange some intelligences, the Venetian could not stop talking of the conquest.

"We should have known from the moment the Borgias began negotiations with Guidobaldo. To think a Pope could be involved in such an inhuman betrayal!" The Venetian tapped his fingers on the desk between him and Nicholas and shook his head. "What is worse is that as usual the Borgias will only profit from their sins. Perhaps we have misunderstood God all along." He smiled at Nicholas, who laughed obediently, but it was clear the Venetian was at least halfway serious.

Nicholas gloried in this outrage; it was delightful to witness, to overhear, and to agree solemnly with it, like a ghost at his own funeral reveling in the eulogies. In the late afternoon, by no accident at all, he came across Amadeo, the merchant, whom he had avoided since Carnival.

Amadeo was taking a glass of wine in the shade of a grape arbor, near the edge of the city. He greeted Nicholas fulsomely enough, and Nicholas asked why he was still in Rome, in the heat of the summer.

"I was in the hills until last week," Amadeo said. He signaled to a wine-boy to bring Nicholas a glass. The shadow of the grape leaves dappled the tabletop between them; heavy ripening cones of grapes hung down over their heads. "But a matter of money brought me back to Rome. For which I am most grateful—else I would not have heard so swiftly and so well of this newest triumph of our prince."

Nicholas lifted his eyebrows. "Valentino?" he said smoothly.

"Yes—of course! The coup at Urbino—brilliant! The Borgia has grown in his mind. He has freed himself of the bonds of common opinion. Who would have thought it? But it was brilliant—brilliant."

The wine-boy set a glass of deep red wine down before Nicholas, who touched his fingers to the stem; he was gorged on Amadeo's praise and had no appetite for anything else.

He said, "There are those whom the act has shocked beyond anything the Borgias have done before."

"Bah. Small-minded folk. I for one am willing to give our prince his due."

Nicholas had to struggle to keep his face bland. He turned their conversation to other things, afraid Amadeo would detect something in his expression. For the first time in his life he did not feel smaller than the run of men.

On his way home that evening, he stopped at the inn where he had taken Miguelito's horse, to pay for its keep, and found that the horse was gone, although the bill had not been paid. While he was waiting for the innkeeper to figure the difference between his coin and the amount due, he heard two men arguing in the nearby common room.

"Valentino is a devil!"

"He is savior of Italy."

"It was the act of a barbarian."

"He must do what is necessary."

"He betrayed his ally."

"Urbino belongs to him—he took it without a costly war. Is that worth nothing?"

His own arguments on the tongue of a stranger swelled his spirit again. He could not keep the smile from his face. The innkeeper paid money into his hand.

"Well," the innkeeper said, "be pleased you have something to be glad over, Messer Dawson—and have pity on the folk of Urbino."

"God have mercy on us all," Nicholas said.

JUAN WAS AT WORK in his garden. Nicholas could hear him singing breathlessly beyond the trees and brush; he heard the strokes of the hoe. Miguelito was gone. The house was empty. Nicholas went to his chamber to put away his coat and shoes, dressed in more comfortable clothes, and crossed the main room to the kitchen for a glass of wine. The soup was simmering in the kettle and a large cheese rested on the wooden cutting surface by the basin; the cloth covering was peeled back a few inches from the edge of the cheese, revealing the mellow white flesh.

Nicholas poured his glass full of the wine. Just an ordinary wine; he wished it were finer, a northern wine, perhaps, to celebrate his triumph. He had never won a victory before. He held the glass so that the light of the lamp shone through the wine, as red as the ruby Valentino had sent him. He sipped from the glass, imagining that he swallowed jewels.

Juan appeared in the door from the pantry. "There is someone at the gate."

"Who is it?"

"I don't know them. Several men, with horses."

He lowered the glass half-tasted, all full of fluttery alarms, and reminded himself that now he was a man of consequence. "Wait. I will get my coat on." He went back into the house and dressed himself and went out the front door.

In the street outside the gate three men on horses waited in a rank; a fourth man, dismounted, was standing with his reins in his hand. When Nicholas opened the gate, this man saluted him.

"Señor Dawson?"

"Yes," Nicholas said.

"You are to accompany me, señor."

Nicholas lunged back inside the gate but before he could slam it one rider leapt his mount through the gate and pinned him between the horse and the wall. The man on foot had drawn his sword. Nicholas put out his hands, trying to hold the horse back, his nose full of the rich animal odor and his eyes fascinated by the glitter of the sword.

"Come with me, señor."

"I demand to know—"

The sword lifted, the broad blade darker at the edge, dulled with use. "Come with me, señor. Pedro—"

The horseman whose mount had Nicholas trapped against the wall reached down to grasp his arm. He recoiled, and the wall slapped into his back. The horse snorted, side-stepping. The sword tapped his arm. He thought he smelled iron, bitter as aloes. He let the horseman take hold of his arm and hoist him up onto the horse's back.

THEY TOOK HIM DOWN half a mile toward the Lateran, and met a dozen more horsemen, leading an extra horse. They tied his hands behind him and put him up on the horse and led him off.

He tried again to find out who they were and where they were taking him, shaping his voice strident with indignation. "Do you know who I am?" Railing at them, he trotted along after them down the street toward the Lateran gate.

It was still early in the evening. The street was deserted; even the cats had gone in to their dinner. They passed below the Lateran Palace, and Nicholas again protested, hoping someone on the ancient crenelated battlement might hear him. The leader of the men carrying him off wheeled his horse around.

"Señor Dawson, keep still or I shall put my feedbag over your head."

After that Nicholas said nothing.

A cart was coming in through the Lateran gate, high laden with hay, and they had to wait while the carter maneuvered his load through. Nicholas worked his hands inside his bonds. They were taking him out of Rome; he began to sweat at the thought of being at their mercy in a place he did not know. He looked from face to face of the men around him. They were of all types, broad and narrow, dark and fair, lively and taciturn. Their clothes wore no mark of their allegiance, no badge of prince or city. They were Spanish. Valentino's men, perhaps, or from the Spanish army in Naples.

The oxen plodded by, dragging the high-piled hay after them. The horses around Nicholas's horse moved off and his mount went with them. They rode out of the city.

He had always feared horses, and he had never learned to ride, not even the rudiments. Even at a walk he slid awkwardly around in his saddle, and he could not use his hands and arms for balance. As soon as his captors left the city, they put their horses into a quick trot. He bounced on his saddle, his spine stiff in anticipation of every jolt so that each one threw him higher yet, jarring his teeth in his head.

They seemed to ride on forever, passing dusty vineyards

and villas with roofs of red tile. Nicholas's legs ached; the ache progressed to a searing pain along the insides of his thighs and his groin. He bounced on his crotch and nearly fell off the saddle, half-swooning from the pain. One of the other men caught him and shoved him back upright.

They rode on into the darkness of the night. The country sky glowed overhead, so thick with stars his dazzled eyes saw shadows of light even in the dark. The soldiers turned into a lane bordered on either side with olive trees. At the far end was a villa whose long low wings enclosed a brick courtyard.

There the Spaniards took Nicholas off his horse and hauled him away. A man on either side of him, they had to carry him, his legs shaking and sore and useless under him. In a small room inside the main building of the villa they dropped him into a chair and left him.

He sat there, too exhausted even to wonder where he was, only relieved that the ride was over. His thighs were scraped raw and bleeding. With his fingertips he pulled the cloth of his hose away from the abused flesh. Now his gaze took in the room around him. It was small, and the only window was covered by a grille of wooden slats. The furniture stood close around the walls, square-cut tables crammed in between chairs covered with rugs in bright colors. Three candles burned in a brass floor standard by the door.

A man came in with a dish and a cup, which he put down before Nicholas, and left without speaking.

Nicholas sat still a moment after the door shut. Finally he leaned down and took the cloth away that covered the dish. A steamy fragrance of beans reached his nose. Suddenly he was mad with hunger; he snatched the bowl and spoon up and shoveled the food into his mouth and gulped the glass empty of its wine.

His stomach soothed, he went off in a circle around the room. The square furniture and the somber colors reminded him of the lodging where he had lived his years in Salamanca. Under such light as this he had learned to hate Aristotle and to love Theodosius. His first heart's love had seduced him in a room like this. He stood absently fingering the blackened wood of the back of a chair. Behind him there was a footstep.

He turned his head. A man with a grizzled beard stood on the threshold of the door.

"So you are the man who has made a fox of the Borgia lion," the grizzled man said, and smiled, and around his eyes the weathered skin pleated in a dozen wrinkles. "I am Gonsalvo."

The Spanish general. Nicholas began to bow and remembered that he had been dragged off to this meeting. He squared up his shoulders.

"My lord, I protest—"

"Of course." Gonsalvo settled himself in the chair opposite Nicholas. He wore a leather tunic over a plain shirt of linen, and might have been an ordinary countryman, except for the heavy signet ring on his left thumb. He said, "My men informed me that you suffered from the ride. That was my oversight—I never considered you might not know horsemanship."

He smiled again, his eyes narrowed in their fans of wrinkles. Nicholas throttled his own impulse to pass the abduction off that lightly; he wanted more than that from this great man. He said, "One would think the servants of the King of Spain—"

"Do what serves their master," Gonsalvo said. His voice was soft but he did not smile. "You did not come when you were requested to come, and so we took you. I regret the necessity. Actually, I have been curious about you since the night I spent in your house in Rome, talking to my little lion Cesare."

Nicholas sat down. "I am ready for answers."

"Now recent events have made my interest more pressing.

It was you who planned the taking of Urbino?"

"Yes," Nicholas said.

"You speak most excellent Spanish."

"I was born in Navarre," Nicholas said. "I studied at Salamanca."

"Indeed. You are of English parentage, by your name."

"Yes."

He realized that he was giving more answers than he was hearing; he touched his mouth with his hand and his gaze slid away from Gonsalvo. His legs hurt.

"Tell me what you think of Cesare Borgia," Gonsalvo said.

Nicholas lowered his hand to his lap, startled at that question; it was impossible for him to answer it without thinking more, and realizing that startled him again. He said, almost stammering, "He is my master, my lord captain."

"Yet as I know him I cannot suppose he made you his servant by any fair means. Are you not still an officer of the Republic of Florence? I fear our gentle Cesare suborned you by wicked means."

Nicholas was wrestling with his thoughts of Valentino. Gonsalvo might as easily have asked him what he thought of earthquakes, or nightmares. He had been too busy dealing with Valentino to pass a judgment of him.

"I desire," Gonsalvo said, "to bring you into my own service, if that finds favor with you."

"For what purpose? To spy?"

"Indeed. We have a bargain, he and I—he and my king. I mean to know even as he decides it if he will betray us."

"I will not betray him," Nicholas said.

"What! Have you not betrayed your city of Florence? Were they not your masters for enough years to bring a boy to manhood? Have you forged a stronger loyalty to Cesare in a matter of months?"

"Not in time," Nicholas said. "In actions—in the taking of Urbino."

He was determined not to yield to Gonsalvo. The Spanish

captain touched his beard with his fingers, his eyes unblinking.

"Money will not sway you?"

"Valentino pays me excellently well."

"Nor rank—the favor of Spain, your homeland?"

"My homeland is Navarre," Nicholas said. "Sometime in the future, perhaps, the Aragonese will swallow up that land and people as he has every other space in the peninsula, but as of now, he has not."

He had forgotten the pain in his legs; he sat up straight and stiff in the chair, cocked forward a little, aiming his words like blows at Gonsalvo. The man he refused glorified his refusal. He exalted in standing against Gonsalvo.

"Then," Gonsalvo said, "will you not consider that Cesare Borgia is a cruel, treacherous man whose highest standard is his own untempered will? A man is only as good as him he serves, Señor Dawson."

"No," Nicholas said.

But he no longer imagined himself ennobled by the argument.

Gonsalvo shut his eyes. "I could keep you here until you agreed."

"You could," Nicholas said. "But the news will reach Valentino very soon that I have been taken off, and it will require little effort on his part to discover where, and by whom, and then I should be of no use to you."

"In any case, I am not a Borgia. I will not keep you here. You may return to Rome." The Spanish captain got lithely to his feet. His smile was gone; a frown twisted his brows, and he looked older, restless with anger. He looked no more at Nicholas. With his fist he knocked sharply on the door.

When it opened, he spoke to someone out in the next room. "Take him back to his house. Be there by sunrise." He tramped out of the room.

A file of soldiers came through the door to Nicholas and took him away. They hurried him through the villa to the courtyard and boosted him onto another saddle. When his skinned thighs closed on the leathers, he groaned in pain. The soldiers mounted their horses and they trotted away.

JUST BEFORE DAWN, as Nicholas and his soldiers rode through the Appian Gate, a dozen men on foot set on them.

The Appian Gate was little used, the soldiers having chosen it for that reason, and the road was bordered in meadows and old ruined walls. From these hiding places more men rushed, and the soldiers shouted and surged across the dirty road. Nicholas was dragged from the saddle. Exhausted, half-crippled, he could not struggle; he felt himself carried off through a fighting mob. A moment later he dropped to the ground.

On hands and knees, his mouth full of dust, he scuttled blindly away from the shouting and fighting and the clatter of hoofs. He scrambled into high grass and came to a wall of brick. Pushing himself to his feet, he ran along the wall until he came to a place where the bricks had tumbled down and left only a few feet of the wall standing, and flinging one leg over this ridge he climbed into the safety and darkness beyond. Crouching down, he put his hands against the cool brick, lowered his head, and breathed deeply of the dusty air.

Farther down the street someone shouted, "This way!" The horses galloped off, and the racket of fighting faded away.

There was a tree growing up just behind him, which explained the darkness. He put his cheek to the brick of the wall. There was no sound; he was alone. He wiped his face on his sleeve. The wind stirred the tree's branches.

Just as he was about to look out through the gap in the wall a foot tramped down on the road outside.

He recoiled, crouching down again in the wall's shelter. His hackles rose. Casting around him he found a loose brick and took it into his hand for a weapon. The heavy footsteps in the road were coming toward him, grinding on the dirt of the road. They reached the wall; they stopped.

"Nicholas?"

It was Stefano. Nicholas lowered his hand and dropped the brick.

"I am here," he said, and went forward through the broken wall.

"THE OLD MAN COULD SAY only that someone had carried you off," Stefano said. He put the chair down beside the tub and sat on it. "What happened?"

"I had an interview with a Spanish knight," Nicholas said. "He felt I needed an escort."

"Then you weren't really in danger?"

"I thought I was," Nicholas said.

He settled down to his neck in the hot water. The soap bit into his lacerated thighs. He shut his eyes. A sense of well-being invaded him with the warmth of the bath; everything now seemed less important and much more entertaining. Juan brought in another bucket of hot water and poured it in over Nicholas's feet.

"I didn't really rescue you, did I?" Stefano said. "Old man, the glasses. The Spanish were bringing you back by themselves."

Nicholas put out one soapy hand to Stefano's. "I feel myself rescued."

Stefano was pulling the cork out of a bottle of wine; Juan stood behind him with glasses in his hands. The cork slid with a *thok* out of the bottle.

"What Spanish knight?" Stefano poured wine into the glasses that Juan held out. "Old man, a glass for you." He gestured broadly to carry his meaning over the gap in language.

"Don't give him orders," Nicholas said.

He was falling asleep. He did not want to tell Stefano about Gonsalvo.

"Let him drink with us," Stefano said. "I am not giving him orders. What do you think, that he is your slave? Your property?"

Juan stood watching them, attentive. Nicholas put out his wet hand again and took a glass from Stefano.

"Bring a glass for you yourself," he said in Spanish to Juan.

The old man bowed and went off across the room to the kitchen. Stefano had not understood; his gaze fixed steadily on Nicholas's face, he did not smile or look easy until Juan reappeared with a third glass. Then Stefano spread his broad smile across his face. He filled Juan's glass and raised his own.

"To—what shall we drink to? To life! To life."

Nicholas drank of the familiar red wine.

IN THE AFTERNOON after he had slept his fill Nicholas met Stefano on the riverbank, near the broken bridge and the place where they had first met. The bank of the Tiber there was thick with trees. Pairs of lovers strolled or sat or sprawled in the shade beneath the branches. Nicholas kept to the narrow sunlit path at the edge of the bank. He and Stefano walked along a hundred feet without speaking; at last Nicholas stopped. From his purse he took the ruby ring that Valentino had given him and held it out.

"Here. This is for you."

Stefano gave him a sharp look of surprise. Taking the ring, he held it to the light, and a low whistle escaped him.

"Four hundred crowns at least. Five, maybe."

"At least," Nicholas said dryly. He started off again down the path.

Stefano walked along beside him, trying the ring on his fingers until he found the best fit. He held his hand into the sunlight so that the ring glittered and the ruby shone fiery red. Suddenly he turned to Nicholas, as if to kiss him.

Nicholas thrust him off. "Not here—with all these folk about."

"You are ashamed," Stefano said.

"This place is full of eyes."

Stefano let out a yell of laughter. He looked broadly about them. "I see no one heeding anything but his own lust."

"They are indecent."

"I do not understand you. You must turn the simplest things into scholars' matter." Stefano spread out his arms and tipped his head back so that the sun shone on his face. "The day is beautiful. We are free men. Care about anything more than that, and you are asking for trouble."

Nicholas laughed at that. He was pleased Stefano thought him complex. They turned away from the river and followed an overgrown path through the trees toward the lower ground. As they left the shelter of the trees, a painted whore approached them.

"Gentlemen, let me serve you, both at once!"

Nicholas went by behind her, Stefano passed before her. They went on down toward the ancient ruins in the meadow beyond. There were two old temples, a few hundred feet apart, in the grass there; one was round and light, and the other massive, its great columns half-sunk into the marshy ground, toppling under their own weight. Nicholas slowed his feet. The ground squelched under him.

He had come this way often but now for the first time the ruins disturbed his mood. It was so easy to look on this airy shape of stone and think: a temple of Vesta. That meant nothing to him, a handful of words in an old book. What the ancients had thought here, who had believed in Vesta, he could no more recover than he could replace the flesh on a skeleton of dry bones. Those who spoke of restoring the antique world to life could believe in that only because there was so little known of that past that it assumed any shape desired of it.

"You are right," he said. "I am a hypocrite."

"What are you talking about now?" Stefano asked. He was admiring the ring again, his arm stretched out.

Nicholas thought of his conversation with Gonsalvo. He had not denied the Spaniard out of loyalty to Valentino. The more he tried to isolate his reasons into a logical order the more confused he became; as he thought about what had happened, his memory of it changed, and he began to wonder if he remembered what had actually taken place or if he were reconstructing what he desired to have done. Not loyalty to Valentino had inspired him, but the will to enlarge himself.

"Well, well," he said, "there is nothing to do but admit it, I suppose. And no one else does any different."

Stefano gave him a sharp oblique look, but he said nothing. On his hand the ruby glinted in the sunlight. Nicholas rubbed his hands together. They were walking down toward the path that led through the marshes where the Circus Maximus had been; goats grazed on the hillside beyond, and their coarse wool hung in shreds on the branches of the thorn brushes all around. Nicholas felt like a fool for having seen so little how the world was ordered by self-interest, because once he accepted that, the chaos of human motive that had always defied his analysis fell into order with a marvelous clarity. Whatever men professed, they did what served them. Nor could he see a fault in it since they would be mad to do otherwise. Stefano was walking beside him, and he reached out and took hold of the younger man's hand.

Instantly Stefano clutched his hand tight. "What are you thinking about?" he said.

Nicholas laughed. They turned onto the path through the marshes.

NICHOLAS KNOCKED on the door to Bruni's chamber, which he did seldom; usually he came there only on the ambassador's invitation. The lack of custom worked at Bruni as well, because when the big man opened the door he looked surprised to see Nicholas there.

"Excellency," Nicholas said, without any formality, "I must ask your attention on a matter personal to me."

"Ah?" Bruni said.

They were still standing in the doorway, with the threshold between them. Nicholas put his hands behind his back.

"Excellency, the Signory has fallen badly into arrears on my salary."

"Ah," Bruni said, and looked distressed. He backed out of the doorway. "Come in."

Nicholas followed him into the dim, over-decorated room. Bruni did not go to his desk but paced up and down across the room a few times, while Nicholas stood just inside the doorway and watched him.

"I can assure you that this is no fault of mine," Bruni said. "In fact the Signory has been lax in paying me, as well."

Nicholas cleared his throat. "Your Excellency's family is resident in Florence, able to bring pressure to bear on your behalf." He happened to know that Bruni had received a bank draft for his back salary within the week.

"For certain payments, yes, but as you must know—" Bruni's back was to him, but he turned his head to look over his shoulder at Nicholas—"being watchful as you ever are, I have been paying the couriers' and scribes' wages out of my own purse, and for that I have not been recompensed."

"All the more reason, Excellency, why you should do your best to see us all paid."

Bruni had stopped at the window and was pulling the draperies apart with one hand so that he could peer through into the yard beyond; there was an alley there, full of horse dung, nothing to look at. He said, "Nicholas, if you need money, I will be happy to loan you any reasonable sum."

"I should rather take my due from the Signory," Nicholas said.

"Every diplomat in Rome is underpaid."

That was true. The Spanish ambassador to the Curia had been paid nothing since his arrival in Rome several years before. Nicholas made no comment on it, curious to see what Bruni would say next.

"Very well," the ambassador said, and turned and faced him. "I will do what I can. But expect nothing, I promise nothing."

"I cannot see," Nicholas said, "why I should expect to work when I am not to expect to be paid."

Bruni's eyes widened, and the corners of his mouth tucked down in an unhappy scowl. "For the Republic," he said. "For the Republic. For the city." His voice fell to a reverent hush. Suddenly, snapping his head back, he spoke in full voice again. "You have my leave to go. I have said that I will do what I can to help you, I have no more time for these matters."

"Yes, Excellency," Nicholas said, and went out of the ambassador's chamber.

THE GARDEN OF CARDINAL ORSINI was perfumed with orange trees. Lanterns hung everywhere in the twilight; the breeze turned them, swaying and bobbing in swarms of moths and mosquitoes. Nicholas, lingering on the edge of the terrace, was wishing that he could go home, take off his clothes, and sleep in the cool of his bedchamber. He raised his glass and lost the perfume of the oranges in the aroma of the wine.

Below him, Bruni was saying, "Alas, my dear Cardinal, the stars are inscrutable. One sees their meaning too late to prevent disaster."

They walked across the grass, Bruni in his high four-cornered hat, and the head of the Orsini family in his soutane, the color blotted out to black in the darkness.

"You will pardon me, most excellent orator," the Cardinal was saying. A page brought him wine in a thin-belled

Venetian glass. "I do not share your enthusiasm for blaming all that befalls us on the movement of a few stars."

Nicholas went after them, keeping a respectful distance. The Cardinal paused to finish the contents of his glass, opened his hand, and let the glass drop. A page scooped it out of the grass.

"What is a star?" the Cardinal went on. His voice was high and feminine. "A crystal sphere, with an angel within to guide it across the sky—no more than that. To understand man, study men, not the stars."

"I cannot believe that God would be so frivolous," Bruni said. "Not—" hastily, one hand raised—"that I call in question a doctrine of the Church."

"None would believe it of you. Will you join a few of us to hear the most excellent Messer Berocchi read his latest work?"

"Heavens. Another heroic narrative verse?"

The Cardinal's soft laughter rippled out. "I fear so. I understand this commemorates the recent triumphs of our splendid Duke Valentino." Abruptly the Orsini stopped, turning, his silk hem sliding across the grass. "Messer Dawson, you will join us?"

Nicholas cleared his throat. Girolamo Berocchi's readings usually lasted hours.

"Excellent." The Cardinal led them on across a lawn where a mass of young men were forming the lines of a dance. In a pavilion by the roses the musicians were tuning lutes and horns. Nicholas followed his master and the Cardinal into the vast Orsini palace.

"The stars," the Cardinal was saying, in his velvety voice, "seem to be preparing another Neapolitan stew for us, if rumor is true, my dear Bruni."

"Ah," Bruni said.

They were crossing a vast hall, prepared for the comedy that was to be played at midnight, to cap off the evening. The stage covered one end of the room; from the paper-plaster arch hung loops of scarlet silk and scarlet ribbons wound down the two Doric columns that supported it on either side.

"Naturally I would not pry secrets from you"—the Cardinal took Bruni's arm in a comradely grip—"yet it does not entirely strain my ability to believe when I hear that the French intend to send a formal protest to Spain over the matter of Naples."

"Such a tedious matter for a gathering of friends," Bruni said. "You should press Nicholas for details, Monsignor—he keeps us all so very well informed on these little border disputes. Nicholas?"

"Excellency," Nicholas said. Bruni knew nothing of the ferment in Naples. He followed the two elegant men ahead of him into the next room, where Orpheus and Eurydice walked and sang and wept across the walls.

There the poet had already begun to read. A clutch of somber men and women were arranged in attitudes of attention around the room, some in chairs, some standing or leaning against the plaster columns that pretended to hold up the ceiling. Nicholas still held his empty glass, but there was no place to dispose of it. Stopping behind an Orsini duchess, he let the Cardinal and Bruni go off to the front of the room. If he stayed near the door he could leave unobserved within a few moments. He put the glass in his hand down behind the chair where the Duchess of Gravina sat, and with his toe nudged it into the shelter of her vast skirts.

Berocchi, the poet, stood at a lectern of wood carved and painted to simulate a Doric column. As he read he gestured with one hand. His fingernails were painted red to heighten the power of this action. His poem, as usual, was in Latin dactylic hexameters. Nothing varied the singsong rhythm, with its strong step and weak steps like a drunk staggering home.

None of the listeners moved. They all appeared to have braced themselves up, even those on their feet, so that if they nodded off no slumping head or dangling hand would betray it. Nicholas stood fidgeting through several relentlessly awful lines.

Capua secessit caesim a verbis Caesaris—

Perhaps it was a subtle Orsini joke on Valentino.

Nicholas began to creep his way toward the door. It was a rare privilege of lesser rank that he could leave, and the Duchess of Gravina, for one, could not. By degrees he reached the door and slipped through into the next room.

Here the walls were painted with wild beasts, tamed by the music of Orpheus' harp. Several other people were gathered in groups by the open windows to talk. It was hot; Nicholas paused to loosen his coat. A man in riding clothes tramped in the door.

This man stopped to look around him. His boots were gray with mud. Behind the mask of dust on his face Nicholas recognized one of Bruni's couriers and hurried to reach him before he could call more attention to himself.

"Messer Dawson," the courier said loudly, and clutched at Nicholas's arm. "Where is my lord Bruni?"

"Keep your voice down," Nicholas said. "In the next room, but he is busy. What—"

The courier strode off, heading straight for the poetry reading. Nicholas lunged after him, trying to grab hold again before the man could put them in the middle of a crowd, but the courier eluded him. He tramped on into the next room. Nicholas looked swiftly around him; some of the others in this room were watching, attentive.

In the next room Berocchi's voice stopped. Someone said, behind Nicholas, "Is something wrong?"

He turned his head; the voice belonged to a slender young man in clothes so picked out with gold lace and pearls that he glittered. Nicholas bowed to him.

"I know nothing of it, Monsignor de' Medici."

The young man smiled. He had pointed eyeteeth. "You know me?"

In the next room, Bruni shouted, "Nicholas!"

"As your Magnificence might know," Nicholas said, trying to sound unconcerned, "I began my career with the Florentine legation here when Florence was under your father."

"Nicholas!"

"You have my leave, Messer Dawson," the youth said smoothly, still smiling. "I believe your present employer calls."

Nicholas started toward Bruni but before he could reach the door into the reading room Bruni was rushing forth, the Cardinal Orsini and others of the audience after him, and the courier on his heels. He gripped Nicholas by the arm. In a voice that probably reached well beyond the slumbering lions and oxen on the walls, he said, "I am recalled to Florence. The mob is throwing up barricades in the streets—"

"Excellency," Nicholas said. "I beg you to lower your voice."

"Piero de' Medici is known to be in Arezzo!"

Nicholas kicked Bruni in the shin. Orsini and his friends boiled over with excitement, and the gilded boy at Nicholas's elbow murmured, "Messer Dawson, you may find yourself again where you began, soon enough."

"By God!" Bruni shouted. "How dare you kick me!"

Nicholas looked away. At least Bruni was yelling on a safe topic. Bruni shouldered past him, shouting for a page. His face was grossly red. He wheeled to face Nicholas again.

"The legation is in your hands. Keep the peace there. I will—someone will send you instructions."

The Cardinal summoned a page, who hurried away with Bruni to find the ambassador's cloak. Nicholas wondered if Bruni would have the wit to save himself in the disordered Republic. Bruni disappeared out the door.

Around Nicholas the others began to chatter.

"Florence may fall! Well, it has not been a sturdy Republic."

"What republic is?"

"Sometimes," the Cardinal said, in a voice like an extended sigh, "it seems to me that the whole world is shattering around me."

"Shattering perhaps," said Giulio de' Medici, "in order to be reborn! Ours is the age of glorious rebirth. We must keep heart at all times."

The Duchess of Gravina elbowed her way in among them; her wide face was stern as any man's, her upper lip feathery with fine white hair and her eyes fierce. "Rebirth!" she said. "Then it is a monster being born. Such men as the Borgias are its precursors, and events like this—"

"My lady." The Cardinal bowed before her, and she clamped her lips shut. The other voices rose.

"We are seeing the end of things."

"No—a new age," the young de' Medici cried again. "A beginning."

"The disintegration of all value—"

That was someone on Nicholas's other side, and a new voice there took up the argument.

"This is a time to return to the great age of the classical world. If we only keep our faith firm, we can!"

Nicholas listened to all this but said nothing. Whatever could be said was by that fact alone too simple to satisfy him. Perhaps none of it was true at all. Perhaps all that was happening was that people were trying to say what was happening to them, and the disintegration was not in things but in their knowledge of things. He struggled with the idea of a world of blind impact and unlaw, the only order a tenuous expectation of consistency from one moment to the next.

"Messer Dawson—"

He stirred himself. "I must take my leave. Serenity—"

Smiling, the Cardinal put out his ring to be kissed.

IN THE LATE SUMMER HEAT every man of consequence fled Rome for the healthy air of the countryside. The Pope withdrew to his castle in the Alban Hills. Every morning Nicholas went to the legation, read the routine dispatches, and gave the clerks and pages what work there was. When they were done he sent them home.

From Florence and Bruni came no news. The crisis there had thrown even the sensation of Urbino into shadow. It was known generally that French troops from Milan were marching to the city, but no one cared to speculate what influence they might have; in any case there were only a few hundred Frenchmen stationed in Milan to begin with.

With the great men of Rome gone, the city was lifeless; nothing happened. No one even carried gossip of any interest. It was as if Rome were surrounded by a wall of silence, like the castle in the tale. By noon of each day there was nothing more to be done and Nicholas locked the doors of the legation and went home.

He dined in the garden. Stefano came to share his meal, nearly every day, and to pass the afternoon with him. They sat under the trees, where Juan burned wet rags to keep off the mosquitoes, and talked idly, or Stefano dealt out the cards of his tarocco deck on the table still scattered with crumbs from their meal.

The cards were becoming familiar to Nicholas. He sat watching them spin from his lover's fingers. The Hanged Man appeared often, dangling upside down by one foot, the other leg crossed over the first at the knee, and a mad smile on his face. The Pope followed him, and the World, and the Lovers, of course man and woman. Stefano had said that the cards could tell the future. Nicholas made up antic interpretations of their order. A pinprick stabbed his neck; he slapped at it in a mindless reflex, his gaze fixed on the cards.

The Devil grinned also, like the Hanged Man, fierce and agonized.

Nicholas scratched his arms, red and lumpy with insect bites. Stefano was turning out the cards again.

"Why do you do that over and over?"

"There's nothing else to do." Stefano waved the deck over the table, where half a dozen faces already lay looking up at the sky. "Shall I teach you the game?"

Nicholas shook his head. "I'll watch. I'm better at that."

In the heat and stillness of the city at the center of the world the cards took on an illusion of meaning. Perhaps they were keys, those cryptic figures with their symbolic names and rings of Hebrew and Greek lettering. Nicholas considered that he should have been a Platonist; then he could pick up the card called the World and put it in his purse, and never more worry about Duke Valentino.

At the thought he laughed, and Stefano's head rose.

"What amuses you?"

"The heat has cooked my brain. Like an egg, Stefano."

"Tell me."

"No—no. It's gone already."

Stefano ruffled the deck with his long fingers. He wore the ruby on his left forefinger. "Tell me."

Nicholas shook his head, smiling, and scratched his itching neck.

"If you ask me, your brain's been soft since your little ride out of Rome last month."

"Really? How so?"

Stefano turned, slinging one leg over the other, and folded his arm over the back of the chair. "I cannot say, to be truthful. Ask the old man. You let all manner of things go on that formerly would have stirred you up to a black sweat. Ask Juan."

Juan was working in his garden. Nicholas could hear his

tuneless singing beyond the box trees. Another mosquito whined in his ear and he covered his ear with his hand. The heat was making him sleepy and lecherous; he smiled at Stefano. He had not known until he lost Stefano how much he loved him; now he was determined to keep him. It surprised Nicholas how that elementary decision simplified their relationship.

"You and Juan do as you like here, and nothing I say has any more effect than to entertain you."

"I am a guest in your house," Stefano said, and put down the cards. "You have never told me who stole you away from Rome, either—was it Valentino?"

Nicholas burst out in laughter. The insect hum sounded by his head and he slapped at it; the body broke against his fingers, spurting blood.

"No. It was not Valentino. It was Gonsalvo da Cordoba."

Stefano's eyebrows lowered over his sunburnt nose. "Who is that?"

"He is the captain-general of the Spanish army in Naples."

"A Spaniard. We have enough of those, with Valentino and the Pope. I am surprised he brought you back again."

"Why?"

"They are all treacherous. See what Valentino did at Urbino."

"What think you of his work in Urbino?"

Stefano lowered his eyes, his eyelids like shells, moist with sweat. "If I were his man, I should never turn my back on him. It was shrewd, I warrant you that. And the lesser men can be thankful, since they took no wounds."

Among the dirty crockery on the table was a napkin; Nicholas took it and wiped his bloody fingers. "Urbino was my work."

His lover's pale eyes widened. Nicholas imagined lions' eyes like that. Stefano said, "What?"

"I gave him the plan. It was my scheme, all of it."

Stefano looked down again at the deck. He turned over the

top few cards one by one: the eight of swords, the Ace of pentacles, the Fool, the Hanged Man. Nicholas wondered if he believed what he had just heard.

"That's where you are getting all the money," Stefano said.

The Hanged Man glided across the table and out over the edge, onto the empty air. Nicholas bent to pick it up from the ground.

"Why did you tell me?"

"Why should I keep it from you?" Nicholas laid the card on the table. "That is the ring he gave me, when the plan worked and Urbino fell to him."

Stefano gawked down at the ring. He shot a narrow look at Nicholas. "Well," he said. "Do not turn your back on him, Nicholas." He raked the cards into a heap and made a square deck of them again.

"It's hot out here," Nicholas said.

"Let's go inside. I have to go soon anyway."

"Soon?"

"We have some time still."

FOR MANY DAYS Nicholas had no word at all from Bruni. One day as he was walking through the horse market near the legation, someone called softly to him from an alley.

He looked; down in the shadow of the alley a hooded man beckoned furiously. Nicholas hesitated to go into the narrow darkened space, and the man called, "Messer Dawson! I have a message for you—" and waved a roll of paper.

Nicholas went down three or four paces into the alley and reached for the roll, but the hooded man hid it quickly in his cloak. His empty hand reappeared, palm up.

"Two crowns."

Nicholas gave him fifty carlini. The man paused only a moment, shrugged, and gave him the message.

Heavily waxed and sealed, it required a strong knife to

open; he took it back to the legation. There was no signature, only a bare page of script.

"My dear friend," the letter began. "Since Saturn holds in his toils that fountain whence we two were wont to quench our thirst—"

Bruni, certainly. Nicholas smiled, and to his own surprise felt a sudden amused affection for the ambassador.

"Know you then that your Virgoan traveler keeps his place here, although with nothing but doubt for tomorrow. The situation, as you might guess, wavers between the Jupiterians of the city and the Mercurians. Certain barbarian influences also make known their presence. I have cast my fate in with those supporting the Father of the Planets, in the person of one whose calls are Pisces Sagittarius. I trust you will unravel this mystery, and give me the benefit of your counsel. Sign me thus: no one."

Nicholas laid the letter down on his desk. Perhaps Bruni was justified; the crisis in Florence might well require exactly this sort of subterfuge, but Nicholas felt that the ambassador could have risked a little more clarity. He laid his two hands on either edge of the letter to hold it flat. The *Jupiterians* of the city versus the *Mercurians:* that eluded him. He thought perhaps the first reference was to the aristocrats of Florence, who had always resisted the broadly based Signory, and the second to the popular Republic, the fickle mob. The *barbarian influences* certainly were the French, whose arrival to defend Florence from the Borgias had been timely enough for the interests of the King of France. In that case Bruni was supporting the great families in their move to take control of the city back from the mob to whom Savonarola had delivered it, many years before. *Pisces Sagittarius* confused him, until he realized that the initials of the phrase were those of Piero Soderini, the dominant politician in Florence.

Nonetheless he wished Bruni had taken the chance of saying more exactly what he meant.

Bruni wanted advice. Lacking knowledge of the planets, Nicholas could hardly employ a similar code, and finally he wrote down exactly what he thought: that Bruni should watch all the sides in the controversy, try to choose the strongest, and support it, because the sooner the crisis was resolved the safer Florence would be.

With this letter in hand he started out of the building, to go find a certain Sienese merchant whom he knew to be staying in Rome overnight. As he went through the workroom, he noticed that the curtain over an archway onto the loggia was open, and when he closed it he noticed the palms on the loggia beyond.

They were wilting in the heat. The tips of their fronds were brown and yellow. Nicholas stood still, one hand on the curtain, his gaze fixed on the row of dying plants, and all his fresh affection for Bruni soured into rancor. He wished he had not seen the plants; now he would have to do something. He felt as if Bruni had deserted them purposely to irritate him. He would not water them himself; one of the pages could be ordered to do that, but the page's work would have to be supervised and his failures reproved. Nicholas started to turn away, the plants like a new burden on his back.

He turned around, full of a frivolous malice. Going out onto the loggia, he looked out, first, into the courtyard below; there was no one there, only a horse tethered at the far end of the yard, a pile of dung decorating the paving stone below its tail. Even the far balcony on the facing wall of the building was deserted, where customarily the old lady sat with her tatting. Nicholas lowered his gaze to the plants.

Going along the row of pots he pushed them one by one over the edge of the loggia. They smashed on the paving below. He went back into the workroom, took his coat, and went down the stairs.

When he emerged into the courtyard a groom was standing there, frowning at the mess of dirt and broken plants, the bits of bright pottery scattered all the way across the court to the far wall. As Nicholas passed, the young man said, "What happened, sir? Do you know how they fell?"

"I have no idea," Nicholas said cheerfully, and without pausing went on his way.

In the Borgia Tower the anteroom to Valentino's chamber was sweltering with late summer heat, the air dense and stale, and the light gloomy. Nicholas sat in the corner away from the fire. He was alone in the small room. He had been waiting over an hour; night was coming; more than six hours had passed since he had received Valentino's summons. In that time Nicholas had considered the summons from every perspective. The message's wording gave no hint why Valentino wanted to see him, a void Nicholas had tenanted with numberless demons.

The door into the inner chamber was on his right. Now he was wondering if Valentino were there at all, if anyone were there.

The moments crept by. He began to stare at the door. No one had come in or out all the while he had been waiting. Surely the room was empty.

If he could go into that room—if he could catch even a glance of Valentino's privy papers—

Now his gaze was fastened to the door. He was sure that the room was empty, but what if someone came in suddenly and surprised him there? He did not want to have to explain that to Valentino. Still, he would have no chance like this again, to look through Valentino's privy papers. He could open the outer doorway so that he would hear anyone coming. Immediately he rejected that. Anyone passing by would see him where he should not be. He would have to take the chance. Only a few seconds. Just a look.

He went to the door and stood with his hand halfway to the latch, gathering up his courage. Just a few moments. He opened the door.

The room beyond was dark. On the table a single candle burned. Behind the table sat Valentino.

Nicholas startled down to his heels. He said, "Magnificence. Your pardon."

Valentino left his chair. "What will you do with my pardon?" He sauntered around the table to the door and shut it. "What a mean-stomached mouse. You waited an hour and twenty minutes merely. Better be honest, mouse, you are too cowardly for the other. Make something of this."

He swatted with his hand at a pile of letters on the table. Nicholas moved nearer the candle. Valentino had waited, sat there and waited, to see if Nicholas would steal into his room. Nicholas's hands were wet. His neck burned with embarrassment. He remembered it as if he had watched it from above, himself fidgeting in his chair on one side of the wall and on the other Valentino waiting. He took a napkin from his sleeve and dried his hands. Behind him, Valentino laughed.

The three letters in the pile were short notes, nearly identical, in cipher. Nicholas saw the key at once and translated them out in his head.

"These are all notes agreeing to meet at Lake Magione in October," he said.

Valentino returned to his chair. "I managed that well by myself."

"They are all in the same hand. Where did you come by these, Magnificence?"

Valentino was looking off into the darkness. "A friend in Gianpaolo's service sent them."

Nicholas gave a little shake of his head. Into his mind popped the memory of Gianpaolo Baglione, in this very room, horror-struck by Nicholas's plan for Urbino. "It's slight enough," he said, "but it can't be good."

"Then you agree with me," Valentino said. He reached his two hands across the table for the letters and gathered them into a stack. "Take these." He held them out to Nicholas. "Find out what you can.

"Yes, Magnificence."

"I want to know everything as you learn it. Within an hour."

"Yes, Magnificence."

"Where do you suppose you are going now?"

With the letters in his hand Nicholas had backed a step toward the door. "With your leave, Magnificence—"

"I have not dismissed you." Valentino smiled at him.

Nicholas realized that something bad was coming. For an instant his eyes met Valentino's; instantly he dropped his gaze.

"The city of Florence is more fixed against me than ever," Valentino said. "Although as you predicted the state fell. You must have known that it would not fall to me."

"Magnificence, no one is always right—"

"I don't believe you, my dear mouse."

"I assure you, Magnificence—"

"Bah."

Although Valentino never raised his voice Nicholas fell still. He passed the cryptic letters from one hand to the other. That raised his spirits; having work for him, Valentino was only going to scold him. He took a deep breath, half sure, and took the jump.

"Magnificence, you know everything—I throw myself at your feet for mercy."

"Henceforth you serve me alone, mouse."

"I ask nothing more than that, Magnificence."

The candlelight gleamed strangely on the prince's eyes. His smile parted his lips. He was feeding on these cringes and scrapes. Nicholas bent his knee a little more.

"In your service I can make good use of my position with Florence. Only guide me to your purpose. I am your tool."

Valentino was silent. Nicholas touched his lower lip with his tongue. He had spoken too broadly, the prince would take it for satire. The chair scraped on the floor; Valentino was rising.

"What do you mean?"

Nicholas raised the handful of letters. "If these mean some conspiracy among your captains, as it could be supposed to mean, then your enemies will know of it long before your friends."

Valentino said swiftly, "You think it's that? They conspire against me?"

Something in his voice brought Nicholas to stare at him, surprised. It seemed as if Valentino were afraid. His gaze met Valentino's back. The Borgia was standing in the darkness looking down through the window. Abruptly he wheeled smartly to face Nicholas across the candlelit table.

"Then find out what they conspire to do. Stay with the Florentines. Do they pay you well?"

"Poor and late."

Valentino broke into a sudden sunny smile. "I pay well. You'll learn to love me. Now go and bring me something to convince my father."

"Magnificence, I will do what I can."

"Oh, no." Valentino cocked up his sun-bleached eyebrows and pointed his finger at Nicholas. "You will do what I say. Now go."

Nicholas bowed and left the room. In the antechamber he paused a moment, there in the deep brown darkness by the outer door, far from the candle, and sorted through what he had just seen.

He understood more of Valentino now, enough that he no longer feared him. He saw how Valentino was to be managed. Great as his power was, yet he could not trust it; he feared so for it that the cringing of as low a man as Nicholas was true comfort to him. That was how to lead him. Nicholas saw it as clearly as a problem in mathematics. Whoever made a king of Valentino would hold him.

He saw himself, not the king but the king's minion, whispering in his ear.

A sound beyond the door brought him to himself. Footsteps. Someone was coming up the stair outside the antechamber. Valentino would come out of the inner chamber and Nicholas did not want to see him, not now, with the new knowledge shining in him. Hastily he went out the door.

In the morning he had a dispatch from Florence, in two pieces: a letter giving him temporary power to receive diplomatic communications in the name of the Republic, and a short order concerning Astorre Manfredi.

"It is known to us," the letter ran, "that the Borgia having seized the city of Faenza took into his power the youthful prince Astorre of that city, and that since the return of the monster to Rome this young man Astorre has been flung into the dungeon of Sant' Angelo. We require that you do all possible to achieve his release, in the name of the Republic of Florence."

That was all, save the signature; yet the signature told Nicholas much, because it was that of Niccolo Machiavelli. Machiavelli was Piero Soderini's man. Nicholas spent several moments weighing out what it meant that a henchman of Soderini's should already be signing letters to Florence's most important legation.

The Fortress of Sant' Angelo stood like a tumulus on the bank of the Tiber just upriver from the Vatican. Its battered round walls were high enough to shadow the street around it, and the two new towers that Pope Alexander had added to it gave it an awkward, horned look. Nicholas loathed the place. He remembered his meeting here with Lucrezia Borgia and hoped that he could find some way as effective in the case of Astorre Manfredi. He presented himself at the gate of the fortress and was let in.

Thick with soldiers, the cramped open spaces of the ancient building were threaded through a bulk of solid stone. Nicholas imagined that an anthill must be as crowded and as cold. A guard took his credentials and letter of introduction and led him to the gallery where he was to meet Astorre.

The gallery, pierced with windows, was as bleak as the rest of the fortress. Not even a woven hanging covered the raw stone wall. The oval windows were barred with a grillework of wrought metal, coiled like rose vines, and studded with iron thorns. Astorre appeared at the far end, among the shadows, and stood hesitantly until a guard came forward to direct him to Nicholas.

Nicholas bowed, knelt, and kissed the young man's proffered hand. The guard read off his name, mispronounced as only a Romagnol could mispronounce it, and his station. Folding the letter, the man propped himself against the wall to watch.

"You are gracious to come, Ser—Doo—"

"Messer Nicholas Dawson, Magnificence."

Astorre smiled. He was a handsome boy, his hair soft and pale, hanging in curls over his ears like a carved Cupid's, and his innocent eyes wide-set. The smooth lips smiled too easily. The dungeon had not corrupted him yet. He listened to Nicholas's speech of friendship and concern with his head inclined a little to one side.

"You of Florence are ever kind to me. There was no need of this visit to assure me that you will not desert me now."

Nicholas said something about ransom and asked what amenities the prince might need to soften his prison stay. At the word "prison" Astorre moved, his hands rising from his sides, his eyes shifting away.

"Prison. I am not in prison here."

He turned toward the window, through which he and Nicholas could see the Tiber.

"I am a guest here. He—my lord Cesare—he has never used me as a prisoner. Only as a guest. He has said it often."

"Magnificence, the Duke Valentino enjoys the power of soft words—"

"He would not deceive me."

The boy put his hand on the grille, his fingers curling through the open work, among the iron thorns.

"I can leave whenever I wish."

Without moving his head, Nicholas glanced at the guard, listening to every word. Was the boy saying all this for the guard's sake? Or for his own?

"Nevertheless, Magnificence, I beg you, do not attempt to leave before we have arranged the formalities."

"Oh, you diplomats." Astorre, smiling again, looked over his shoulder at Nicholas. "He is right—without your little rules you are lost."

"Then, Magnificence, for our comfort, allow us to believe that our little rules are of some value."

"As you wish."

The guard was coming toward them. The interview was over. Nicholas knelt again. Again he paid the prince the usual compliments and assurances. He touched the pale fingers to his lips. He hoped that Astorre's trust in Valentino went no deeper than that. He hardly dared look into the boy's beautiful, trusting face.

The guard took away the prisoner. Nicholas went as swiftly as he could make his way down the cramped driveway to the courtyard.

There Miguel da Corella was dismounting from his horse. Nicholas paused, uncertain whether to greet him, Miguelito's moods being utterly beyond prediction. To his surprise the soldier saw him, burst into wreaths of smiles, and hailed him over to his side.

"Messer Nicholas. What do you here?"

"In fact, I am going out," Nicholas said. "This place haunts me."

Miguelito pulled off his heavy riding gloves. "You are a fantast."

"No, never, for God's love. I have no such imaginative fever, I assure you."

A smirk crossed Miguelito's face. He stuffed his gloves into his belt. The buckle of the belt was in the figure of a Gorgon's head. "Maybe so. Whom did you come here to see?"

"Don't you know?" Nicholas said, certain of it; as if Miguelito had told him outright, that question warned him that the soldier was here to plumb what he knew of Astorre.

The other man worked one shoulder up and down. His olive complexion was darker by a film of dirt. Nicholas put on a polite face of waiting for an answer.

At last Miguelito said, "What do you think of him?"

"Of whom?"

"Ah—you wiggler—Astorre! The pretty boy."

Nicholas glanced at the gate, longing to go. "He is certainly that."

"You find him attractive."

"That I never said. He is—soft. What do you intend for him?"

Again Miguelito's lips parted in a leer. "Yes, that, very soft. You are right." He began to walk, going to the gate, walking Nicholas to the gate. "He yields too readily. I love strength in a man—something I can test my own power against. Otherwise one might as well love women. Isn't that so?"

Nicholas lowered his eyes to look at the rough paving stones. "What do you intend for him?"

"I don't decide such things. Ask someone else. Have you learned any more about those coded messages?"

"I know whom they were to be sent to," Nicholas said.

Miguelito's eyes widened. "Who?"

"I should tell Valentino."

The soldier flung a sharp look to either side of him to see if anyone watched, and stepped closer, his head thrust forward. "Tell me. You know I am my master's right hand and right eye and right ear."

He stank. Nicholas moved backward, away from him, smiling. "Not close enough to him, though, to know what fate he intends for Astorre."

Miguelito grunted, and his lips curled down; that angered him. "Well," he said, "come tonight to the palace. Attend on him at supper."

On the last word he wheeled and strode away. Nicholas began to call after him but there were too many strangers in the courtyard. Half of Rome would know with their breakfast if he waited on Valentino at his private supper. He wondered how the Signory would construe that. Miguelito had gone. Nicholas went back to his legation.

On his way to the Vatican that evening he fell in with another servant of Valentino's, a Spaniard named des Troches, who was buoyant with speculations. "The Pope is to dine tonight with Valentino. We shall all have to look smart."

"Why?" Nicholas asked.

"Well, I for one have hopes of a certain office in the Pope's household that I happen to know will soon come vacant. A very nice pension."

Nicholas glanced sharply across at the other man. Paste jewels sparkled in the Spaniard's sleeves. His beard was oiled to a point. They came to the doorway and Nicholas stood aside to let des Troches go ahead of him. There at the threshold to the dining chamber, where already a dozen courtiers hummed and buzzed, des Troches paused a moment, his face intense. His hands darted over his costume, touching his clothes into place, as if he were putting himself together. He walked forward with a new strut in his gait. Nicholas followed, half-amused, feeling drab.

They entered a room full of noise. No one sat at the table near the window, and Nicholas could not make out how many places had been made ready. It was commonly known that Valentino preferred to dine by himself. A number of other men were already talking and moving around the room when Nicholas and des Troches came in, and des Troches was greeting them, some casually, some with the intensity of a lover. Nicholas went off along the edge of the room.

There were four sets of gold dinner plate waiting on the table. He wandered away, reluctant to be so much in the eye of the room.

"Messer Dawson." A man in a red coat put himself forward into Nicholas's path. "We met at the Cardinal of Siena's Christmas, some years ago, you must remember." He put out his hand and said his name, which Nicholas recognized vaguely. He shook the hand fluttering at him.

"I have never spent Christmas with Piccolomini."

"Never mind. It doesn't matter, actually—everyone knows who you are." The man in the red coat smiled, showing the gaps in his teeth. He leaned forward a little to smile into Nicholas's face. "You will know me better soon enough."

Nicholas's face went hot; he hoped he was not blushing. He said, "I am sure of that. Your leave, sir."

He started around the man, but before he could get away Valentino's pages came in announcing him.

All around the room the court bowed, and a few moments later they were all kneeling while the Pope came in. With Alexander were his son Joffre and Joffre's wife Sancia, a princess of Naples, who was wearing shoes so steeply heeled that she teetered along on her boyish husband's arm.

Miguelito strolled across the room toward Nicholas. "Good evening, Nicholas."

"And to you," Nicholas said.

The soldier lowered his voice. "Now tell me what you would not tell me at Sant' Angelo."

They were standing almost within one another's arm.

Nicholas saw des Troches watching them from a short distance away and stared at him until des Troches turned his head and walked off.

"Gianpaolo had the notes written to send to Oliverotto and two of the Orsini, but he met them in person before they could be sent. I understand they agreed to a secret meeting at La Magione. That is all I know."

Miguelito said, "You are sure?" He spoke a broad Navarrese oath. "Those devils."

Nicholas cleared his throat. Miguelito's passion was interesting to him; there was something religious in this outrage. Miguelito nudged him with his elbow.

"How did you find this out?"

Nicholas shrugged, not answering. Miguelito glared at him. "Wait here."

Nicholas looked toward the table where the Pope sat with his family. The most favored of Valentino's court were serving their supper to them. "Let me go with you," he said.

"Isn't that careless?" Miguelito said. "What if the Florentines hear you are so friendly with us?"

Two hours ago Nicholas had worried over the same matter, but now he longed to put himself within hearing of whatever was said at that table. "I am accredited to the Pope's Court," he said to Miguelito. "It's my work to be friendly with you." So he could argue it to the Florentines. Miguelito grunted.

"Come, then."

Nicholas could not withhold his smile. His hands clasped casually behind his back, he went after Miguelito across the room. He knew all the court watched, envious. It was important to look as if he did this at his will.

Miguelito went to stand behind Valentino's chair, and for a moment Nicholas stood there alone, out in front of everyone, but unnoticed by the Borgias. He circled around hastily to the wall. The Pope was telling his daughter-in-law Sancia a ribald story about the Cardinal d'Este. Valentino was eating fish.

The Pope exploded with thunderous laughter. Sancia gave a mocking shriek. Clutching his arm she leaned forward and whispered in his ear. Valentino picked a small bone like a needle from the tip of his tongue.

"Telling someone else's secrets, pretty sister?"

Sancia whipped her head around. "Only yours."

"Peace, my children," said the Pope. A servant offered him sauce for his fish and he turned to regard it.

Sancia was still staring at Valentino, her head thrown back. "What do you think I told him, Cesare?"

"My children," the Pope said, smiling, "peace."

Valentino cut his fish with a leaf-bladed knife. Sancia lowered her head.

Nicholas stood by the wall, his hands behind him, and his gaze pinned to the family around the table. He wondered how many others of their court understood them, since the Borgias were speaking Spanish. Probably many others. Valentino would recognize him, sooner or later—he told himself that several times, as the servants took dishes away and brought new ones, and the Borgias ate of the rich food. Miguelito stepped forward once, to sip from Valentino's glass. They feared poison. Or were only being careful.

The Pope spoke of Lucrezia, from whom he had received a letter announcing that she would bear him a grandchild in the spring. He delighted in this news, rubbing his hands together, and again and again saying his daughter's name.

"Well, Sancia," Valentino said, "now it's your turn."

"He is intolerable," Sancia said.

"Cesare," Alexander said. "Become tolerable."

"I've been," Valentino said, "eminently. But that didn't work either."

Miguelito hooted with amusement. At the other side of the table, Joffre lifted his eyes a moment from his dinner, his face blank, and returned to eating. By the wall, Nicholas wondered if Valentino had intended the pun—while he was a Cardinal, he had been Sancia's lover—and decided that he had.

The Pope said mildly, "You are insulting nearly everybody, Cesare."

"Although of course he's only made a daughter," Sancia said loudly. Her strong drawling accent made her speech comical; in the Roman shadow-puppet show, the whores were always Neapolitan. "And knowing the bride to be French, I suspect it was a virgin birth anyway."

"I decline the obvious retort," Valentino said, "in view of the defenselessness of the target."

His glass was empty; a servant filled it up again, and again Miguelito came forward to sip from it. Nicholas let his eyes leave Valentino to follow his dark henchman. The tasting was ceremonial. Valentino would never risk losing Miguelito. As he watched, Miguelito took his place against the wall again.

Sancia was saying, "What you mean is, Cesare, that you won't risk angering me to the point where I might say something."

The Pope said, "I will not hear any more of this quarreling!" He looked from Sancia to Valentino.

"This is my table," Valentino said, "if Your Holiness will recall that."

The Pope was no longer smiling. Vast in his rich robes, he sat between Valentino and Sancia with his head settled on his shoulders like a Spanish bull's. To Sancia, he said, "Keep your place, woman." His head swiveled toward his son's. "Would you be here, save for me?"

Valentino beckoned to his steward, and the servants bustled in with the game course. Through this business the son and the father eyed one another grimly. Valentino looked away first, but now the Pope's forehead gleamed with sweat.

Nicholas watched all this with his whole attention. He had known for years, all Rome knew, that Sancia and Valentino hated one another. This rivalry between Alexander and Valentino Nicholas had never seen before. But he remembered something now, another argument between the two men, arguing over Lucrezia's marriage. Then he had not gotten the impression that Alexander was afraid of Valentino.

There was some use for knowledge like that. Nicholas could not see it yet, but like all the other courtiers he weighed every word the Borgias spoke.

Over the compôte of apricots, Alexander turned to Valentino and said, "The cook's excellent, but the master of the revel's gone out to dine, I take it? Or are you and Sancia the sole entertainment?"

"I waited only for your word, Papa." Valentino lifted his voice. "Des Troches! Speak to us mellifluously in some other man's tongue."

Des Troches was clearly ready as a spurred cock. He sprang forward, and posing in the center of the floor before the Pope dipped in a low bow. Speech poured from his mouth.

"Your Beatitude, all Christendom kisses your feet. The past does nothing but prefigure your reign, the future shall only reflect it. Let me therefore restore to our memories the deeds of the earliest Romans, whose virtue yours is the fullest flowering of." He thrust one arm out in a statuesque gesture. "Arma virumque cano . . ."

There was an audible mutter of dismay through the courtiers. Uneasily Nicholas wondered if des Troches had the entire poem by heart. After a dozen lines Alexander turned to his son again.

"Is this how you lull yourself to sleep on campaign? Please, relieve me of it—you know Mars is not my star."

"Would you prefer Venus, Papa, or Jove?" Valentino scanned his court, his brows curled, as if he had not already decided. He turned to look around him, which brought Nicholas within his range.

"Messer Dawson." Valentino sat forward again; his voice turned lively with mirth. "Step forward and address us with a few lyrics of Horace to his Cynthia."

"Propertius," Nicholas said, automatically.

At once he wished he had not spoken. Valentino twisted around in his chair again.

"What did you say?"

Nicholas walked around to the front of the table, so that the prince could hold him in his gaze without the effort of turning. He made a deep obeisance to the Pope and faced Valentino again. "Cynthia was the love of Propertius, as your Magnificence surely knows, meaning to test my learning, shallow as it is."

Valentino slapped his hand down on the table. "Well, then, Messer Dawson, since you know the ladies so well, let us hear you address some fortunate lover with a speech of seduction. To Sancia. Make courtly love to Sancia."

Nicholas stiffened, his gaze moving to the princess, on the far side of the table from Valentino. She was frowning, but with puzzlement; probably she recognized the tone of an insult without understanding the substance. She watched him—they were all watching him, expecting him to obey. He had to obey. Fortunately her name fitted easily into the only love poem he knew well enough to recite.

He bowed to the princess. "Vivemus, mea Sancia, atque amemus." In a plain speaking voice, without gestures, he recited the lovely verse.

When he had done, the Pope patted his white palms together. "That suits me very well, especially all those kisses." He laughed, ebullient, his round face bright again with good humor.

Nicholas bowed again and withdrew to the wall. The Florentines would buzz if they heard about this. Everyone around him was watching him covertly; he saw the gleam of their eyes, the nudges and the mutterings. Valentino had made a fool of him as well. He pushed himself against the wall, his head down, and tried to look as if he did not care.

A FEW DAYS LATER Astorre Manfredi's corpse was turned up by the wheel of a mill on the Tiber Island. Nicholas went to the watchtower where the body was taken, so that the Signory of Florence would have first-hand knowledge that their friend was dead.

The river had destroyed the boy's beauty. After one glimpse of his face Nicholas swiveled his head away. The old custodian followed him to the door.

"Poisoned, he was—mark me." The old man grinned. He had no front teeth.

"Spanish poison," Nicholas said. Around Astorre's bloated neck the mark was still visible of the garrotte. He had been warned. Nicholas touched his throat. There was no use in innocence. He had been warned. He fumbled at the latch of the door, and the old man, hut-hutting in his throat, reached past his elbow to help. Nicholas went out to the sweet autumnal air.

PERHAPS HE SHOULD HAVE DONE more for Astorre, exercised some slight influence in his favor; or perhaps he had done too much, showing interest, and led Valentino to eliminate a potential threat. Life was unjust. Nicholas took an absurd comfort from that. Not his fault, but life's itself.

Across the room from Nicholas sat Stefano, eating up the last of his dinner. Juan came in and took away the empty glasses.

Nicholas watched Stefano wipe his fingers on his napkin and slide back in his chair. He had eaten twice as much as Nicholas. His appetites were enormous. That gave him his distinction, in one sense, his zeal, his vitality. In another sense it was his ruin. Already he was going to fat. He sat there with his hands on his paunch; Nicholas half-expected him to take a sliver from the hearth and pick his teeth. In a few years he would lose his looks, coarsen into a plain middle age. That thought was another absurd comfort to Nicholas.

Stefano turned his head suddenly and glared at him.

"Why are you staring at me? You are worse than a woman, sometimes—gawking at me."

Nicholas put his elbow on the arm of his chair and set his chin on his fist. "I enjoy looking at you."

The younger man stirred from head to foot, shifting in his chair, looking in the other direction. "Sometimes I think I liked you better when you did not like me half so well."

There was no answer to that, and Nicholas made none.

"This place is like a church. There's nothing to do here."

"What would you like to do?"

"You never take me with you to the Vatican any more. Why—are you afraid I'll embarrass you in front of those clerks?"

"Not at all," Nicholas said, uneasily; he saw what Stefano wanted. He pulled nervously on his chin. "You are never an embarrassment."

"God's bones—I cannot even pick an argument with you any more."

"Do you want to go to the Vatican? Why?"

"They have a lot of money there, and no skill at cards."

Juan came in again with glasses of another wine. Stefano lunged out of his chair. He took the glass from Juan and paced off around the room.

"There is nothing to do here. You even took away the only thing worth looking at, the pictures on the walls."

Nicholas said, "We can go to the Vatican, if you wish. Not tonight, the Pope is otherwise busy, but soon."

"Thank you," Stefano said, but the look he gave Nicholas was still angry. He raised his glass and drank the fine wine as he drank all wine, sluicing his throat. Nicholas took his eyes from him. The more he tried to please Stefano, the less he pleased him. There was a certain symmetry to it; he remembered how at first Stefano had pursued him, and he had resisted. He did not want to think how it would end. Raising the glass of wine, he closed his eyes and drank.

AFTER RIOTS AND EVEN ATTEMPTS at murder of high officers of the Republic, the city of Florence re-formed the state, placing at its head a Gonfalonier elected for life. The first man to enter into this office was Piero Soderini, a man of ancient and honorable family whose brother, Cardinal Soderini, was the leading churchman of Italy. The great ones of Florence had triumphed over the little people. Savonarola was truly dead now.

"None here of good mind," Bruni wrote, "but believes that His Excellency the Gonfalonier will restore our Republic to its height of eminence enjoyed in the past. He is a man of highest purpose, very firm of mind, and unutterably set against the Borgia beast."

Nicholas marked that with a dot of ink from his pen.

Bruni followed with a long paragraph describing the disposition of the stars at the time of Soderini's election and their interaction with the stars of Soderini's birth. He added, "I have met with His Excellency in numberless private sessions, and was able by reference to my past dispatches to argue that, while seldom heeded, my advice and understanding of events have always proved as accurate as a rendering from life. My dear Dawson, be confident in my assurances that I pressed them with reports of your faithful service to the Republic."

There followed a detailed list of the other offices created and filled in the reform of the government. Nicholas let his gaze slide over this assemblage of names he hardly knew. The letter ended in a volley of astrological advice. Nicholas laid it down.

He knew Soderini well, by reputation: a clever man, honest, astute, but uninspired. The Republic having suffered much from flights of fancy in the recent years, such a stolid man might serve well. At least the contrast would be refreshing. Nicholas folded the letter up and put it away in his desk.

As he was doing this there was a knock on his door. He went to answer it and a young man in a fashionably flat hat invited him down to the workroom, where the young man's master waited.

This was a banker from Florence, a member of the Albizzi bank. Nicholas shook his hand. They exchanged the usual greetings and Nicholas escorted the rich man down to Bruni's office, where he would have room to sit down. Nicholas himself stood before Bruni's desk, a sort of proxy.

"What may I do to help you here in Rome?"

The banker removed his hat, and the young man took it to hold for him. "Messer Dawson, I have been in Naples, and for reasons obvious to us all I am eager to return to Florence as soon as possible. I have certain letters to be delivered here in Rome and elsewhere. If you will do me the great favor of seeing to their delivery, I shall be the sooner on my way to Florence."

"I shall do as you require, Excellency."

The banker took a thick packet of papers from his coat and gave them to the young man, who conveyed them to Nicholas. The banker folded his arms over his chest.

"There are five letters. Four are a simple matter of taking them on to the name written on the front. The fifth requires a certain delicacy."

Nicholas made a noncommittal sound in his throat. He laid the packet down behind him on the desk. The banker stared at him a moment.

"The Orsini are great enemies of our Florentine state, as you well know."

Nicholas made another throaty noise, this one signifying understanding. He said, "I have contacts with the Orsini."

"We know that," the banker said, acidly, "which is why I have trusted you. However, it's not so simple as that. If Florence hates the Orsini, the Orsini are none too pleased with Florence. It might prove embarrassing to the recipient of my letter if his family knew of this correspondence."

"I understand."

"I happen to know that Gravina will be at San Leo Fortress in Urbino within the month. You will arrange to have the letter sent there."

"Gravina," Nicholas said, stupid.

"Yes, the letter is for the Duke of Gravina."

"I shall see that it arrives there," Nicholas said.

"Very good." The banker rose. Again he and Nicholas shook hands, and this time Nicholas shook the hand of the young man, who turned out to be the other man's son. They left. Nicholas shut the door behind them and let out his breath in a windy sigh.

"HAS GRAVINA ANY REASON to visit San Leo, sometime in the next month?" Nicholas asked. "Any good reason?"

Miguelito frowned at him. "San Leo. The fortress in Urbino?"

Nicholas nodded his head. They were standing off to one side of the Pope's sitting room, where surrounded by their familiars the Borgias were playing cards. Directly under a clump of blazing candles was Stefano's burnished head. He was playing tarocco with the Pope himself, and smiling, obviously winning. Miguelito was pulling on his moustaches. His wrist was flea-bitten above the frayed cuff of his shirt.

"He has not been assigned there, if you mean that."

"I have been told to send a letter to him there. By a Florentine with Orsini connections."

"You think this has something to do with the La Magione meeting?"

"I put that color on it, yes. San Leo is a key fortress. I

think they are conspiring to drive Valentino from the Romagna."

"They. Who are they?"

Nicholas shrugged his shoulders. "All his captains seem to be implicated. Whoever is the ringleader would have offerred the suggestion to them all, and not one of them has come to Valentino to report it. Has anyone come?"

"No." Miguelito scratched furiously at his wrist, his face drawn tightly into a frown. "Who is the ringleader? Gianpaolo?"

"I do not know the man. Nor any other of Valentino's captains."

"The meeting is on Monday," Miguelito said.

Nicholas looked across the room again at Stefano, in time to see Valentino just settling himself into a chair at the table, and he took in a deep breath. He hoped Stefano had the sense to lose. He yearned to go over and watch the playing. Miguelito was eying him unpleasantly.

"Your logic is flawless, as usual," Miguelito said. "But what does it stand on—three letters with no address and one letter with the wrong one."

Nicholas was edging away from him. "By your leave." He started across the crowded room toward the gaming table, and Miguelito sauntered after him.

Stefano was sitting there with the Pope, Valentino, the Pope's friend Adriano Corneto, and a Spanish Cardinal far along in his wine. Valentino had the cards and was dealing them. Nicholas took up a place behind Stefano, where he could watch the play as Stefano saw it.

He knew the game very little. The gaudy cards were meaningless to him. Other elements of the game fascinated him: the deft economy of the gestures of the players, the repetition of the sounds, of cards sliding on one another, coins clinking. The players spoke in a sort of code. Nicholas enjoyed the purity of this form, a ritual in and of itself, like mathematics. He understood why folk believed the cards could tell the future. It was hard to believe such an intricate miniature world could have no purpose but to rearrange a supply of money.

Valentino dealt several times. Nicholas saw that Stefano bet very little and lost hardly anything. On the fifth deal at last Valentino lost, and the deck of cards passed on to the drunken Cardinal on his right.

"You have very fine hands, if I may say so," Stefano said, on his left.

Valentino and the Pope both turned on him, one on either side of him; the Pope demanded, "Do you suggest that my son cheats?"

"I have lost nothing." Stefano's face was blandly cheerful, a mask he put on over card games. "I enjoy the art, of course."

A brief silence met this, while everyone watched the Pope, to see how he would take that. Then Valentino erupted with laughter. He leaned out and clapped Stefano on the shoulder.

"As one artist to another, I accept the compliment."

At that, the Pope began to laugh, and the laughter spread rapidly around the room. Nicholas relaxed, pleased. He was glad Stefano had won Valentino's respect even if it were only for cheating at cards.

As the laughter subsided around the room Miguelito leaned down and murmured into Valentino's ear. A few moments later the Pope and his son left the card game, and with Nicholas and Miguelito went into a small room nearby.

There Nicholas repeated the fact he had learned and the conclusion he drew from it, reciting like a schoolboy with his hands behind his back. Valentino heard it impassively, but the Pope cursed the Orsini in very round terms.

"This time I shall see every last creature of that name sent down to Hell."

Valentino got out of his chair and paced around the room,

his hands on his hips. His head was bowed and he looked angry. Nicholas followed him with his eyes. He marked a little sore on the prince's upper lip and guessed Valentino entertained the pox.

"Well," Valentino said, "I shall learn who my friends are, shall I not?"

Alexander laid his broad fat palms on his knees. "Who besides the Orsini have you tied to this?"

"My other captains," Valentino said. "This news Nicholas brought us now is the first sign that it's spread beyond them."

"Do you think it has?" Alexander swung his head toward Nicholas. "Your city—does it support this blasphemy?"

"I don't know, Your Holiness, if it please you. Vitelli is a blood enemy of the Republic. I doubt they would deal with him even against my lord Valentino."

"We will find out who is involved when the revolt breaks," Valentino said. He came back to this chair. "San Leo will go to them—I cannot prevent that, they hate me there and I have no army close enough to hold it."

"No army at all, if your captains rebel," the Pope said.

"Still I can hold the other fortresses in the Romagna, if I act quickly enough. I shall go to Cesena. There I will be close to everything."

"You have no men," the Pope said.

"Then give me some money, to raise more soldiers. Miguelito will go with me."

"Magnificence," Nicholas said, "if it please you, your allies the French have one hundred lances in Florence. Two hundred in Milan."

Valentino gave a throaty growl of amusement. "The French are in Florence to protect her from me. Let's hope they are flexible."

"It's time they learned how we do things in Italy," Nicholas said, and the Pope lifted his head to laugh.

Nicholas spent half an hour more in the little room, listening to Valentino and his father haggle over the amounts of money to be spent, and where it was to be raised, and when, and how shipped where. The Pope's resources were vast. Nicholas had not realized before how easily Alexander could shuffle money back and forth, like dealing out cards, some here and some there from a stock never sounded. Against that, the rebel captains gathering at La Magione could muster only their private armies. Nicholas's skin tingled with a sudden excitement. For the first time he saw how foolish the conspiracy was. Valentino had said it himself, that soon he would know all his enemies, and they would reveal themselves at a time when he had the power to overwhelm them.

Nicholas saw something else, too, that in one stroke a whole swarm of Valentino's advisers would fall, and he himself would stand that much closer to the prince.

They dismissed him. He went out to the open room again, where the courtiers talked and played. He stopped to watch Stefano play cards. The Spanish Cardinal slept; only Corneto remained opposite Stefano. The dealing of the cards reminded him again of the Pope's dealing with money. The game was a little symbol of the play of power, the rise and fall of men, and the fickle breath of luck. A man of skill could win at the game without luck, a man of art, like Valentino. He felt sure that Valentino would win the bigger game.

In the darkness before dawn, he and Stefano walked back through Rome toward his house. Nicholas said, "You are fortunate Valentino did not take the insult from what you said to him. Whatever did you have in mind?"

Stefano laughed. He was more than a little drunk, and he had won; he swaggered along like a pirate. "God's bones. He likes a man around him, Valentino, now and then, that's all. After all you little bootlickers."

Nicholas's temper rose; he was tired, and his nerves were

raw. "It was his whim to laugh. Be careful he doesn't take the whim to do otherwise."

Stefano made a rude noise with his tongue against his teeth.

OLD JUAN ASKED, "What is this of a rebellion against the Borgias?"

Nicholas unwound his woolen neckcloth and gave it to his servant. It was the middle of the day but an early winter chill numbed the October air; his cheeks still burned from the walk back to his house from the legation. He unfastened the front of his coat. "Where have you learned of that?"

"In the market." Juan helped him remove his coat. "They were all buzzing—it was easy to catch their drift. The whole of Valentino's army has gone against him—is that it?" He folded the coat over his arm and laid the neckcloth neatly over the coat.

"Yes," Nicholas said. "All Valentino's condottieri have broken faith."

"Come sit down, I will bring you wine."

Nicholas went into the center of the room. The fire had been laid but not lit, and without its heat to draw the damp from the air, the house was wretched as a cave. The wind leaked in through every window and the marble floor gave off a chill like an emanation. Nicholas sat in his chair, the wood creaking with the change of weather, and Juan served him.

"Perhaps it is the end of Valentino, then," Juan said, while Nicholas sipped the steaming red wine and warmed his hands on the cup.

"Valentino's army is nothing without him. Why have you left the hearth cold?"

"There is only enough wood left for the evening fire."

"When is the woodcutter coming?"

Juan shook his head; he put a dish of sausage and lentils down on the table. "When he gets here."

"There is wood at the legation. We shall purloin a little."
An aroma of garlic and onions rose from the stew to make
his mouth water, and he picked up the spoon. "Superb."

"What is Valentino without his army?" Juan said.

"The Pope's son."

"The Pope is old."

"Exactly why Valentino's enemies should have waited.
Now they have betrayed themselves to him and yet they
have small chance of overthrowing him. Please allow me the
pleasure of eating my meal."

Juan withdrew a few steps and stood, his hands clasped
before him, to watch his master eat. Nicholas ate slowly,
enjoying the rich flavor of the stew, and keeping Juan in the
corner of his eye. The old man wanted to talk; the expression on his face grew strained with the effort to obey his
master and keep silent, until at last words burst from him.

"Will Messer Stebano come tonight?"

"This is Wednesday—tonight is the all-preceding tarocco
game at that damnable taverna."

"I forgot."

"You always forget," Nicholas said. "This is an excellent
sausage. I pray you give me the opportunity to eat it in
peace."

Juan closed himself into an unwilling silence. He watched
Nicholas's every move, his eyes following the motion of the
spoon. Although he had spent the morning out to market he
could not have spoken above two or three words. As soon as
Nicholas let him, he would rattle off again. Nicholas reached
for his wine.

The gate bell jangled.

"Go see who that is," Nicholas said.

"Stebano." Juan made for the door at his best speed.

Nicholas pushed his plate away. The stew had warmed
him, or he had gotten used to the graveyard air of the house;
he stretched out a little, content. His eyes shifted to the blank

walls of the room and he debated how to cover them, when he had the money. That led him to the problem of his finances. The ugly suspicion was growing in his mind that the new state in Florence meant to repudiate the debts of the old one, which included his past-due salary. With his tongue he worried a bit of food trapped between his teeth. He should have kept aside some of the money Valentino had paid him.

In the front door Ercole Bruni strode, his traveling cape sweeping after him, a broad smile on his face, and his arms out to Nicholas like a father's. Nicholas stood up, surprised, and suffered Bruni's ebullient embrace. The ambassador's black furred cloak still carried the chill of the outdoors.

"Excellency," Nicholas said. "What a surprise. I had no idea you were coming back to Rome so soon. Juan, light the fire. Sir, permit me to help you with your cloak."

Bruni began to shed his clothes. "We thought the current problem required my presence here, near the Pope." He lowered his voice, rolling his eyes toward old Juan, who was crouched over the hearth. "This fellow here—trustworthy?"

"He speaks no Italian," Nicholas said, gathering up the armful of Bruni's outer clothing. "Sit, please. He will bring you a cup of hot wine. Excuse me a moment."

He took Bruni's cloak and hat and gloves off to the cupboard in his bedroom. When he came back, Juan was handing the ambassador a steaming cup of wine and Bruni was thanking him profusely in words and wide gestures to illustrate. Nicholas went to stand beside his chair.

"You may go, Juan."

The old man left. Bruni was drinking the wine; he lifted his beaming face above the cup.

"So. What do you think of this newest twist of events?" Bruni held up one finger, to keep Nicholas still. "The La Magione rebels have asked the support of Florence in their revolt against Valentino. Hah! What do you think of that?"

"To be expected," Nicholas said. "May I sit?"

Bruni's joyous face lost a little of its glow. "You expected it? Yes, sit."

"I suppose they have asked Venice to support them as well," Nicholas said. "Little doubt what the Serenissima will respond to that."

"Little doubt at all, of course," Bruni said hastily.

Nicholas's glass stood empty on the little table, along with the disorderly relics of his dinner. "By your leave, Excellency," he said, and getting up again put the spoon and the dish and its cover and the glass all in a heap and carried them away to the kitchen.

Juan was sitting in the pantry with a candle to warm him, mending clothes. Nicholas filled his glass with wine from the jug and took glass and jug out again to the sitting room.

"What has the new Gonfalonier to say to the rebels?" Nicholas asked.

"He has not answered yet," Bruni said. "I am here to gather news and gossip for him, to assure the proper answer. Uhh—what do you suppose Venice will say?"

Nicholas cocked his eyebrows, assuming a look of mild surprise. "Surely no established state will support such a witless enterprise against the Pope himself."

"Ah." Bruni's smile popped back into place, broad as a baby's. "As usual you agree with me. I am happy to be so intelligently seconded."

Nicholas leaned forward across the little table to pour more wine into the ambassador's glass. The fire was going out and he went to poke it alive again. "Has Soderini any private opinion of the rebellion?"

"He has sent Machiavelli to Cesena," Bruni said, "to observe Valentino. I thought that was rather shrewd." He sipped noisily at the wine. "To see how Valentino behaves himself."

"Indeed."

"The stars are ambiguous," Bruni said, "but Mars is retrograde. I foresee disaster for one side, either the rebels or the Borgia. Someone is going to come out of this very sore. What do you think?"

"Are the French troops still in Florence?"

"Yes, and eating out of the Republic's pocket, I may add. Making pigs of themselves."

Nicholas nodded his head. "You must be hungry. Forgive me, I am most remiss." He raised his voice for Juan.

Bruni began to rise from his chair, his hands on the arms. "I can go to an inn."

"Not at all. Let my man serve you. Our fare is modest but of an excellent flavor, I assure you. Juan—" he rattled off instructions to the servant in Spanish, and the old man went out again to the kitchen. Nicholas sat down, reaching for the jug of wine. "Excellency?" He poured the ambassador's glass full again.

GORGED ON LENTILS and sausage and wine, and tired from traveling, Bruni fell asleep in his chair. Nicholas bundled himself up again in his coat and neckcloth and hurried to the door.

Juan walked out to the gate with him. Nicholas said, "If he wakes again before I am back, give him the note I left on the table."

"We shall need wood, now that you've burnt it all up for his sake."

"I will hire a carter to bring some here from the legation supply." Nicholas opened the gate.

Juan put out his hand to hold the gate open for him. He turned up his long face, graven with lines. "If Valentino falls, what will become of us?"

Nicholas's jaw fell open. He had never guessed that Juan might know. He must have inferred it all long since, as he did everything, watching and dreaming.

"Valentino will not fall," Nicholas said. "Don't—"

He shut his mouth again, looking out to the street; he had intended to warn the old man to keep the secret, but that was fatuous. Juan pushed the gate open a few feet.

"Don't worry about the wood," Nicholas said, and went out. In the street, the first gusty rain of October was beginning to fall. Hunching his shoulders, he put his face into the wind and walked across Rome to the Vatican, to report what Bruni had told him to the Pope.

NICHOLAS WOKE WITH A START. His mouth tasted stale and foul. He was still in his chair in the sitting room; he had fallen asleep there, by the fire. The first thought into his wakened mind was that Stefano had not come.

He stirred himself, his stiffened limbs protesting. The hour was late. Juan had gone to bed; the kitchen was dark. It was very late. Perhaps Stefano had fallen into a game, although on Thursdays he always came to Nicholas's house. Nicholas padded around the room in his stocking feet—his shoes lay under the chair where he had slept—to pour himself a glass of wine and wake himself up. When the game was done Stefano would come, however late the hour; he always came on Thursdays.

The fire had gone out. Nicholas fed it bits of wood and blew on it and nursed the first little flames into robust life. He crouched in the warmth and light of the fire, enjoying the baking heat on his face.

When Stefano came he would be hungry. They could warm his dinner over the fire.

He made another circuit of the room, putting on his shoes. Stefano was often late. He had no sense of time or the propriety of being on time. But he always came on Thursdays.

He remembered the first Thursday, when Stefano had

come very late. That time he had been waylaid leaving the game. Nicholas stood by the fire again and poked furiously into its heart. Stefano was a big man, and hard. He was always in fights. If Nicholas began worrying about such things he would never stop. He forbade himself to worry what had befallen Stefano this time. He would learn it when Stefano came.

He drank another glass of wine. He forced himself to read a few pages of a book. The fire died down, and he fussed over it again, reviving it.

The hour could not be all that late, after all—he had not heard the midnight bells, or the watch pass. At that moment he heard or thought he heard a cock crow, off in the distance, the cock at the end of the street. It was a myth they only gave voice at dawn; they crowed all night. The Sforza of Milan even took a family name from that, *Galeazzo*, because when the first Galeazzo was born the cocks crowed all night. Nicholas went back to his chair and his book.

He drank the last wine in the jug, thinking to fill it again from the keg in the kitchen, when Stefano came.

He could not read; he was too sleepy. He thought of putting his head down and napping, but instead rose and walked around the room again and prodded the fire, and he took the jug out to the kitchen to fill it.

He had to light the candle, to fill the jug, and while he was standing there scratching his knife over the flint in his tinderbox, the pantry door opened and old Juan padded into the kitchen, yawning, a candle on a dish in his hand.

His eyebrows rose like arches over his eyes. "You are early to rise."

Nicholas said, "No—it is still the middle of the night."

"But it is dawn," Juan said. "Look—see the window?" He pointed into the pantry, at the pale shape of the window in the far wall. The flame of the candle danced in his eyes.

He said, in a different voice, "He did not come?"

Nicholas closed the lid of his tinderbox with his thumb. He went out again to the sitting room.

HE ALMOST WENT into the Trastevere, instead of to his work, to find out what had happened to Stefano. He saw the folly of that. Youths let their longings trick them, not men like Nicholas. Above all he would not make a fool of himself over any man, even Stefano.

When he reached his office there was a slip of paper on his desk.

He pounced on it. It read: "Come at the second hour after nones to the lane behind the candlemakers' market, near the Piazza Navona, and wait by the olive tree for a man in a red hat."

He read it over half a dozen times, trying to make sense of it, and finally sat down at his desk and spread it out between his hands on the surface and read it over again. It was absurd. Was it from Stefano? It had to be from Stefano, or concern him. A ransom, a tryst? He folded the note and put it in his wallet.

When the legation shut down for the afternoon, instead of going to his house for his dinner, he set off across the heart of the city toward the Piazza Navona. The streets were crowded with folk going home, loaves of bread tucked under their arms. The shops were closed or closing. He passed a hatmaker belatedly locking his door. In the lane behind the candlemakers' market, stinking of tallow, there was no sign of a man in a red hat.

Nicholas loitered by the only olive tree, his head turning to direct his gaze to either end of the lane. He was sure now this was a game of Stefano's.

A spot of red appeared, bobbing toward him from the direction of the piazza, and on coming closer resolved itself into a red hat perched on the head of a very tall man. It was no one Nicholas knew. He met the fellow with a smile and a joking remark, which the stranger's sour look quickly cut off.

"Come with me, please."

Nicholas grunted. This had nothing to do with Stefano. Yet he was curious enough to follow the red hat on down the lane. At the corner the man removed his signal from his head and stuffed it under his coat.

They set off on a mad course through the deserted streets, turning every few feet into another alley or lane, and circling back over their tracks, until Nicholas lost patience.

"What fool's errand is this?"

The stranger said, through tight lips, "I am to see you are not followed."

"Very well," Nicholas said. "Assure yourself." His stomach growling, he thought with regret of his dinner, which by now Juan himself would be eating. He refused to let this hugger-mugger pique his curiosity. In the end it would be a joke of Stefano's or something else petty. They crossed a piazza below a ruined wall, where a fountain streamed green water from a bronze shell and crowds of pigeons waddled around the paving stones pecking at the debris left from the morning's market.

In the next street was the Pantheon. The stranger drew Nicholas to the steps of the Roman relic.

"Go in. A man will come and ask you for a carlini—you must say you have only crowns. He will take you on."

"This is absurd," Nicholas said heatedly.

He said the last word to the stranger's back, as the man turned and walked away. Nicholas hesitated, one foot on the ground, one on the worn marble step. He looked up at the battered columns. At last he went into the building.

From outside it looked massive, worn, and undistinguished, but inside all the mass dissolved into the vast upward-arching space below the dome. The coffering on the inside of the dome increased the sensation of height and space. Below the oculus in the center of the dome, the marble floor was still puddled with water from the previous night's rain. Nicholas walked slowly around the edge of the room. Once statues of all the gods had stood in niches around the walls, but the walls were blank now, the niches empty; there was nothing to keep the eye from following the soaring line upward, and like any foreigner he could only look up, gaping.

He wondered if anything built in his own time would endure so long and so well as this; the banality of the thought made him smile, and he let himself wonder next at the innocence of the ancients, who had imagined all future time would be like theirs. It was hard to remember that in history old was young, and that the Pantheon came out of the childhood of the world.

"Have you a carlini?"

He lowered his eyes to a slight homely man who stood before him. "I have nothing but crowns."

"Come with me, please."

They left the Pantheon and again went roundabout through the streets. Nicholas decided not to be put off again. When they reached the stopping point on this journey he would demand to be told what was going on, or he would go home.

Probably it was a joke. Once again he considered that Stefano was playing a game with him. Or someone wanted him away from his house.

Treading after the slight man, he came to that idea with a jolt. That was the answer: they were keeping him from his house. Almost he turned in midstep and rushed away across the city to the rescue of his house. While he was gathering the resolve to do that, the slight man stopped.

They had come to an archway between the walls of two

buildings. Nicholas reached out and took a handful of the smaller man's coat.

"Who are you? What does this mean? By Heaven, I will not let you go until I understand everything!"

"Go down there, to that door, and knock."

"You will come with me to the watch."

The slight man pointed through the archway. "Go there!"

Nicholas looked, his hand still fisted in the cloth of the other man's coat. The archway opened on a narrow alley between two high featureless walls of yellow travertine. Somewhere water was dripping. At the end of the alley there was a door with a lamp hung over it. Nicholas frowned at the man in his grasp, determined to have one at least of these people to take to the watch.

"Come with me."

The man shrugged. He led Nicholas down to the door and rapped on it with his knuckles.

Nothing happened. The two men stood expectantly before the closed door a full minute. Abruptly Nicholas said, "No, per Baccho!" He turned, walking away from the doorway, to go back to his house.

"Wait!"

He stopped. The slight man knocked heavily on the door again, and this time the door opened at once.

"Go in," the slight man said to Nicholas.

Nicholas went up behind him and pushed him. "You first."

The slight man went in and Nicholas followed. They entered a gloomy little cellar, windowless, with only a table and a few wooden chairs for furnishings. A candle burned on the table. The slight man sidled away from Nicholas, going toward the door. In the big chair behind the table was a man wearing a black velvet mask; he watched Nicholas, his eyes glittering through the holes in the mask. He had the broad shoulders and narrow waist of a horseman. With a gesture he dismissed the slight man, who went out the door into the sunlight, and shut Nicholas into the room with this stranger.

Nicholas stood fixed in his tracks, unknowing what to do, or what was about to happen. The tall man removed his mask. It was Gianpaolo Baglione.

"My lord," Nicholas said, amazed.

The Baglione dropped his mask on the table. "I bid you a great good day, Messer Dawson."

Nicholas looked swiftly around him. They were alone in the room, but other doors led out of it than the one he had entered in by, and behind them crowds of armed men might be waiting for a signal from their lord. He faced Gianpaolo again; he had always suspected Gianpaolo of leading the conspiracy against Valentino.

"My lord," he said, "may I ask you the purpose of this gaming?"

"Gaming," Gianpaolo said. "I would it were a game, Messer Dawson. It's a little more than just a game. I want a message taken—no, that is wrong."

He pushed with his foot at the table, looking sour.

"We swore to destroy him," he said. "All his captains together, in one voice, we vowed to rid Italy of him. Well, Messer Dawson, I am sorry I swore it. I want to be his friend again."

Nicholas's tongue slid into his cheek. He made a surprised face for Gianpaolo's benefit. "That may be difficult to arrange. Why have you come to me?"

"Bah. I heard you talk to him, that time, when you told him how to take Urbino. He'll listen to you." With a rush of activity Gianpaolo stood up and walked off into the shadow at the back of the room. "The Valentino I knew—grew up with, damn him!—he was like me, he loved horses and swords and thrashing one's enemies. You don't understand that, do you? Little scribbler, city man, you have no idea what war is supposed to be. To take a city by guile—that isn't war."

Gianpaolo sat down again, this time on the table, with the candle behind him, so that he loomed up before Nicholas like a black beast.

"That's the nobility of war, to use force, to force your enemies down on their knees. Not to take from them when they aren't looking."

Nicholas took a step backward, away from Gianpaolo. "Valentino decided everything, not I."

"He's always been a cheat," Gianpaolo said. "But not like this. Go tell him I'm sorry."

"I will do what I can."

"It was a stupid notion, anyway. I don't know why we thought Venice or Florence would help us. And the French in Milan—go tell him I will come to his side again."

"I shall. How may I find you?"

"I will find you." Gianpaolo moved in the dark, an indeterminate movement, and suddenly Nicholas found himself gripped by the arm. "I will find you." The tall man slid off the table, took his mask, and went out, leaving the door open.

Nicholas stood where he was, full of thoughts. Before he left, he pinched the candle out.

WHEN NICHOLAS CAME to his gate that evening, he found Stefano there.

They mumbled a greeting at each other; Nicholas could not look Stefano in the face and bent his attention to finding his key and using it in the lock. They walked in under the trees. Ahead, a light showed: Juan had opened the house door. Nicholas was walking first, ahead of Stefano, so that he did not have to look at him. Stefano had come only for a free meal and a bed. With every step Nicholas told himself to save his dignity and send Stefano away but he knew he would keep him there as long as he could, suffer much to keep him there.

Juan stood on the threshold, his face locked into a grimace

meant to be expressionless. He said, "Shall I bring you supper?"

"For both of us," Nicholas said.

Stefano had gone to the hearth. "The place is like a dungeon. Why has the old man let the fire go out?"

"The woodcutter has not come in yet. We are very short of wood."

For an instant, in the course of this casual talk, their eyes met; and Stefano's flinched away. Nicholas sat down. Stefano felt it, too, then, the ruin of their friendship.

"Where were you last night?" Nicholas asked.

"At the Vatican."

Nicholas jerked his head up, surprised; he imagined Stefano in a gilded suit, playing cards with the Pope. "Really. Did you win?"

"No, in fact. His Holiness won. And Corneto. It is the game, to come in second. Did you wait for me?"

"Yes."

"I'm sorry. The message said to come at once, I had no time to send to you."

"Who sent for you?" Nicholas said, expecting the name of one of the Pope's household. Alexander summoned only princes in his own name.

"Someone named des Troches," Stefano said.

"Des Troches."

Valentino's man. Nicholas rubbed his hand over his mouth. Juan brought in the steaming plates of soup, flavoring the room with a fragrance of cabbages. Silently he laid their supper down before the two men by the fire, and they began to eat.

The silence weighed heavier every moment. Nicholas hunted frantically for some topic light enough to break it; he could think only of the long night he had passed waiting for Stefano, falling asleep in his chair.

"Keep losing to the Pope," he blurted, "and you will play often at the Vatican."

Stefano wiped his mouth on a napkin. "I did not lose apurpose."

"I did not mean to imply you had."

"He plays shrewdly. And well. It is a good game. I am to go back again Friday, in the afternoon—is that what you wanted to know?"

"I—"

"Do you think I belong to you? I'm my own man, Nicholas. I have my own life, and when the chance comes to better it —a chance like this—"

Nicholas left his chair and walked away from the table. Halfway across the room from Stefano, he stopped; he pinched the bridge of his nose between his fingers, wondering what he could say next. Behind him, the other chair grated roughly on the hard floor.

"Look," Stefano said. "This is no good. I'm sorry. I owe you a lot—without you I would never have gone past the gate over there."

Juan hurried out of the room, plates in his hands. Nicholas said nothing.

"I'm going," Stefano said.

"No, stay." Nicholas turned toward him again.

Stefano hesitated for a moment, his coat in his hands. His mouth worked up and down at the corners, indecisive. Abruptly he started to the door again.

"Goodbye."

"Please."

Stefano went out the door. Nicholas stared after him, drained of will, his muscles slack and his mind empty. Through the open door came a distant clang as the gate was slammed shut. Numbly he went to his chair and sat down again and put his face in his hands.

VALENTINO LINGERED in Cesena, drawing together what troops he could to face the army of his rebellious captains. In the first weeks of the mutiny much of the territory of Urbino had gone over to the side of the rebels, but since then no more of the Romagna had deserted Valentino, and the great powers of Italy supported him, a prince against rebels. Nicholas sent word of Gianpaolo's offer to change his loyalties.

A few weeks later the Pope summoned him to the Leonine City.

"I was dispatched a note to give you," Alexander said. "I destroyed it. I am not my son's courier."

Nicholas bowed, one foot behind the other, in the Spanish style. He had never before been alone with the Pontiff. They were in Alexander's reading room; the walls were painted with figures of grazing bulls, the Borgia emblem, and the marble floor was worked with the Papal tiara above the crossed keys. Somewhere nearby someone was practicing on the lute, the same tune, over and over, with the same mistakes.

"Your young friend plays a brilliant game of cards," Alexander said. "Do you still keep company with him?"

"No, Your Holiness."

Alexander looked keenly into his face. "I am sorry. I had noticed you never came with him."

"No, Your Holiness."

"Well." Alexander rubbed his nose; his tone turned brisk. "Perhaps it's for the best, my English friend. That is a sin, you know, you risk your soul. The Lord despises sodomy."

"Alas."

"The Lord loveth increase," the Pope laughed, his ebullient humor swelling up again, infectious. "For see how I am blessed, and my only virtue, Messer Dawson, is that I have been fruitful and multiplied."

Nicholas had to smile at him; Alexander's high spirits defied his age and made him seem to Nicholas no older than he was himself. "Yes, Your Holiness."

"Save that Cesare is no replica of me." Smiling, Alexander

picked his nose with his forefinger. His fingers were plated with jeweled rings. "The note was brief."

"Was it, Your Holiness?"

"He sounded very smug, my son. He wishes you to know that your goose is not the only gander to waddle away from the gaggle, but soon they shall all rejoin one another, roasted in a fine sauce."

As the last word left him, Alexander's restrained laughter bubbled up again, and he gave himself over to a thunderous peal of mirth. Nicholas, watching, his head bowed slightly in the proper deference, wondered if the metaphor were Valentino's or his father's.

"You are to tell your goose to keep faith as he will and wait to be summoned. That is all." Alexander rolled the gatherings of his nose into a ball and flicked it with his forefinger away across the room. His smile sagged; he was morose in an instant. "A man is measured by his enemies. I hope—I pray that my son has not found his true enemy, and that these—fleas and rats are not the measure of my son."

"Your Holiness, he shines above them like a star."

The Pope was looking past him. His lips squeezed together into a pout. He heard so many flatteries; how could he believe anything that anyone told him? Nicholas took his leave with many a ceremonious phrase and went out.

THE WHORES WERE ALL NAKED. Some of the more drunken men had boosted women up onto their shoulders and were running up and down the middle of the great room, pretending to joust, the women on their backs shrieking with laughter and striking at one another with their open hands. As Nicholas came into the room a page got into the way of a whore and her mount, who ran him down. They all fell, and the rest of the crowd roared with laughter and threw sweetmeats at them as they lay groaning on the floor.

Nicholas stayed nearby the wall. The Borgia court had

always made him feel dull as a village priest, but now they made him feel old as well.

He saw Stefano on the far side of the room, playing cards. His profile to Nicholas, he kept his attention on his game; he would not notice Nicholas watching him. He wore a coat of red shot with silver. His attendance on Valentino had not improved his dress. Nicholas looked elsewhere.

The Spanish courtier des Troches came up to him, talking. "Your friend is doing well, Messer Dawson, that was shrewd of you there."

"Very shrewd," Nicholas said. Two couples strolled past him; he followed them with his eyes, absorbed in the contrast between the naked women and the dazzling court clothes of the men.

"Do you play?" des Troches was saying.

"Play what?"

"Tarocco." Des Troches's face put on a mild surprise at Nicholas's ignorance. "It is a marvelously useful skill, you know. The Pope does many a good work over a deck of cards." His long white face slipped for an instant into a smirk.

"Does he indeed."

Valentino's dwarf was coming through the room toward him; like a rat in the weeds he parted the court as he passed. He was coming straight to Nicholas, who moved a step away from des Troches.

Des Troches followed, pressing the matter of tarocco. "You ought to have your friend teach you."

"I understand it takes years to learn," Nicholas said. The dwarf plucked on his sleeve. "I beg your pardon?"

"Come," the dwarf said, and Nicholas followed him.

They left the noisy hall and went into a little room, gloomy in the light of two candles. Miguelito was sitting in a cushioned chair in one corner. Nicholas went in, rubbing his hands together; this room was cold after the sweaty warmth of the sala grande.

"Have you talked to Gianpaolo again?" Miguelito said.

Nicholas shook his head. "I have not even delivered the answer yet to his first message."

Miguelito's eyes widened. "It's been a month. Why not?"

"I have no way to reach him. He said he would come to me."

The door flew open and Valentino strode in, pulling off his gloves. "This place stinks of incense. Light some candles. One of you light a fire, my father will be here immediately."

Nicholas went around the room with one of the lit candles, putting the flame on the wicks of the candles set in sconces on the walls, and the room grew steadily lighter and apparently larger. Miguelito was standing by his chair. He did nothing; perhaps he thought it beneath him.

"What do you know of Niccolo Machiavelli?" Valentino said.

Nicholas glanced over his shoulder to see if the prince was talking to him; he found them both staring at him. He went to the hearth and knelt to light the fire laid there.

"A very interesting man, the creature of Soderini, the Gonfalonier. He's been in the chancery for years." The fire caught on a twig in the hearth. He laid it in among other twigs and puffed on them to spread the fire over them.

"Have you ever met him?" Valentino said.

"No, never. But I've read thousands of his letters." Nicholas sat back on his heels and put more wood on the fire.

"He has a lot of opinions. Ideas about history and the abstracts of statecraft."

"Yes," Nicholas said.

"What do you think of him?"

The Pope came in, ringed by little pages who brought his cushion, his cup, a shawl. They bustled about getting him settled in the biggest chair in the room. Nicholas looked above the pages' heads at Valentino.

"Actually, I understand he's rather gullible."

Valentino laughed, and the Pope looked up, his face sharp with curiosity. "Who is gullible? This room is clammy as a well. Messer Dawson, I pray you, do not block the heat of the fire."

Nicholas moved away from the fire so that the Pope could enjoy its warmth. Valentino walked up to the hearth.

"We were discussing a certain Florentine diplomat I have been wooing like a bachelor. I went to see Lucrezia, whose love I am to bear you."

They talked about Lucrezia a moment. Nicholas watched the fire, which he would have to feed to keep alive.

"So," the Pope said. "You find time in the middle of plots and counterplots to visit your sister. That makes me very happy. What exactly is your situation in the Romagna?"

"I have been in touch privately with each one of the men who signed the contract against me at La Magione," Valentino said. "I have assured each one that I will make peace. Vitelli and the Orsini are attacking Urbino for me, to retake the fortresses that rebelled against me."

The Pope grunted. "God's holy love, the treacherous bastards that they are. And when you make peace with them, what then?"

Valentino laughed again, and shot a look across the room at Miguelito. "Then I am going to kill them, every one."

"The Orsini among them? You cannot kill two of that blackhearted tribe without drawing the rest of the scum down on you." The Pope leaned forward, his dark eyes glittering. "Take them all. Now is the time to ruin the Orsini, once and for all."

Valentino turned, swinging his head to face Nicholas. "What do you think?"

Nicholas coughed a little into his hand. "His Holiness is infallible, of course. By that same reasoning, it would be disastrous to attack the Orsini and fail."

The Pope reached out and clutched Valentino's arm. Valentino was standing, and the Pope sitting, and with the shawl draped like wings across his shoulders the old man looked hellish, hunched there, gripping his son by the arm.

He said, "I mean to do it! I have waited years for this revenge. Since Juan's death I have waited to avenge him. The
Orsini murdered him! I will see them all dead."

A movement in the corner of Nicholas's eye brought his
head around; Miguelito had folded his arms across his chest
and shut his eyes.

Valentino said, "Had my brother lived, I would still be
a Cardinal, and Juan would be Valentino. I have no revenge
to take."

"Do not speak so!" The Pope wrenched on his son's arm.

Nicholas glanced at Miguelito again, who was still standing in the corner with his eyes shut and his arms crossed, as
if he had gone to sleep. Shrilly, the Pope ranted against the
Orsini, cursing them for the murderers of his son. That
young man had died nearly ten years before; Nicholas remembered very little of the murder, done at night, like so
many others, and the body dumped in the river. Valentino
was watching his father impassively. His whole course had
turned on that death. Would he have left the pivot of his fate
to chance? Nicholas wondered if the Pope did not hate the
Orsini the more because he feared they might not have
killed his son than because he knew they had.

"We will see what is to be done," Valentino said at last.

The Pope seemed to have tired. He sat slumped in his
chair, drawing the shawl around him, and stroking the fringe
between his fingers. "Ah, well," he said, "that is all I can
expect."

Valentino turned to Nicholas again. "I want to know what
Machiavelli is saying of me to your Gonfalonier. Find out."

"I need not. Excellency—he is advising the state to support you. It is the scandal of the chancery."

A smile spread across Valentino's face. "Excellent. I knew
I had judged him right."

The Pope was rising, complaining of the cold again, and
with a start Nicholas saw that the fire had died down. The
meeting was ending, anyway. Valentino went with his father

to the door, talking to him again of Lucrezia. In the corner, Miguelito opened his eyes.

Nicholas went out behind the Pope and his son, back to the great room where now under the masses of blazing candles the whores danced in rows with rows of gilded gentlemen. The Pope's humor brightened. He spread his hands in an exaggeration of the blessing and said an obscene rhyme in Latin. He clapped Valentino on the shoulder, and with a new life in his walk started off across the room.

Nicholas watched him go, circling the rows of courtiers who all bent down on one knee as they saw him, so that Nicholas could easily see him even on the far side of the room, at the table where Stefano was playing cards. Stefano was kneeling too, of course. The Pope took his place at the table, and the other players rose.

Stefano saw Nicholas; hastily the young man turned back to his chair, putting his back to Nicholas.

Valentino said, "Do you miss him? What an ass you are."

Nicholas twitched, startled, and his ears and neck grew hot. Valentino was standing right behind him. He poked Nicholas hard in the side with his forefinger.

"Forget him. I removed him from your sphere because I want nothing to distract you from your service to me."

He poked Nicholas again and strode off across the room. A moment later, nimble as any courtier, he was dancing with a whore down the middle of the figure. Nicholas's face was still burning with embarrassment. Under lowered lids he looked from side to side, to see who might have overheard Valentino's remarks. Dozens must have heard, dozens of other men. He sidled away to the nearest door.

IN EARLY DECEMBER Nicholas found another note on his desk, this one commanding him to attend Mass at Santa Maria in Aracoeli the following morning.

He went reluctantly. The steep steps that climbed the hill

to the old church were obstacle enough; and he had nothing
to tell Gianpaolo except lies. All the world knew now that
Valentino had made a truce with his rebel captains; surely
Gianpaolo knew it, and Nicholas found it idle of him
even to have arranged this meeting, idle and devilish.

Midway up the Plague Steps, he decided that he would
not lie to Gianpaolo.

His legs hurt him from thigh to ankle and there were
dozens of steps still to be climbed. He tried to lose himself in
thoughts but his aching muscles nagged him back to the im-
mediate moment. He paused to rest. Below him the broad
piazza lay, its dusty oblong empty even of street vendors at
this early hour; dawn had just broken, and darkness still
obscured the broad expanse of the Barbi Palace across the
way, although the sunlight picked out every brick on the
face of the Aracoeli. Nicholas trudged on. He thought over
this warm-heartedness toward Gianpaolo Baglione, Stefano's
cousin. He wondered if he would have been tempted to
betray Valentino with any other of the rebels.

The church bell began to toll. He dragged his feet from
step to step. The strokes of the bell shivered in the air above
his head. He heard the chanting of the Franciscans inside the
church.

The vast, dim hollow of the building enveloped him.
On either side a line of columns towered up to the distant
ceiling. The columns did not match, having been brought
here centuries ago from all over the city, some fluted and
some plain, and some still bearing inscriptions from the
classic age on their scrolled heads. The Plague Steps had been
brought here also from somewhere else, he forgot exactly
where. Plundered from an earlier Rome. The bell stopped
tolling, and at the far end of the aisle between the columns
the Mass began.

"Oremus."

Behind Nicholas, footsteps sounded. Expecting this, Nicholas did not startle when a low voice murmured, "Outside."

Gratefully he left the church. Beside the building was an arbor of grapevines, covering the walk over toward the Palace of the Senator on top of the Campidoglio hill. The grapevines, pruned to a web of twigs, let through a watery confusing light. Nicholas removed his hat and went in among the crisscrossing shadows; a man in a mask stepped forward from the shelter of the church wall.

"Well?"

Nicholas glanced behind them; the way back to the church stretched out empty into the sun. He faced Gianpaolo.

"I sent your message to Valentino, my lord. He said that you should keep faith as you would, and come to him when he summoned you."

The black mask hissed. "Is that all?"

"No more than that."

"You know that he has signed a truce with us? That we are all to meet at Senigallia, to talk over a new alliance?"

Nicholas inclined his head. "That is certainly apt, isn't it? Senigallia—*the camp of the Gauls.*"

Gianpaolo said a round oath, one Stefano had used once. He took off his mask. "What do you mean by that?"

"You have a young cousin, named Stefano."

Gianpaolo put his head to one side. "I understood that you had my cousin, Messer Secretary."

"Not any more. Valentino has seen to that." Nicholas paused a little, considering this; Gianpaolo was looking at him with distaste. He said, "The Gauls were great loppers of heads, Messer Rebel. Heads will fall at Senigallia."

He turned and walked down the sloping path under the arbor, expecting to be called back; Gianpaolo seemed unsubtle to him. But no one called. When he reached the steps, he paused to put on his hat, and looked quickly back over his shoulder. Gianpaolo was gone.

Nicholas blew out the breath in his lungs, wishing he had not done it, and yet delighting in it. He knew he was a fool to betray Valentino, and Gianpaolo was careless with secrets: Valentino could well learn of it. Even while he realized that, stiffening at the thought of the consequences, he longed for Valentino to find out and make the vengeance perfect. He hurried down the Plague Steps. Perhaps this would exorcise Stefano from his thoughts. He strode away down the pavement of the Corso; he was already late to his desk.

IN JANUARY OF 1503 Cesare Borgia met with his rebellious captains at Senigallia, and there his faithful men surrounded the rebels and took them prisoners. Oliverotto da Fermi and Vitellozzo Vitelli were strangled at once; Don Miguel da Corella noosed them with a cord. The two Orsini, Paolo and the Duke of Gravina, were made prisoners until such time as the rest of their family could be dealt with. Gianpaolo Baglione did not come to Senigallia.

Everyone expected that Cardinal Orsini would flee Rome or be arrested with his kinsmen. Yet one evening in the dead of winter Bruni received a summons to dine at the Orsini Palace.

"It's madness," Bruni said. "The man's gone mad."

Nicholas lifted the invitation by the corner of the page and read it through again. He said, "I hope they do not kill the fatted calf. He'll have to invite all Rome to have company on either elbow."

"I certainly cannot go," Bruni said. "Our position with the Pope is already ambiguous. I cannot risk displeasing His Holiness."

Nicholas put the invitation down again. Alexander had brought a young man's energy to the task of arresting the Orsini. His men were seizing every member of the family in Rome, even women and children. It was said that Alexander personally had signed the documents for each seizure and that he kept on his person a stack of warrants for the execution of every one of the Orsini, as soon as they were all collected.

Bruni said, "You must go."

"I," Nicholas said, astonished.

"Cardinal Orsini has always been most friendly to me. I will not reject his invitation entirely."

"What about offending the Pope?" Nicholas said. "What about my neck, if it comes to that?"

"You know everyone in Rome," Bruni said, with a little twitch of his hand. "Even the Borgias will forgive a visit to a friend."

Nicholas said, "I shall be ill. Much too ill to go to an evening dinner."

On the other side of the desk, Bruni planted his elbows firmly down and hunched his head and shoulders between his hands. He gave Nicholas a broad, kind look. He said, "I expect to write soon to the Gonfalonier. Perhaps I will mention the salary due you—a considerable sum, is it not? A few thousand crowns?"

Nicholas put his lips firmly together. Although he refused to yield out loud, he knew at once that he would go to the Cardinal's supper. Bruni knew it, too; with an indulgent smile he took the invitation and folded it and put it away in a drawer of his desk.

"You may leave, Nicholas."

Nicholas left.

THE GREAT ORSINI PALACE looked almost as if it were deserted. The front gate was unattended and Nicholas could not find a porter to admit him, although he shouted through the grillework into the courtyard and banged on the knocker. When he leaned on the grille to look into the corner of the yard, the gate swung open. He went in by himself across the brick yard.

There was garbage heaped in the corners of the court-yard. A scarred cat sprawled across the marble balcony above the left-hand wall of the palace. Even in the right-hand wing, usually let out as dwellings, there seemed no life stirring. Many of the windows were open to the wind, the shutters gone. He went up to the door into the Cardinal's palace.

"Messer Dawson."

The door cracked open enough to allow a man inside to look out and identify him. It was the porter. Nicholas said, loudly, "I am here in the name of His Excellency the ambassador from Florence."

The door opened wide. The aged porter let him into the palace. He had been a source of news and gossip to Nicholas for years; in fact he knew the servant better than he knew Cardinal Orsini. He gave the old man his hat.

"What is happening here? Has he been taken, then?"

"Don't say it." The old man rubbed his nose. He led Nicholas across through the hall. The black and white marble floor was tracked with dirty footprints, all leading toward the double door on the left. The footman was leading him there too. Nicholas tried again.

"Why has he not left the city? He's been implicated in the plot, I know that. The Pope surely—"

The old man cleared his throat in a report like a cannon, silencing Nicholas halfway through the word. He opened the double doors in a dramatic gesture.

"Messer Nicholas Dawson, of the Republic of Florence."

Nicholas went into the great room beyond. For a moment, in the vastness of the hall, hung with figured rugs and tapestries, and painted with scenes from Roman myth, he did not notice the few living people who were there. The banquet tables, reaching the length of the room on either side, were set for guests, but the benches and chairs were empty; no one moved or talked. It was like a haunted room, or one visited by plague. Then he noticed the dozen men seated at the head of the table, and he relaxed. Suddenly the room seemed warmer.

Cardinal Orsini in his red soutane rose to greet Nicholas.

"I might have supposed that you would come. I sent five hundred invitations—you see how many answered."

"Your Excellency, you ought to be well away from Rome."

The Cardinal laughed. His voice was mellow and soft as usual. "You are not original, Messer Dawson. Each of these who preceded you here has said very nearly the same thing. Will you sit and join us?"

Nicholas bowed and mouthed appropriate greetings to the half dozen men who sat around the table. He barely knew any of them; they were private men, of lesser rank than the bulk of the Cardinal's friends, low enough to escape the scythe. A servant in the Orsini livery took him to his place and brought him wine.

"Where were we?" the Cardinal said. He swept up his silk skirts and took his chair again. "Yes, Raimondo, you were tempting the muse. Successfully, may I remark."

Raimondo was a minor member of another old Roman house. He stood up in his place and began to recite in Latin. Nicholas searched the other guests with his eyes. If the worst happened, he could claim that he was here to report on this utterly strange event for the Borgias. As soon as the notion formed in his mind he was ashamed.

Under the distraction the servants brought in the meal. Nicholas hardly tasted the fish, the soup, the roast doves in a sauce of wine and mushrooms. There were few servants and the pace of the meal lagged; the man on his right was carving meat from a dove while the crisp-skinned fish, turning cold, was still on Nicholas's plate. Raimondo had done with his bad Latin and another man rose and began to read a sonnet of Petrarca from a small leather-bound book.

Nicholas could not shake his mind free of the image of the plague supper. Every time the servants' door creaked he expected news of a dead rat; the smell of the place was like a death house. He longed to get away into the open air.

A thick compôte of fruit and honey passed before him untouched. One by one the guests rose to recite. Soon his turn would come. He sat still in his place, panicked, wondering what he would say.

The man beside him at the table rose and mouthed an indifferent sonnet and sat down again. Nicholas found himself on his feet. He fastened his gaze on the Cardinal, at ease in the midst of his friends, and the words of Solon came to his tongue.

"Count no man happy until he lies safe in his grave."

He sat down again. Everyone was staring at him. From the far end of the table a rumble of angry comment sounded.

"Bad form. Very bad manners!"

"Throw him out."

The voices tumbled together. He paid no heed; he wished that he could go. With a gesture the Cardinal stopped the talk.

"No—he is right, and I honor what he is. Poor Nicholas, your career will not last long. Diplomats must never tell the truth."

Then he raised his voice, calling across the vast, half-empty hall. "I am ready."

The side door opened. Four or five men with swords came into the room. Their long coats were figured with the Borgia bull. They came around the table and stood on either side of the Cardinal Orsini.

"My friends," the Cardinal said, "I bid you goodbye. His Holiness commands me to put myself into his custody, because of my part in the insurrection against Duke Cesare Borgia. Let my fate be a source of illumination to all of you."

With those words he let the soldiers lead him away. Stunned to silence, the dinner guests sat over their plates, and no one turned to his neighbor even to share a look. Nicholas left as quickly as he could.

The Cardinal Orsini was arrested in January. It was several weeks before the Romans heard of his death.

SOMEONE HAD DRAWN in chalk on a ruined wall near Trajan's Column. The steady rain had washed away all but the smeared outlines of a bull, grotesquely crowned with the tiara, vomiting something indistinguishable. Nicholas pulled his hat down to shield his eyes from the rain and turned into the narrow tree-shaded lane that led toward his house.

Ahead, a man shouted, in the rainswept darkness under the trees, and he stopped. The shouting grew louder. There were men fighting down there, and even as he started back the way he had come, there was a scream of terror and a whoop of triumph and a tide of men ran down the lane toward him. He dodged into the shelter of the trees.

The men ran awkwardly, twisted to look behind them; they carried cudgels. Passing Nicholas, they began to throw their weapons down and face forward so that they could run faster. Nicholas pressed his hands against the trunk of the tree that hid him. Out of the shouts and the pound of the rain he picked the thud of oncoming hoofs, and several horsemen galloped down past him. He sucked in his breath. The horsemen rode up on the heels of the men fleeing on foot and leaned from their saddles and stabbed with their swords. Nicholas's chest constricted. The fleeing men shrieked. They had reached the piazza; with the horsemen trampling them down, they scattered across the open ground.

Nicholas let out his breath, his throat sour with nausea. There were men lying in the lane only a few yards away from him. He lingered there behind the tree, afraid to show himself. In the piazza, the racket of the fighting seemed dim and fading. At last he stole out from the shelter of the tree and went to kneel beside the nearest of the bodies in the lane.

The man was dead; his skull was crushed. Nicholas's stomach heaved. His eyes averted, he knelt there in the rainy grass a good while before he could trust himself to stand up again. There were two or three other men lying still in the lane, and he went quickly from one to the next, to make sure that they were beyond any help of his, before he let himself go home.

As he passed by the Colosseo, he came on a man scrawling words on a brick wall; brazen as a whore, the man paid no heed to him, even when Nicholas slowed to read what he was writing.

ORSINI KEEP OUT!—DEATH TO ALL ORSINI!

Which explained the man's boldness. Nicholas went on his way.

ONE DAY, FINDING HIMSELF near the Pantheon, Nicholas went in again. The day was fair and the cold sunlight shone down through the gloom to an ellipse on the muddy floor. Although the noon hour had well begun, three or four beggars were sleeping against the foot of the wall. Dark jagged streaks stained the ancient marble behind them. The air smelled of urine. Nicholas turned around and walked back out again to the street.

LATER THAT DAY HE MET Bruni at a reception for the Spanish ambassador, de Rojas. When they had presented themselves to the Spaniards and exchanged the distantly formal greetings expected of an ally of France, Bruni hustled Nicholas off to see a painting somewhere else in the palace. Bruni had little interest in art; Nicholas wondered what he wanted to talk about. In fact Bruni could not wait and began talking excitedly as soon as they were out of the Spaniards' earshot.

"Well, now, have you heard about Machiavelli? I could have told you this would happen."

"What?" Nicholas said. They were in the hall, and too far from the nearest people to be overheard.

"Well," Bruni said tautly, his face glowing, "there's nothing yet really one could cash at a bank, but rumor has it he's about to be charged with spying for the Borgia."

Nicholas's head popped up. "Who? Machiavelli? Good God!"

"Remember, I said nothing official yet."

"Of course not."

Across the hall walked three young men in the livery of the Pope, going toward de Rojas's receiving room. Nicholas followed them with his eyes. "I am sure it is not true," he said.

"Oh, nonsense," Bruni cried, and hastily lowered his voice again. "Of course it's true! You know what everyone's been saying."

"Do you really intend showing this dreary painting to me, Excellency? The sun will be down before an hour, and I have a long way to walk."

Bruni started off toward the front of the palace, to leave. Nicholas fell into step beside him.

"Of course he is guilty," Bruni said. "You know the Borgia—how he will have his man, one way or the other, have him or get rid of him to some advantage."

This was so close to Nicholas's experience that he grunted in surprise; he fought the urge to blurt something out that would give himself away to Bruni. It was folly to do that. Probably it meant nothing. Bruni talked so much that mere chance would bring a truth out of him sooner or later.

They had come to the courtyard gate, where another man was waiting with the porter.

"Messers," the porter said. "I know you both, and this gentleman, too, who is a Venetian. Will you take him company with you, so that he will not have to go alone, with the streets so dangerous?"

"By all means," Bruni said. "Where are you going?"

The Venetian gave an address halfway to the Florentine legation; they went off to take him home. Bruni said, apologetically, "You must think us barbarians worse than the French, our streets are so unsafe."

"Worse than the Spaniards," the Venetian said, but with a smile, saying he wanted it taken for a joke. Bruni laughed; Nicholas laughed.

They walked quickly along the street, Nicholas keeping just behind and to one side of the other two men. A cold wind was blowing. The street was empty save for them. Usually the Romans lived in the street, but they were indoors now.

The Venetian said, "I am told the Pope's men are hacking the heads off every Orsini they find, even babies. He's another Herod. What think you of this French king—will he bring another army down to Naples?"

"He will have to," Bruni said. "Gonsalvo has taken every city south of Gaeta, and will have Naples herself soon."

Ahead the street narrowed, and they paused. Bruni looked around them and pointed to an alley.

"There is the faster way, but excessively narrow and dark."

"And a bad neighborhood, Excellency," Nicholas said. "If I may say so. We would be safer to go straight on."

"Straight on, then," the Venetian said, walking swiftly off, and Nicholas and Bruni followed. The Venetian smiled warmly at them over his shoulder.

"The Pope is Spanish, is he not? A passionate man. One presumes the Orsini have given him reason to hate them. I have not, I am sure."

"Nor I," Bruni said.

Nicholas kept them in the corner of his eye and walked with his head down, pretending to pay no attention. They came to the end of the paved street and picked a way through the mud, stirred and pocked and pooled with the prints of men and horses. The rain had washed down the tall fronts of the buildings on either side, turning the yellow travertine to a dull dark gold.

The Venetian said, "Recently I chanced to buy some very fine chairs, fit for any gentleman's finest rooms. They used to be in a palace of the Orsini and they are delightful. I would keep them, but I am pressed somewhat—I will sell them for a thousand crowns."

There was a long silence. They walked through a piazza where a fountain flowed. Three or four women were filling jugs at the pool, while a man stood by with a club on his shoulder to protect them. They stood staring at Bruni, Nicholas, and the Venetian until they were well past.

Bruni said suddenly, "I am going to pretend you did not say that. I do not want to hear what you just told me. Nicholas, is this not the street he told us?"

It was. Nicholas gave the Venetian directions to the house. The Venetian got angry; he swore at Bruni, called him a hypocrite, and stamped furiously away through the mud puddles. Nicholas and Bruni set off again.

After a moment, Bruni said, "I am not a hypocrite, am I, Nicholas?"

"Excellency, you were a friend of Cardinal Orsini."

"Then you think I behaved properly?"

"Irreproachably, Excellency."

Bruni seemed content with that; he straightened, lifting his face, and smiled. They crossed the Corso and reached a paved street again.

"Well," Bruni said, "if the French do come, they will make short work of Gonsalvo."

Nicholas said nothing.

"You think not?"

"Excellency, the Spanish will defeat the French."

"You're mad. The French have the greatest fighting men in Christendom, the finest military minds of our century. The most money."

Nicholas again made no answer, and Bruni gave him a quick, concerned look.

"You do not believe it?"

Nicholas said, "It's a sad day in Rome when the greatest question is whether the French can defeat the Spanish."

"The Pope is the French king's ally! The Borgias never lose—they never make mistakes like that."

They had come to the side door into the legation; Bruni had rooms in another part of the sprawling palace. He rang for the porter and turned back to argue with Nicholas again.

"I forgot that you have Spanish connections."

"Excellency," Nicholas said, "you asked me my opinion."

"Oh, well." Bruni put his hand on Nicholas's arm. "Forget that. But listen to me, Nicholas. What we talked of before, when we talked of Machiavelli—" he said no more, only patted Nicholas's arm a few times, with a certain weight, and gave him a piercing look. The porter opened the little door and let him in and closed the door, and he was gone from Nicholas's presence.

What they had spoken of before, when they spoke of Machiavelli. Nicholas remembered abruptly how Bruni had seemed to know his connection with the Borgia. Known it, forgiven it. Was it a warning, what he had just said? Nicholas found himself staring at the blank locked door in the wall. He walked away, hurrying now, with a long walk before he was home, and the night coming.

Bruni knew, then. Yet that changed nothing in the matter; Valentino still had the power over Nicholas that had forced him into the service of the prince in the first place. Nicholas could only do as he was doing.

He felt himself a homunculus, with no heart or will of his own.

A guest in the monastery where he had grown up had owned such a thing, and Brother Leo had taken him to see it, in secret because the abbot thought such things were heresy. Nicholas had expected a living miniature man, dressed in hose and doublet. The bottle shocked him. The greasy-looking foggy liquid that filled it, the shriveled baby floating in it, sickened his stomach. He left the room at once. Brother Leo came after him in the yard, but they never spoke of the homunculus again.

Nicholas had seen the thing only for a moment, and long ago, but he could bring a clear image of it instantly to mind, the lids sealed like shells over the eyes, the webby nubs of fingers and toes: an unfinished being, incapable of life. He knew himself to be like that, powerless save through Valentino.

Action was the Borgia's virtue. He would not wait for chance to bring him an opportunity, and anyone who did wait would fall behind. Nicholas did not mean to fall behind. If Bruni knew of his treachery, his position with the Florentines was shaky at best. His only hope lay in the hopes and dreams of Cesare Borgia.

BY HIS SERVANT NICHOLAS DAWSON.

TO THE MOST MAGNIFICENT AND ILLUSTRIOUS
DUKE VALENTINO,

My lord, I have heard the certain news that the French king intends to lead an army to the relief of those fortresses in Naples to which the Spanish army has laid seige. The French claim this army will be the greatest ever to cross the Alps into Italy, and they expect to add to it the support of their allies here, among whom you are now listed.

All this is as it may be, but in your Magnificence's interest I ask humbly to be allowed to direct your Magnificence to consider that the Spanish may very well win the contest. My judgment depends on my knowledge of the Spanish commander, Gonsalvo. In short, it is commonly known that Gonsalvo built the Spanish armies according to his own design, and therefore fits his instruments better than the French commander, who, although I do not yet know his name, will beyond doubt be chosen because of his titles of nobility, rather than any particular understanding of the army.

At any rate, you will lose less in the event of a French victory, if you are the ally of Spain, than you will lose if a Spanish victory takes you in the arms of France. The Spanish fight for God, and consider their enemies the Devil, and therefore when they have beaten them, want no more than to exterminate them, and not to make alliances with them. As for the French, they have fought in Italy for years, and have been corrupted by our more practical Italian traditions. Your Magnificence, you are master of the heart of Italy, which any man must have in trust who dreams of an Italian crown. Now let the foreign crowns take notice of it.

I send you this letter, Magnificence, even though it would destroy me if the Florentines should see it. Therefore let your servant ask you to commit this to the flame.

Some days after he sent the letter to Valentino, Nicholas was in the Pope's audience hall to hear a spokesman for the Romans ask the Pope to stop his feud with the Orsini. The Pope looked angry at the beginning of the plea and his face reddened and his breath came short at the end of it, when the spokesman mentioned that the fighting was liable to ruin the Carnival, when the Roman shopkeepers made their greatest profits.

"Merchants," the Pope said, disgusted. "You think only of money."

Another of the Romans went up beside their spokesman to say, "Your Holiness, we rely on you to keep the peace in our city! When it is your men who do murder—"

"Leave off!" the Pope cried, and heaved his bulk up out of his chair. All around the crowded room the onlookers stiffened to attention, watching, like soldiers. Nicholas glanced around him and saw the same anxious look on every face; in such a mood, Alexander could be rash as a boy. But the Pope only flung his hand out in a violent gesture at the air.

"Murder, you say—have I not suffered murder at the hands of the Orsini? Have I not waited years for my revenge? No! My only regret is that my son Cesare prefers to hunt and drink and gamble over his sacred duty to avenge his brother!"

In the hush that followed his words someone gasped. Nicholas stroked his fingers back and forth together. The Pope walked in a circle around his chair, his bulk emphasized by the heavy swaying of his ceremonial robes.

"Need anyone ask what I mean?"

No one spoke. The booming voice resounded off the walls and the ceiling. Nicholas thought, He will not let us go, able to say we are ignorant.

"Over ten years ago," Alexander cried, "the Orsini slaughtered my eldest son, Juan, and threw his body in the Tiber. Now I will take the right of any father to avenge his grief."

He struck his chair with a blow that cracked in the silence as if he had broken the chair. Surprised, Nicholas saw tears on the old man's broad-veined cheeks. "My son!" he said. He groped for the chair and sank down into it. "My son!"

Before them all he covered his face with his hands and wept. Nicholas lifted one hand before his own eyes. It was painful to watch this, to see what should be happening only in the Pope's privy chamber.

Alexander was recovering himself. His head and shoulders hunched forward over his knees, he lifted his face. With his fingers he wiped the slime of tears from his cheeks, and his fingers modeled his expression into the solemn stately face of a public man. He straightened up, his back to the back of the chair, and his chin lifted.

"You are dismissed from my presence," he said to the Roman suppliants. "I will hear no more of this. If the Carnival is ruined, so be it. Go."

The Romans slunk away. Nicholas lowered his hands and slid them behind his back. The Pope looked around him for the next petitioners, and a page came forward to announce them.

When Nicholas left the Leonine City to go to his house, he found his way blocked by a spreading battle between the men of the Borgias and the Orsini. He circled it, going endlessly up and down streets looking for a clear way through, but there was none, and finally he retreated back to the legation and slept the night there.

LATE AT NIGHT the jangling of the gate bell stirred Nicholas from a deep sleep. Out in the street he found Miguelito and a dozen other masked and mounted men.

"Did we wake you?" Miguelito said kindly. "The sun has hardly set." He raised his voice to reach the men behind him in the street. "Here he is in his nightshirt like a clerk."

Among the men behind him was Valentino. And Stefano.

"I hope you aren't looking for a place to play cards," Nicholas said. The night was cold and dank; he shivered in his dressing gown and low house shoes. He avoided looking at Stefano. "And I'm fairly out of wine."

Miguelito leaned down from his horse to speak into Nicholas's ear. "We only came to tell you that my master will see Gonsalvo here in one week's time. You will arrange it with Gonsalvo. Go back to bed."

"In a week? He may not have the opportunity."

"Arrange it." Miguelito swung his horse around, and the other horses skittered and wheeled in the close quarters, manes and cloaks fluttering. Stefano rode well, to Nicholas's surprise, who had never seen him near a horse.

Valentino caught him staring at Stefano. Valentino reached out and palmed Stefano's shoulder. "See how he pines for you. Go give him a kiss."

The prince was in his teasing humor. Nicholas turned quickly to the gate.

"Leave off," Stefano muttered.

"Give him a kiss!"

The other men were laughing. Stefano's horse jumped, its jaw pressed open by the rider's hard hand on the reins. "By Cock, leave off!" Stefano cried.

"Bah." Valentino spurred his horse, which leapt sideways, and with a backward sweep of his arm knocked Stefano out of his saddle. The prince galloped away down the street, his followers streaming after him; with their dark cloaks spread on the wind of their passage they seemed like a flight of bats.

Falling, Stefano had kept hold of his reins. His horse plunged, fighting to run with the others. Stefano struggled to make it stand and when it stood, bounded into the saddle.

"Damn you!" he shouted at Nicholas. He raced his horse away down the street after Valentino.

NICHOLAS DRANK the last of his wine and set the glass down. Juan, standing behind him, held out the linen napkin so that he could wipe his lips.

"You must not be here tonight," Nicholas said. He dropped the crumpled napkin on the table beside the remains of the bread. "Have you somewhere you might stay?"

"When may I come back?" Juan asked.

"Tomorrow morning. I will give you some money, if you need it."

"No—I can stay at the church," Juan said. He began to gather the dishes and silver from the table.

"Let me give you a purse. You could go to an inn." He

imagined Juan sleeping on the stone floor of a church, head to foot with a painted saint.

The old man was shaking his head; his stoop curved his head and shoulders forward over the clutter of dishes. "I would rather stay in the church than in some filthy common bed. What will you do—are you staying here?"

"Yes." Nicholas hitched himself up on his left ham and pulled his purse from under his belt. He counted a hundred carlini onto the table. "Here—at least you can have some wine."

"This is business of those other people," Juan said.

Nicholas did not answer. Juan, superstitious as a child, would not bring Valentino's name to his lips.

"You should not be here then either," Juan said. He started away with the dishes.

Nicholas made a rude noise with his tongue against his teeth. "You sound like Bruni. Tell me the stars foretell disaster." He pushed at the table, rattling the legs against the floor, to cover the old man's answer. "Take this money and get out of here. I will expect you back tomorrow to serve me a cold breakfast." Rising, he went across the room to his bedchamber. When he came out again a few moments later with his good coat in his hands, Juan and his money were gone. Nicholas put his coat on by himself.

Now, alone in the house, he fell into a whirl of impatience. He went around the room twice, moving one chair an inch, and sliding his hand over the scarred front of the cabinet in an effort to hide its flaws. He went into the kitchen to put the wine into the jar and found that Juan had done that, and even set out half a dozen glasses on the sideboard. Nicholas grunted, displeased. Living in his imagination, the old man was taking of late to acting on what he imagined as if it were perfectly real, which set Nicholas's teeth on edge. As he came out again from the kitchen into the main room, the gate bell sounded.

He went out into the late twilight and opened the gate for

two men wrapped in cloaks and hoods. They were on foot. Halfway down the path through the trees to the house, Valentino put back his hood and stopped.

"He has not come?"

Nicholas said, "Not yet, Magnificence. He sent to me that he would come by sundown. He wanted a guide through the city and I sent him des Troches."

Valentino hawked as if he were peeling off the inside of his mouth and spat white into the shadow under the trees. "Why des Troches?"

"Of late he has pestered me often to do me small favors."

"You should have gone yourself. Des Troches will get him lost." Valentino made an impatient face. "Still, it works out well, for me. When he comes, meet him, sit him down and give him drink, and draw him into talk. Is there somewhere in your house where I can listen secretly to him?"

"The bedroom," Nicholas said.

"The kitchen would be better," Miguelito said.

They had been speaking in Italian but Miguelito used Spanish, and henceforth they spoke in that language.

He went on, "There is a way out from the kitchen—when you wanted to join the captain-general, you would only have to go around the house and enter by the front door."

Valentino was already moving toward the house again. "Excellent," he said.

Nicholas followed him in through the front door, and when Valentino hesitated, directed him toward the kitchen. Dark as an imp in his black cloak, Miguelito followed his master. The gate bell rang again.

On the stone threshold of the kitchen Valentino said, "Des Troches will be with him—you can trust des Troches to help you draw him out."

The door shut. Nicholas went out to the gate, his armpits wet.

Again, two cloaked men waited for him; these men led

horses by the reins. Nicholas stood aside to let them pass by him. He considered what his neighbors were thinking of this gathering. An orgy, perhaps. He circled after the newcomers, avoiding their horses, and spoke in Spanish.

"Excellency, let me thank you for allowing me the honor of sheltering you once again." He bowed to the burly man on the left. "Unfortunately, I have no groom to take your horses, but if you will tether them under the trees—"

"Allow me the honor," said the slender man, and taking the reins of both horses led them away into the shade.

The heavy-set man facing Nicholas drew his hood back and opened his cloak. Smiling, he said, "The pleasure belongs to me, Señor Dawson, and the happy anticipation of entertaining you once more, as well."

Nicholas could not hold the older man's sharp eyes. He said stiffly, "I am at Your Excellency's disposal," and bowed and held out his hand toward the house.

Gonsalvo da Cordoba laughed under his breath. "Well, we shall not speak of it." He started toward the door. "Has my young friend arrived?"

Nicholas, following at his heels, was filled with the suspicion that the Spanish captain-general knew that Valentino lay in wait for him. He held the door. Des Troches was tramping through the high grass toward them, his cloak over his arm.

"No," Nicholas said to Gonsalvo. "He has not arrived yet."

Gonsalvo nodded his head once and went into the room. Three strides inside the door, he stopped and exclaimed.

"You have painted out your mountains."

Nicholas said, "They bored me, Excellency."

Gonsalvo faced him, moving like a dancer on the balls of his feet, his tufted gray eyebrows up. "You found them more boring than plain white walls?"

"They fix the imagination," Nicholas said. "Against white

walls, I can see what I please." He smiled at Gonsalvo, who was exactly his own height, eye to eye with him; he had remembered him much taller. "Actually, I am trying to accumulate enough money to have them painted again."

"With what?"

Des Troches had come in. Nicholas glanced at him. "There is wine in the kitchen, there," he said, and pointed to the door. Des Troches left them.

"I don't know what I shall put on the walls." A gesture of his hand offered Gonsalvo a chair; they both sat down at the same moment, half-facing one another. Nicholas crossed his legs at the knee. "Perhaps scenes of your victories in Naples?"

Gonsalvo pushed his boots out in front of him. "Not by Italian artisans."

"It would require the talents of a Perugino, at the least."

"The Italians hate me. Hate all Spaniards, even—" he paused to take a glass from des Troches, who had come back from the kitchen—"our divine Cesare. Is that not so?"

Des Troches burst into speech. "Not so! All Italy rings with praise of my lord's virtue and good fortune."

"Besides," Nicholas said, "my lord Valentino is half Italian."

Gonsalvo put the glass down untasted. "All the same, one hears the most bitter words of him, from some men."

Des Troches had left the kitchen door halfway ajar. Nicholas touched the bell of his glass with his fingertips. Gonsalvo was saying nothing that Valentino wanted to hear.

Des Troches had leapt into words again like a greyhound. "Those whom he has destroyed may speak against him, but many more, whose lives he has restored, will sing his praises."

Nicholas lowered his glass. "Guidobaldo da Urbino was much loved, and how many of his people rose to defend him? You see him hounded over Italy. You yourself, my lord —your image in little hangs over very few Italian hearths."

"I do not seek power here for myself," Gonsalvo said.

"What you do not seek you may receive. You are the king's vicar in Naples. You have driven out the French completely, now—"

"They still hold Gaeta. This is a fine wine, Señor Dawson, but I recall you have fine appetites."

Nicholas met the other man's pale direct stare a moment, and Gonsalvo smiled again, showing teeth below his grizzled moustaches. What he meant was clear: if Nicholas pushed him, he would mention Nicholas's visit to him, a hard thing to explain to Valentino.

Des Troches was saying, "Gaeta! Who doubts the Spanish pennant will fly from its walls before summer?"

"I doubt," Gonsalvo said, "until I see it."

Des Troches leaned forward, his smooth face earnest. "Most excellent of captains, your caution graces your reputation. Yet surely you are waiting only for the proper moment to give the French their final humiliation."

"I only wish I could agree with you, señor."

Nicholas could not hold his tongue any longer; he felt Gonsalvo's unspoken threat like a challenge. He said, "Yet you are certain enough of the power of your rule in Naples that you left your army to return to Spain—last month, I understand, and for some time."

Gonsalvo's eyes half-closed. "When my king summons me, I go." He reached for his glass on the floor by his boot.

"And of course the defenders of Gaeta know that the French king is bringing an army to their relief," Nicholas said. "Which surely accounts for their resolve."

Des Troches cleared his throat in the racket of a stuttering cough. "The French will be no match for the battle-hardened veterans of Spain."

Nicholas was staring intently into Gonsalvo's face. "The French army," he said, "will be the largest to invade Italy since the hordes of Attila." Let Gonsalvo see that Nicholas feared neither him nor Valentino.

"Attila also failed," Gonsalvo said mildly. "You are well informed, my dear Dawson."

"My post with Florence gives me access to much French information."

"As your post with my lord Cesare gives you access to information on the other side?" Gonsalvo did not look angry; the webs of lines around his eyes were crinkled, as if he suppressed a smile.

"I do what I can," Nicholas said.

That pomposity brought Gonsalvo to laughter. He raised his glass in a satirical salute. "I am sure of that."

Nicholas felt Gonsalvo laughing at him; like an ass he had let the Spanish captain lead him deftly into revealing how seriously he took his own part in this. His ears burned when he remembered Valentino listening. Des Troches leapt into the spreading silence with a flurry of words.

"King Louis loiters in France. Who knows if he will even come to Italy? What use to spend more French blood in pursuit of a fantasy?"

There was a knock on the door, and des Troches jumped straight up from his chair. Nicholas relaxed down to his heels. He leaned over the arm of his chair and put his wine on the floor.

"Let them in," he said to des Troches.

The other man sped away across the room. Nicholas sat back, his shoulders slumping, and found Gonsalvo's eyes on him.

"Señor Dawson, a draw, I think."

Nicholas could not answer that. The door creaked; Valentino came into the room, Miguelito at his side, and des Troches behind him.

For several moments no one spoke save the two great men, smiling at each other, and giving one another compliments and assurances of love. Nicholas, des Troches, and Miguelito stood around them, motionless. Nicholas found himself drawn to the differences in the two men—Valentino taller by a head, young, and fair as the sun in its glory; and Gonsalvo, weathered more than aged, square-set and solid. Valentino stood with his head thrown back, and every motion of his hand caught and held the eye like the gestures of a magician.

They sat. Nicholas and des Troches went to bring them wine.

"What think you of our Spanish captain?" des Troches said, in the kitchen.

Nicholas poured the red wine into a glass. "He loves the contest."

"Pah! He is a soldier, that is true of the breed."

Nicholas thought not. The soldiers he had experience of all loved to win, and avoided even the threat of a test. He put the tall Venetian glasses on a tray and took them out, des Troches going ahead to hold the door.

In his chair by the fire Valentino was talking of some feat of arms; Gonsalvo sat hunched to one side listening, his chin in his hand. Nicholas took the wine in between them. Valentino took a glass and drank and plunged back into the recital of his deed, but Gonsalvo's gaze strayed, and he held the wine up to the light.

"Excellent," he said, when Valentino had come to the end of his story, "most excellent, and your successes show how well you know your craft. For myself, I would be proud to own such fortune as attends you."

"Fortune," Valentino said. "I have shaped my destiny in my own hands, señor el capitan, and whatever becomes of me, I shall neither blame nor thank fortune."

Nicholas went to the hearth. A damp chill was creeping into the room, and he sank down onto his haunches and put a log on the rails and stuffed tinder under it. Behind him, Gonsalvo was asking questions of the country north of Rome—how the French army would have to march south. While Nicholas was scraping the flint over the steel in his tinderbox, Miguelito knelt beside him.

"Here—you are ruining my nerves." He took the box and struck sparks into the tinder flax. As they knelt over the fire, he said, "You seem to know one another—you and Gonsalvo."

"What?" Nicholas said.

"Oh. You are so fiery with him. I have marked it in you, Nicholas—you are mild as a mouse on first meeting, it's only later you show teeth."

"My lord said—"

"I heard." Miguelito rose and leaned himself up against the wall again, his face turned away. The fire was glowing in the tinder; Nicholas bent down to blow on it.

After a while he took the empty glasses and filled them in the kitchen. The two men by the fire talked back and forth; Valentino talked most, while Gonsalvo spurred him on with questions.

"Of the French army," Gonsalvo said at last, "what do you know of their commanders?"

"Less than I know of yours." Valentino smiled. His hands, which had been busy with gestures, suddenly fell still on his knees. "Among whom I would number myself, if we can agree on the terms of the contract."

Nicholas lifted his head, alarmed. It would not help Valentino's cause with Gonsalvo to bargain. Gonsalvo sat motionless for a moment, his gaze on Valentino, and his face smoothed clean of expression above the masking beard. Finally he held out his empty glass to Nicholas.

"The Italian condotta is something foreign to me—I do not understand the principle or the practice. What terms do you require?"

Reluctantly Nicholas went to fill the glass, his ears straining behind him to hear what they said. Valentino spoke lightly, almost carelessly. "I must protect my territories. After all, my domains lie between the French king and you. I will be placing myself in mortal jeopardy. The situation is delicate. My father's very safety may be at stake."

"These are your terms?"

Nicholas had come to the kitchen door and had to go in after the wine. He heard nothing more. The door swung shut behind him. One of the candles in the kitchen had gone out and the long narrow room was gloomy as a church. He found the wine jar empty and took it into the pantry to fill it again. Valentino knew Gonsalvo little, to put a base price on service to him. Pouring the wine into the glass, he took it out again to the front room, where Valentino was saying, "—Florence, of course."

"My superiors rather favor the de' Medici."

Valentino sat unmoving as an Egyptian king in his chair. "I said my terms were high."

It was Tuscany he wanted. Nicholas put the glass into Gonsalvo's hand, rough as old wood.

"Then there is the matter of Venice," Valentino said.

Gonsalvo sipped the wine. He licked his lips with the tip of his tongue and brushed his damp gray moustaches back. He said, "Under the circumstances, my young friend, I think we can stop with the matter of Tuscany."

"Ah?"

"I am not prepared to accept your contract."

A wash of dark color flooded Valentino's face; his eyes blazed. "You have not listened to me."

"I have."

"I will not accept one inch less than what I have demanded!"

"I am offering you nothing," Gonsalvo said.

Valentino exploded up from his chair; he stalked across the room, carrying the attention of the other men with him. Halfway to the far wall he wheeled, all his leonine beauty glowing with his rage.

"You will force me into the arms of King Louis."

Gonsalvo remained in his chair, drinking his wine in slow sips. His face was gravely indifferent; he slouched on the arm of his chair.

"You shall have me as an enemy," Valentino said, in a shaking voice. "Then perhaps you will learn to respect what I am."

He strode out the door. Miguelito followed, slower, leaving the door open. The draft fluttered the candles and blew a gust of smoke from the fire into the room. Des Troches hurried over to shut the door. His face was furrowed with distress like an old hound's. In the dimness before the candles recovered, Nicholas looked down at Gonsalvo and saw the old soldier smiling.

Des Troches came back, looking much worried. He gave Nicholas a quick glance, as if seeking agreement, and said to Gonsalvo, "My lord, I shall escort you out of Rome again."

Gonsalvo nodded. Silently he rose and gathered up his cloak and bundled himself into it, and with des Troches he went away into the garden. After a few moments Nicholas heard them leading their horses through the thick thorny brush toward the gate.

Nicholas poured another glass of the wine and sat down before his fire. What he had just witnessed still unnerved him. It was not merely that Valentino had so misplayed his part; that could be reversed. Something more fundamental showed through the whole argument, something irreconcilable between the two men. In Italy no man ever turned another down; the princes smiled and made their contracts and broke them later, when they could win some advantage thereby. Everyone knew that and accounted for it. Everyone expected to lose something here to gain something there. Gonsalvo had said that the condotta was foreign to him. He might have said as much of the whole Italian practice of war, fought on paper and paid for with promises, the credits of diplomacy. Gonsalvo bought his victories with blood.

Nicholas filled his mouth with the ripe stony wine. For the first time he doubted that his way could contain Gonsalvo's.

It was well before ten o'clock. He thought of going down

into the city for a late supper and a boy. At the same time he remembered Juan, sleeping on the hard floor of the church. It was a long way down to the tavernas, and already ten o'clock. He went out to the street, hailed a passer-by, and gave him ten carlini to go to the church and send Juan home.

He waited by the gate, standing inside the post where the chilly spring wind did not reach. The moments dragged on; he began to wonder if his messenger had taken the ten carlini straight into the nearest wine shop. Then at the end of the street, in the night shadows, a shadow moved, walking toward him. He went outside the gate and gestured broadly. The old man raised his hand in answer. Nicholas went up the path toward his house.

VALENTINO WENT OUT of Rome again, to hunt in the campagna. He sent no word at all to Nicholas Dawson, who realized uneasily that he was blamed for the humiliation the Borgia prince had suffered at his house. Nicholas considered writing another letter to Valentino, suggesting another approach to Gonsalvo, and instantly pushed the thought out of his mind. He was a little afraid of bringing himself to the Borgia's attention. The French were gathering an army to cross the Alps; perhaps when every southbound road in Italy fluttered with the lily banners, Gonsalvo would change his mind and open the matter again himself.

In May a dispatch came from Florence to the legation in Rome that repeated almost by the word the meeting between Valentino and Gonsalvo da Cordoba at Nicholas's house.

The Florentines attributed their knowledge of the secret meeting to a French dispatch. Nicholas read it with a feeling of panic. He stood in Bruni's chamber, under Bruni's eyes, and struggled to keep his fear from showing in his face. He himself went nameless in the report, which only said that the two captains had met at a private house in Rome. He laid the dispatch down on Bruni's desk.

"Valentino has made a mistake," he said.

Bruni emitted a skeptical sound. "Gonsalvo, don't you think? Or do you imagine Valentino's support could not help the Spanish?"

"I mean only that a man in Valentino's place would profit more by keeping news like this secret as long as possible." Nicholas touched the thick pale paper as it lay on the desk. "I wonder how the French came by their information."

"They have their sources, naturally. They could not do otherwise."

"Indeed." Nicholas's eyes were fixed on the dispatch; he longed to take it away to his own desk to copy. He could foresee circumstances when he might need every evidence he could find of what it said.

"What does that remark mean?" Bruni scowled at him. "By the Mother of God, Nicholas, you are becoming cryptic as a sibyl."

"I mean," Nicholas said, lifting his gaze to meet Bruni's, "that it serves the interest of the French far more than anyone else—that we should learn now of this falling out between Valentino and Spain."

Bruni's eyes widened. Above the shaved edges of his beard, his cheeks sucked hollow. "Do you mean that they have falsified this? That it is untrue?"

Nicholas shrugged his shoulders. "It's foolish to accept anything at face value, these days."

"By God." Bruni slapped his desk with both hands. "You may be right."

Nicholas could think of no excuse to have the dispatch to himself for a while, since he had already read it. He lingered a moment, trying to make up a plausible story, but suddenly Bruni rose to his feet and took the dispatch in his hand.

"I'll see to this." He folded the paper and stuffed it into his wallet. "Good morning, Nicholas."

Now Nicholas could only take his leave of the ambassador. Bruni called for his servant; he was going somewhere, taking the dispatch, perhaps to the astrologer he favored so often. Nicholas went back to his chambers.

At noon he left early, fifteen minutes before two bells rang, and walked through the swarming Monday markets toward the bridge to the Leonine City. It was the height of the morning and the city's wives were bargaining for lettuce and fresh strawberries and eggs. The pulped leaves of vegetables littered the street and the air reeked bitterly of burned garlic, oil, and roasting chickens. Nicholas kept one hand on his wallet. He skirted the masses of beggars and children that rushed at every passer-by. Even the balconies and windows of the ramshackle buildings along the river were crowded with folk at market; they let down baskets on ropes to the vendors who pushed their carts of asparagus and oranges, almonds and cheese along the Tiber's muddy bank.

On the broad upright post at the foot of the Ponte Elio there was scribbled: DOWN WITH THE POPE! and ORSINI! ORSINI!

Nicholas passed over the bridge and made his way down the narrow street from Castel Sant' Angelo to the Vatican. There were no markets here, but the little open-air tavernas along the way to Saint Peter's were thronged with foreigners and churchmen, and on the street were the vendors, selling oranges and nuts, vials of blood, the knucklebones of saints, little crosses wearing the name of Rome. A file of barefoot Franciscans was walking briskly toward the basilica.

At the Vatican, the guard knew him and waved him in past the gawking foreigners at the gate. Nicholas heard them exclaim at that, as if he might be someone great. He hurried away from the gate and their awed murmuring. Ahead the palace presented its broad wall, checked with banks of small windows. By contrast to the stone, the gardens on either side of the path and along the foot of the palace were softly splashed with beds of the first spring flowers, primroses and little white clumps of lily-of-the-field.

The Borgias would learn in time that someone at that meeting had betrayed them. He had to seem honest then by being honest now. That thought whipped him on; he was walking as fast as his legs would carry him. Across a bank of daisies he saw three or four of the Pope's pages, loitering in the shadow of a tree. Nearby was the little garden house, covered with ivy. Cutting through the rows of flowers, Nicholas made his way there.

Before he reached the garden house, which was set up on a little slab of white marble with steps all around, like a pedestal top, a page had gone inside to announce him. Nicholas waited, his hands behind his back. The pages eyed him but did not speak. One was eating marzipan. The odor of almonds reached him. The first page returned.

"Messer Dawson, His Holiness desires you to leave. The time is inappropriate."

"Ask the sublime Vicar of Christ to grant me a moment's patient hearing on a matter of importance to the Magnificence Duke Cesare."

The page went inside the garden house again. Nicholas turned his eyes toward the flowers and the dark ugly mass of the palace beyond them.

This time he was let into the presence of the Pope. He knelt, kissed the jeweled cross on Alexander's shoe, and made another little bow to Giulia Farnese, sitting on the Pope's right. One table before them was set up for a meal but there was no food on the plates.

"What is it, Nicholas?" the Pope said. "Can you not send this matter directly to my son?"

"Your Holiness, I ask your pardon, my resources are limited."

"As whose are not, may I ask?" Alexander pouted. He squirmed in his chair; fat as he was, he could not sit comfortably. Nicholas had heard it said that in their congress Giulia sat on top of him, like Mohammed on the mountain. "What is it, Nicholas?"

"This morning from Florence we received a message that gave all the details of the meeting between Duke Valentino and the Spanish captain Gonsalvo. Specifically it spoke of the quarrel—that Gonsalvo denied him, and that my lord Cesare walked out."

The Pope had raised his huge bull's head. His black eyes glittered.

"From Florence, you say? Did the dispatch offer any source?"

"A French dispatch."

"Ay, ay," the Pope said calmly. "How wicked is the world! We are betrayed again."

A page entered. "Your Holiness, the platters from the kitchen—"

"Wait outside." Alexander motioned with his hand. He brought his head around again to face Nicholas. "Who was there, at the meeting?"

"Valentino, Gonsalvo. Miguel da Corella. Des Troches d'Avila and I."

"You have a servant?"

"He was gone—I sent him off."

"One of you, then. Miguelito I cannot suspect. You or des Troches."

"Or Gonsalvo," Nicholas said.

Alexander stirred, all his silk robes hissing like a gown of snakes. "You do not trust Gonsalvo?"

"It is not beyond possibility that he could find some value in betraying us."

Nicholas stirred, as he said that; he knew Gonsalvo would not betray his honor by using another man's secrets.

"Us," the Pope said, with peculiar stress. "What of you yourself, Messer Dawson? You are much more suspect to me than a knight like Gonsalvo."

Nicholas said, "Whether I am innocent or not, I will still maintain it. It seems tedious to belabor the issue."

Alexander lifted his cheeks into a brilliant smile. "Yet you are clever enough to do it, and to come here with the announcement of it. Well. I shall send word on to my child at his play. You may go."

Nicholas knelt again and kissed Alexander's shoe. "Thank you, Your Holiness."

NOT LONG AFTERWARD, Valentino sent des Troches to Siena on an errand of diplomacy. Even as the man was traveling, the order went out to arrest him on a charge of leaving Rome without Valentino's consent. Des Troches fled. Valentino's agents hounded him from Siena to Genoa, from Genoa to Corsica, where he was taken, and on board a galley brought back in chains to Rome.

As Nicholas was passing beneath the hill of the Campidoglio, one evening on his way home to his supper, Miguelito came toward him from the shadow at the foot of the hill. "Come with me," he said, without any other greeting. "Duke Cesare wants you."

Nicholas's back tightened. "Why? What does he want?"

"Just come," Miguelito said, and put on his thin smile, seldom seen. "Don't look so green. We will see you home tonight, sitting down to your supper. The old man will keep it hot for you, won't he?"

In the thickening dusk they went along behind the hill, past the Mamertine, the loathsome prison of the ancients, and crossed the marshes toward the Tiber. Mosquitoes in clouds rose from the damp ground to meet them. The scrubby brush grew up around chunks of marble, the heads of buried columns, fragments of old buildings. Down the slope some way, the flickering light of a fire and the murmur of voices marked a lime kiln. Nicholas groped with his feet on the dark path, afraid of falling. A cat hissed and yowled and raced away ahead of them.

They came to the river's edge. In the river was moored a small covered boat.

Miguelito put out a plank from the shore and they boarded the boat. It rocked under Nicholas's feet. He put out his hands to balance himself. Ahead, the other man pulled a hatch up and descended into a low cabin, and a swatch of lantern light shot out across the deck. Miguelito doubled the hatch up on its hinges and laid it on the roof of the cabin.

"Go on."

Nicholas went down through the hatch three steps into the cabin, ducking his head under the ceiling, which was high enough only for the man seated beside the lantern. This man was des Troches. Seeing Nicholas, he lunged forward, but he was tied hand and foot and could only move a few inches. His face was ash-colored, as if he were already dead; he said nothing.

Miguelito came into the cabin. Nicholas crouched awkwardly between them, the sweat popping out all over his body. The cabin gave off a reek of putrid fish and the smoke of the lantern stung his eyes. He pressed his hands to his thighs. He knew why he had been brought here. He knew what was about to happen. He glanced once around the tiny cabin.

Des Troches screamed out suddenly, "How do you know he didn't do it? He did it!"

On either long side of the cabin were two narrow windows cut into the very top of the bulkheads. Three of them shone back the lantern light but the fourth was dark. Its oilskin cover hung below it. Nicholas lowered his eyes. Valentino was out there.

Des Troches screamed and screamed, accusing everyone. Miguelito eased past Nicholas, his back to the bulkhead, to the black window. His face was composed as a saint's. Between his hands hung the loop of his garrotte. He got behind des Troches, who screamed and screamed, and slipped the loop over the thrashing head. Nicholas could not breathe. His head whirled. He thought des Troches was still screaming, but that was impossible, the loop was tight, digging into the flesh of his throat, and his face was turning dark. His eyes bulged. Above him Miguelito's face twisted with the effort of his work. It seemed to go on for hours.

Miguelito lifted his hands, and des Troches fell forward. Nicholas sighed.

He was determined to show them nothing, not even interest. His back hurt from the unnatural posture the low cabin forced on him. The cabin seemed large enough now with des Troches dead. With his fingertips Miguelito dug the garrotte up out of the rut in des Troches's throat and removed the thing over the dead man's head.

"May I go now?" Nicholas said. "My supper will be cold."

Miguelito put the garrotte away inside his coat. His eyes were dreamy, his mouth a little slack. His head swayed toward the dark window. Remembering, he faced Nicholas again and nodded.

"Well, go, then."

"Thank you. Both of you." Nicholas pushed the hatch open and went out onto the deck.

The boat rocked back and forth and he walked with his feet wide apart. The plank had fallen down into the water. Kneeling on the gunwale of the boat, he leaned over, got his fingers on the slimy rotting wood, and pulled it back up into place. He knew they were watching him. He felt removed from what he was doing, as if he watched too, from one side. He walked down the plank to the shore and started away on the path.

He went at an ordinary pace. He did not look back. He had seen men die before, of sickness, of age, of violence, but never in such a way as des Troches's dying. He struggled with words for it, but he could not reduce what he had seen to the abstraction that made words possible. His feet plodded over the soggy marsh, where the ancient Romans had raced their chariots. He remembered Miguelito's face, tuned fine and taut, and wondered what drove him to that unshielded contact with the last absolute.

He longed for that moment again, to live in that moment, beyond the frame of words.

BRUNI CALLED HIM IN. Bruni would not look him in the face.

"I have the unpleasant duty of telling you that the Signory no longer desires your service."

Nicholas held his breath a moment and let it out again audibly. "May I ask why?"

The ambassador twitched a piece of paper toward him. "It seems that it has been you betraying us, and not Machiavelli."

Nicholas did not have to take the paper; he could see at once what it was. His own even handwriting covered it, beautifully legible, his one manual skill. It was his letter to Valentino, suggesting the advantages of the Spanish alliance.

"I warned you," Bruni said. "You cannot say I did not!"

His hands wrung together, and he avoided looking even in Nicholas's direction, but spoke to the dark end of the room.

"I am still owed a considerable sum of money," Nicholas said. "Nearly four years' salary."

"The Signory has provided me with a draft on the Pazzi bank for the sum of six hundred crowns. You will have to wait until the Republic's purse is a little fatter before you look for the rest."

Bruni opened a drawer and took out a long yellow slip of banker's paper. He held this out to Nicholas, who took it, and for a moment over the voucher Bruni at last let his eyes meet Nicholas's.

He said, "How could you do this? It will ruin me. My family—everyone."

Nicholas folded the voucher in half and put it away in his wallet. "I was forced, Excellency."

"Forced to serve Valentino, maybe—but to be caught—ah—"

Bruni's gaze slid away toward the dark at the end of the room, and again his hands scrubbed one over the other; deep lines pulled at the corners of his mouth. "You may use the remainder of the morning to remove your personal belongings and neaten your chambers."

"Good day, Excellency."

Bruni grunted at him.

Nicholas went out to the corridor. There was nothing here that belonged to him, and he knew no duty to neaten his chambers. He went down to the workroom, where the scribes were only beginning to take up their work, and getting his hat and coat from the rack he left.

THE SWELTERING SUMMER HEAT slowed the pace of life. The French army loitered below the Alps on the vast plain near Milan. Rome was quiet. The Orsini had withdrawn into their impregnable fortresses in the campagna, and the Borgia Pope's soldiers no longer swaggered in the city streets.

Valentino made a formal entry into Rome.

Nicholas went to see it, and stood with a hundred others on the grassy slope of the Gianicolo opposite the Colosseo. They waited nearly an hour before they heard in the distance the brassy heralding of horns. The sound grew louder and louder, until the first rank of the trumpeters strode into sight down the road from the Lateran. All the people watching shouted, overjoyed that the wait was over.

After the trumpeters came heralds, very expensively got up, who walked along reading loudly from scrolls. The topic seemed to be the achievements of Valentino; Nicholas caught only a few words. The sun was high in the sky, and he was wondering why he had come here to sweat along with dozens of other people to the enlargement of Duke Valentino.

Valentino's men in their gold and black livery marched by, some on foot and some on horseback. Halfway through the line rode Valentino himself, wearing black from head to foot, and riding a black horse. He looked bored.

As the Pope's son went by, the people around Nicholas shouted and whistled and waved their caps, making a good show; the courtiers coming in the prince's train were throwing coins and sweetmeats. Nicholas stood silent, his hands gripped together behind him. Valentino passed by toward the Arch of Constantine. Showers of money and sugared fruits pelted Nicholas and the people around him.

"Carlini," muttered a man behind him. "The Borgias are poor again. We'll see some new cardinals soon."

Stefano rode after Valentino, one of a group of young men. Nicholas lifted his head so that he could watch Stefano beyond the crowd. Ahead, the progress had reached the ancient Arch, where an old man, a nun, and two children would present Valentino with flowers and tokens of faith. Stefano drew rein. He was behind another man, so that Nicholas could not see his face. He slouched in his saddle, his elbow thrust out. His horse sidestepped so that Stefano's back was to Nicholas. The sunlight glanced off a medal pinned to the sleeve of his black and gold coat.

"Señor Dawson," a man said, behind Nicholas.

Nicholas turned. It was Gonsalvo, in a dark hat, smiling at him.

"I stopped by your house. Your man said you were here."

Nicholas glanced once again at Stefano and began to sidle his way through the crowd. Gonsalvo followed him; the others were all leaving, anyway, some going down to hear the speeches at the Arch, and some drifting away to their work. Nicholas and Gonsalvo started away toward his house.

"If you have come to bargain with Valentino," Nicholas said, "you must find another go-between. He's turned me out."

"So I have been told."

"And betrayed me to the Florentines, so they've turned me out as well."

"That also I've been told," Gonsalvo said placidly.

There was a wine shop in the next street. Nicholas turned them in that direction, and buying a jar of wine took it across the street to a bench in the sun. Gonsalvo did not sit beside him but stood facing him, his back to the street. Nicholas offered him the jar and he took it and drank.

"In fact," Gonsalvo said, "I have no need of Valentino, who is unsuitable, shall we say, to the purposes of my king. Have you found other employment?"

"I have a little money," Nicholas said. He retrieved the jar and drank from it. The street was busy. In the shop where he had bought the wine two girls were filling jars with oil; the cats were gathering on the corner for the old woman who fed them there every noon. Nicholas tilted his head back to talk to Gonsalvo again. "There is always some use for a secretary who writes a fine hand."

"A secretary," Gonsalvo said. "Your talents would be wasted."

"When you have taken Italy," Nicholas said, "my talents will be irrelevant."

"I disagree with that," Gonsalvo said. "Enough to offer you a place in my service."

That startled Nicholas; he put his hand up to his face, rubbed his nose, and imagined himself great again, restored to eminence; able, perhaps, to revenge himself on Valentino. At the thought of Valentino his vision underwent some adjustment. He lowered his hand again.

"I think myself the godchild of fortune that I am still alive," he said to Gonsalvo. "I shall not tempt Valentino."

Gonsalvo still held the jug. He raised it to drink again and handed it back to Nicholas.

"Valentino is unimportant. The ultimate end of all we do is the Crusade—to redeem the world for Christ as we have redeemed Spain. Nothing is more important than that—we ourselves are nothing."

Nicholas dashed the jar down and leapt to his feet, face to

face with Gonsalvo. "Are you mad? That was Valentino's purpose, you know—to save Italy."

Gonsalvo's face settled, and his smile disappeared behind the grizzled droop of his moustache. Softly he said, "I am not Valentino."

"That is simply a matter of degree," Nicholas said.

Gonsalvo flushed deeply, his eyes glittered, narrowed and direct, and he stood straight as a sentry. Quietly, he said, "I see I have misled myself. I ask your pardon. Good day." Turning on his heel, he walked stiffly away down the street. Nicholas, feeling tired, went back to his house.

NICHOLAS BROODED on the words he had used against Gonsalvo. He of all men had no place making a judgment of Gonsalvo da Cordoba, as great a man as anyone in Christendom. He might have talked his way into a position Valentino himself would have envied. Now he was considering the necessity of putting some of his furniture out for sale to buy bread for himself and his servant.

A few days after his angry talk with Gonsalvo, Miguelito da Corella nearly rode him down in the street near the Colosseo. Nicholas dodged out of the horse's way, and Miguelito wheeled his mount around.

"Go to the Torre Nona," Miguelito shouted. "If you want to save your pretty boy from the galleys."

He galloped away across the meadow again, toward the lane that wound around the foot of the Palatino. Nicholas scrubbed his hands against his thighs, wondering anxiously what Miguelito had meant, and making sure of his wallet started off across the city.

The Torre Nona was across Rome in a quarter of wretched huts and ruins. Nicholas walked more than an hour to reach it. When he entered the courtyard a crowd already filled the margins of the long narrow yard, waiting to see the executions. At the forge in the middle of the court the executioner's knave was pumping on the bellows and the executioner himself lounged on the tower step eating his dinner. The city prison occupied the bottom floor and the underground rooms of a crumbling tenth-century tower. The upper stories were vacant, their rotting wooden floors too treacherous to walk on.

Nicholas went up to the executioner, who was eating onions; when he turned, Nicholas took a long step backward from the stench on his breath.

"Have you a man among your prisoners named Stefano Baglione?" Nicholas asked.

"Maybe I do." The executioner reached for a piece of cheese on the step at his feet. He was a lanky man, half Nicholas's age, with blue eyes so pale they looked almost white.

Nicholas tipped his head back to look up at the tower. The Borgias knew him well; they sent a messenger with a handful of words, and he scurried reliably away to this human sump, his tongue hanging out.

He only wanted to see Stefano miserable. To have his revenge on Stefano, who had cursed him and made him miserable. He put his foot up on the step to the door.

The executioner grabbed the tail of his coat. "Where are you going?"

"To see if he is in there."

"I'll tell you who's in there! No one goes in there but me." The man's broad blackened palm thrust out. "Twenty carlini."

Nicholas thumbed a gold crown out of his wallet and held it up into the sunlight. "Is he there?"

The executioner grunted.

"If he is there, what will become of him?"

"Branded. On the face. He's a thief. The magistrate sentenced him last night. Taken in the act, he was." Now the executioner rose to his feet, drawn by the gold; from the creases of his leather apron bits of his dinner sprinkled down to the dirt. He reached for the coin.

Nicholas gave it up. He knew why Valentino had sent him here, to put him to this torture. He could walk away, go away and never think of it again. Never let himself think of Stefano again. The situation squeezed him like a vise. He took another crown from his purse. Precious, the money was, almost all he had, and he thought it over again for a moment. He remembered how Stefano had cursed him, the last time they had talked. How Stefano once had tried to rescue him from Gonsalvo.

He showed the coin to the executioner, who grunted again.

"What's that for?"

"Don't brand him," Nicholas said.

"Two crowns."

"I'm sorry," Nicholas said. "I have no more. I'm not a rich man. This or nothing."

For a moment the man was still, his idiot eyes fixed on the coin. The blast of his breath was making Nicholas sick. At last he reached out for the coin.

Nicholas stood at the edge of the yard, where the crowd was thin. Half a dozen prisoners were brought out for their punishment, but Stefano caught the crowd's interest immediately, or perhaps they knew him. They began to wail and call out to him, and a woman near Nicholas beat her hands together and shook her head and said, over and over, "Ah, such a beauty, such a beauty to be spoiled by the brand."

Nicholas's hands were sweating. He watched the executioner's knave put the brands into the fire and turn them.

First they branded another thief. The screech made the crowd gasp. Nicholas's lips were dry; he wished he could go away, go back to his house. Now it was Stefano's turn. The executioner made him kneel. He chose a brand and stamped it down into Stefano's face.

There was no scream, and the crowd sighed, disappointed. Someone yelled angrily, "There's a cheat." Stefano rose up, holding out his shackled hands to be freed. On his cheek was a great black T. Nicholas clenched his teeth, starting impulsively forward, ready to denounce the executioner for taking his coin, but as he came nearer Stefano he saw that the brand was only smudged char. The executioner had used a cool iron.

Stefano saw him; his face thinned and hardened with anger. Nicholas went to the gate out to the street. Stefano had to go out that way, and so they met there.

"What happened?" Nicholas said. "How did this come to pass?"

Stefano would not look at him, but glared away down the street. "Valentino sent me to break into someone's house."

"Whose house?"

"Cardinal Corneto's palace."

"Corneto," Nicholas said. "Why?"

"Never mind that," Stefano said. "How did you find out where I was?"

"Miguelito."

They were walking down the street toward the piazza, where, the day being Monday, a number of farmers from the campagna were selling produce from their wagons. Stefano slowed his pace. Before they reached the crowded square, he stopped and faced Nicholas.

"Why did they send you?"

Nicholas's gaze slid away from the younger man's face. "They have reasons, I suppose."

"To humiliate me. To humiliate you."

Nicholas made some indefinite sound in his throat.

"Doubtless he could not pass it up—the economy must have appealed. He is a devil. Why do we do it? Why submit to it?"

"For our own advancement," Nicholas said.

"Well, I've advanced to the Torre Nona. I won't submit any more."

"I doubt he'll give either of us another chance to do so."

"Help me."

Nicholas looked back into Stefano's face, still blackened by the cold brand. "Don't be a fool. What do you mean to do?"

"Between us we know enough of what he's done—we'll denounce him."

"God's heart, Stefano! He is Valentino. Everybody knows what he's done. The problem is that no one can bring him to justice for it."

"The Pope can," Stefano said calmly. His face was bright with resolution, his eyes snapping and his cheeks flushed. "I can reach Alexander and give him certain evidence of everything. What Valentino meant to do to Corneto, for one."

"He meant Corneto some harm?" Cardinal Corneto was the Pope's close friend.

"Come with me. We'll destroy him."

"He'll kill you," Nicholas said.

"Bah." Stefano strode away from him. "I'll do it alone."

"Stefano!"

The younger man never turned back, but plunged straight on into the crowded piazza. A team of white horses came between them and when the wagon had passed, Nicholas could not pick him out of the passing mob. Nicholas's hands were shaking. He rubbed them together, as if to brace them against one another, wondering what he could do. There was nothing he could do. Valentino's men would throw Stefano out of the Vatican if they saw him. He knew Stefano's willful resolution too well to hope much for that to save him. All at once he realized that he should have gone with Stefano. It was too late now, with Stefano already on his way there. Too late. He knew it was not too late, that he could go to the Vatican and find him there, but at the Vatican he would also find Valentino, and instead he went home.

"YES," NICHOLAS SAID. "I know him." His own calm amazed him.

"What was his name?" the watchman asked.

Nicholas reached out one hand to the curling russet hair, fouled with the Tiber's yellow mud. "Stefano Baglione."

The watchman half-smothered a gurgle of laughter. Nicholas ignored it. Stefano's hair curled itself around his fingers. The garrotte had abraded the skin of Stefano's neck, and his hands were bruised. He had fought them, not like des Troches.

"Shall I send to the Baglioni to come for the corpse?" the watchman said, with a fine sarcasm in his voice.

Nicholas pulled the ragged cover up over Stefano's head again. "Bury him with the beggars. It won't matter to him."

His icy calm began to thaw, and before it evaporated he took himself quickly away, out of the shed, out to the bank of the Tiber, the graveyard of Rome.

WHEN NICHOLAS REACHED his house, Juan was out, probably at the market. Nicholas sat down in one of the chairs by the hearth. The morning had exhausted him. His mind rested on the surface of the moment. The white walls of his house shouted at him. He had always meant to have them painted again but had never had the money. He should have filled them with people, faces, hands, eyes, mouths, to give him company now, when he was so ruined a man he could not even feel his grief.

Juan came in, a pail of milk in one hand. "You are back," he said. "You were gone this morning. What happened?"

Nicholas turned to look at him. "Stefano is dead. His body was washed up on the riverbank last night."

"Dead," Juan said, and reliably crossed himself.

"I should have gone with him," Nicholas said.

The old man dropped the pail and the milk ran across the floor. He rushed forward to Nicholas's side and kneeling down gripped his arm with a younger man's strength. "It was them, was it—those other people?"

Nicholas moved his arm in Juan's grip, without freeing himself. "I should have gone with him." All his life he had shirked and cheated so that when the one important thing he might have done appeared before him, he had failed it.

His reason caught him by the hair; nothing would have been served had he gone. He would have died too. Juan was shouting at him. Stefano had fought them, hurt them perhaps, while Nicholas sat in his empty house.

"Revenge him," Juan was shouting. "It is your duty."

"Ah." He shoved the old man away and got up from his chair.

The floor was puddled in the white milk. Old Juan knelt by the chair and began to speak prayers. Nicholas swayed on his feet, his legs weak as a newborn's. He remembered what Stefano had said of Cardinal Corneto.

He realized that he had already decided to do something; now he saw what he could do. He turned again to Juan.

He said, "I am going. I may very well never come back again. If I don't, the house is yours. It may be sold for a good amount—Amadeo will buy it. You could live on that money. Go back to Spain."

"Where are you going?" Juan asked.

"To Cardinal Corneto's," Nicholas said. He took his hat from the stool by the door and went out.

Behind him Juan gave a long canine wail and lapsed again into prayer.

"You are lying," Corneto said. He swiveled his body in his chair, turning his knees away from Nicholas, and crossed one leg over the other. "Rodrigo Borgia and I have been friends since the eighties. What are you telling me—that he would suffer harm come to me?"

"Not Alexander," Nicholas said. "Valentino. He needs money. You are a Cardinal; when you die he can seize your wealth for the Church."

"Why do you tell me this? For my sake, or for revenge? I know the Borgias have cast you off."

"I cannot see that the motive matters very much. The end is the same."

Corneto's broad pale face was furrowed with lines, and his white hair rose in a shock above his forehead. His eyes were shielded behind his hooded lids. His expression was set, completely unreadable. Abruptly he folded his arms across his chest.

"Valentino does nothing without Alexander's agreement. I say you are lying. They cannot mean to harm me."

Nicholas saw how he had knotted himself up: obviously Corneto did believe it. Had he not believed it he would have thrown Nicholas out already. There was more evidence to give him.

"Your house was broken into, a night or two ago," Nicholas said.

"Yes."

"It was Stefano Baglione who did that. Do you know why?"

Corneto glared at him. "The Pope sent him away. Caught him cheating at cards. He thought he could get some revenge."

"Stefano told me Valentino meant something to be done to you."

"Then bring Stefano here, to answer for what he says."

"Stefano was dragged out of the Tiber this morning."

For a moment, glassy-eyed, Corneto did nothing. Suddenly he burst up from his chair and struck at Nicholas. Nicholas saw the blow coming; he ducked, and Corneto's fist struck him glancing on the cheek. Nicholas staggered and fell.

Over him, Corneto boomed, "By God, this is the foulest kind of lie! Every question answered, ah? By God, I don't believe you!"

Nicholas sat up. His cheekbone hurt. Corneto paced around him, shouting down at him.

"Don't you know that this has been tried before—how many times before people like you, schemers, lying scum, have come here and told me scandals, trying to separate me from my old friend? No! I will not believe this. You will come out to the country with me today, and say this to Alexander's face."

There was a virtue in that. Content with it, Nicholas touched his cheek with his hand. Corneto's servants came to take him away.

HE WALKED OUT OF ROME with the rest of Corneto's party, following the Cardinal's litter. They left Rome by a gate overgrown with flowering vines; the road led them away over a rolling hill and down to skirt the edge of the swamp, buzzing with mosquitoes. Just behind Nicholas walked the man set to guard him, a big man with a head so narrow it seemed no wider than his neck, who now and then poked Nicholas in the back with his walking stick.

Corneto's vineyard grew on a hillside high enough to over-look the sea. Elm trees grew around the cave where the wine was stored to age. When the Cardinal arrived, Nicholas in his train, some others of his people were making a table ready in the meadow nearby. Nicholas was taken into the cave full of barrels and told to sit beside the wall. He sat down, glad of the dank cool of the cave after walking through the heat of August.

Brisk young men in Corneto's red livery dashed in and out of the cave, bringing in the banquet which Corneto had transported out from Rome in hampers. In the cave there was a large table, where Corneto's cook opened the hampers, arranged the food on platters, and sent it off to the table in the meadow. Nicholas sat by the wall watching. He was hungry, and his nerve was weakening: he dreaded facing Valentino. Finally he rose and strolled over to the table.

The cook was slicing carrots and radishes into flowers to set about a platter of cold chickens. When he saw Nicholas, he paused long enough to hone the edge of his knife on his leather apron.

"What do you want?"

"I'm hungry," Nicholas said. Directly before him on the table was a jellied soup, kept cold in a basin of snow. Packed down from the Alps, he supposed, in huge barrels or boxes so that there was still some left unmelted when it arrived in Rome in the heat of August. That was the power of a Pope. Next to the basin of snow, in fact, was a cask of wine with the Pope's seal on it.

The cook said, "Here," and gave him a slice of the chicken.

"Thank you." Nicholas did not take his attention from the cask. He ate the chicken without noticing the taste. "The Pope brought his own wine? Isn't that unusual?"

"Duke Valentino brought it," the cook said. "A gift to my master the Cardinal. What are you here for?"

"The entertainment," Nicholas said, staring at the cask. It was not Valentino's seal. There was an adage about new wine in old casks, but it hardly fit this situation. There was another about Greeks bearing gifts that did. Nicholas swallowed the chicken.

"Excellent," he said. "Excellent indeed."

The cook shrugged. "I did not roast it."

A few minutes later the narrow-headed man with the walking stick came to bring Nicholas out to the party. He went willingly but the narrow-headed man could not resist pushing him and cursing him as if he resisted. It was hot outside the cave. When Nicholas rounded the hillside and walked out across the meadow, the cool wind off the sea stroked over him and cooled him.

At the end of the meadow, the Pope sat red as a poppy

behind the table. On his right was Valentino, all in black, and on his left was Corneto. Nicholas's heart jumped up in his chest, and he walked toward them with a long stride.

Miguelito stood behind Valentino, his hands folded over his Gorgon-headed beltbuckle. His coat was dirty. His face was bruised. Nicholas sucked in his breath, his blood racing, his mind rushing back to the memory of Stefano's battered hands.

Alexander said, "What do you mean, Messer Dawson, to disturb my dinner in this unpleasant way?"

Nicholas licked his lips. Valentino lolled in his chair, his head cocked to one side. The sea wind ruffled his hair. Nicholas said, "Your Holiness, do you remember Stefano, with whom you played cards?"

"What is this?" Corneto said sharply. "Come to your charges, Messer Liar."

"What charges?" the Pope said.

"Duke Valentino," Nicholas cried, "murdered Stefano Baglione, for no reason at all."

A grunt erupted from the Pope like a puff of smoke from a volcano. He faced his son. "What have you to say to that?"

Valentino put his head to one side. "My father, my lord, I have never done anything that I have regretted. What I do, I must do to achieve my purpose. Let that purpose be the justification for my actions. I mean nothing less than to bring all Italy under one king, and by my great ambition to give Christendom its head again. As for this—" he pointed his finger at Nicholas before him—"what is that but the most wretched of men? What right has he to charge me with anything? He is a misfit, an outcast, like any Jew or Moor. I serve the holy order, while he abhors it, and perverts even the gentle game of love into a stinking sin. What he did with Stefano Baglione is the crime, for which he ought to suffer as the law decrees."

Miguelito said, "Also he has plotted with Gonsalvo."

The Pope was sitting back, his hands on his stomach, and

his lower lip thrust out. "We took you in, and you served us thus. You are an evil man."

Nicholas cried out, "Your Holiness! Let me speak for myself. I know what I am. I ask no pardon for what I am, low and ruined."

Miguelito was coming around the table toward him, to take him. The three men facing him over the table were unmoved. Nicholas gathered his breath.

He said, "But what is Valentino? That we know, do we not, all of us? And knowing him, I dare him to drink the wine he gave today to Cardinal Corneto."

Miguelito reached him in a jump and grabbed him by the arm. With a twist of his body Nicholas pulled free. He faced Valentino again, and saw the prince turn white as candle wax.

There was a little silence. At last Corneto said, "Bring the wine."

The Pope sprang from his chair, his mountainous flesh quaking. "No. I will not tolerate this. You, my friend, dare believe this calumny?"

"Let him prove the lie a lie," Corneto said.

"Papa," Valentino said. He rose to his feet beside his father. Corneto was staring at them both, his grooved face frowning. A servant came up with the little cask of wine. Nicholas swallowed down the excitement in his throat. Beside him Miguelito made no effort to take hold of him again, but only stood, silent, and waited.

"Bring me the cup, by God," the Pope cried. "I will show these liars and scandalmongers that no one can taint my fatherly love!"

"Papa," Valentino said, louder than before, and laid his hand on his father's arm. A servant broached the cask, and Corneto himself stood forward to pour the wine.

Valentino tugged on his father's arm, and Alexander thrust him away.

"I drink."

He took the cup and drank deep from it. In the whole glade no other man moved. Alexander lowered the cup and sighed.

"An excellent Pramnian. Is it from your own vineyard, Cesare?"

Valentino was impassive. Only the pallor of his face betrayed him. He said, "It is, sir. Do you like it?"

"It is hardy and demanding," the Pope said, "but I am not intimidated easily." He held out the cup. "Will you drink with me?"

Valentino put his head back, his eyes half closed. If he refused it, he condemned himself. Amazed, Nicholas saw him smile.

"Aut Caesar aut nullus," he said, and took the cup, and drank what his father had left.

"Now," the Pope said, "we turn again to this traitor."

His men moved in around Nicholas, bound his hands behind his back, and thrust him to his knees. Nicholas bowed his head. His heart was hammering in his side. Now again he grew frightened.

"Let Miguelito deal with him," Valentino said.

The lesser men began to call for Nicholas's death. Corneto rose in his place at the table.

"Not here. I have every hope still of enjoying our now-delayed dinner."

"Let me have him," Miguelito said.

Nicholas raised his head. The Pope and Valentino looked down on him from the height of their chairs. He had misjudged; there was no poison, or else none strong enough to matter to a Borgia.

"Here," someone shouted. "Let him suffer here, now, for what he's done."

Corneto was frowning. He fingered the lace at his throat. "Let's get it done, anyhow."

The Pope stood up.

"Take him," Valentino said to Miguelito.

The Navarrese soldier stooped over Nicholas, who saw the garrotte slide out of Miguelito's coat like a serpent from his breast. He sucked in his breath. He felt the weight of the crowd's look on him.

The Pope gave a low cry. He fell forward over the table.

A yell went up from the underlings. The Pope struggled to push himself up and slumped forward across the table again. His men crowded around him, supporting him as he thrashed and shoved at the table, the front of his red robe plastered with bits of food.

"It is the heat." Alexander gasped at the air; his eyes bulged. "The heat—" he fell forward again, plunging down through the arms of his servants.

Corneto roared, "Quickly! Bring the litter—" half the servants bolted away across the grass.

Valentino still sat in his place, his face like steel. Now Nicholas saw that he was clutching the table. He saw the sweat gathering on the Borgia's forehead. Miguelito had gone to him again. The Pope's litter was hurrying down the green slope toward them; its curtains fluttered. Miguelito bent to speak to Valentino, slid one hand under Valentino's arm, and helped him rise.

The Pope's servants carried him to the litter. Alexander was still aware; Nicholas heard him say, "It is the heat." His face was gray. He was surely dying. Leaning on Miguelito, Valentino dragged himself step by step toward the litter. They would have to share it, father and son; Valentino clearly could not ride.

Someone kicked Nicholas. "What about this one?"

At the table Corneto still sat, his mouth screwed up. He shook his head.

"Let him go. He did nothing."

Nicholas pushed himself onto his feet. The Pope and Valentino had disappeared into the litter. Surrounded by their crowds of servants, the little room swayed away across the slope toward the gate. Someone cut Nicholas's bonds. He put out his hands in front of him. Corneto was watching him, pensive.

"You did not do that to save me," he said to Nicholas. "I see no duty to reward you."

Nicholas said, "If you would do me one favor, I would be rewarded beyond my dreams."

Corneto's head rose, his eyes sharp beneath the steep pale brow. "What?"

"Recommend me to the Medici. The Signory of Florence has dismissed me. I am in need of employment. The Medici shall find me a valuable servant."

"That I shall be glad to do." Corneto nodded.

Nicholas forgot to bow, to ask for leave. He felt light with new life. He wanted to laugh, and he could not laugh here. He strode away from the elm grove, to the road.

When he reached the highway, the litter was far ahead of him, climbing a hill on its way to Rome. Swarms of bright-coated courtiers surrounded it and trailed after it. At this distance they looked tiny, and their tiny lamenting voices were no louder than the crickets in the grass. Soon they would be over the top of the hill and out of his sight.

Alexander had drunk only half his poisoned cup, but he was an old man, and any poison was enough. Without his father's power and the power of his father's purse, Valentino was beaten, destroyed by his own greed. He thought he had escaped nature, but in the end his own nature had over-mastered him, as surely as the returning swing of the pendulum.

Nicholas laughed.